# A NATURAL CAUSE

## BY LESLIE WIENS

 FriesenPress

One Printers Way
Altona, MB R0G 0B0
Canada

www.friesenpress.com

**Copyright © 2023 by Leslie Wiens**
First Edition — 2023

All rights reserved.

No part of this publication may be reproduced in any form, or by any means, electronic or mechanical, including photocopying, recording, or any information browsing, storage, or retrieval system, without permission in writing from FriesenPress.

ISBN
978-1-03-919641-4 (Hardcover)
978-1-03-919640-7 (Paperback)
978-1-03-919642-1 (eBook)

1. FIC031080    FICTION, THRILLERS, PSYCHOLOGICAL

Distributed to the trade by The Ingram Book Company

To Terry
Mere words shackle the expression of my love for you.


With thanks to:
Val S., Arthur P., and Mark D. for your honesty and integrity.
Sandra K. and Leona W. for your never-ending support and enthusiasm.

# Prologue

Beth looked down at the glove compartment in front of her. She wondered if there was a gun in it. Or had she just watched too many cop shows on TV?

"Want one?" Detective Groemann offered her a cigarette. His left hand was draped over the steering wheel, with an unlit cigarette in his fingers.

"N-no thanks Ken." Beth stuttered. She felt uncomfortable. The fact she was in a police cruiser was part of the problem. *Why weren't they in his Prius?*

"Look, you're nervous. Don't be. If anything ugly happens, I'll just drive away. The uniforms can handle all of this without me. I just thought, you know, that with all the work you did, you deserve to witness this happen. I'm doing this as a favour. You've earned that right. OK?"

Beth couldn't even bring herself to turn towards him. She had told him everything. *Everything.* And they were arresting the man who did those things to her. All she could do now was stare forward at the wipers intermittently working to clear away the light rain that was falling.

Her counsellor had encouraged her to be open with the detective. At this moment, she was wondering if that had been bad advice. But if this all led to an arrest, then she would be satisfied that she had done the right thing. She just wished that she had asked Donna to come along. She could use her comfort right now. Or Sneakers. Or maybe even Tiffany. Yeah, Tiff would have been a better choice for this.

Det. Groemann rolled down his window a small crack and cool air rolled in from the mist outside. "Look, Beth, this guy's gonna get exactly what's coming to him. I'll see to that. I promise."

From the very beginning, Detective Ken Groemann had fit the image of what she expected in a detective. He was huge, over 6'6", and built like he worked out every day. And his voice was deeper than anyone she had known.

He was always calm. Always seemed gentle. But he looked like he could break a person in half if he really wanted to.

Beth stared ahead. Each of the three police cars had left their lights flashing, and combined with the misty rain they created a small lightshow on the windshield. Until the wipers once again swept the slate clear. That is what she needed. Another clean slate. Maybe this would be the start of it.

The uniformed police had forced their way into the house when they couldn't get a reply to their knocks. They had been inside the house for fifteen minutes now. What could be taking them so long?

She started to regret having agreed to this escorted participation. Maybe she should have stayed at home. Ken lit his cigarette and rolled the window down a little further to let the smoke out. Then she saw one uniformed officer approaching their vehicle. The officer knocked lightly on the driver's side window and motioned for Ken to lower it a bit more.

"What's up?" Detective Groemann asked as he flicked his cigarette onto the pavement. It had just been lit. He had only taken one drag. He looked like he wasn't happy to be talking to the officer.

"Uhm. Uh . . . I'm afraid we can't follow through with the arrest, sir. We've run into a complication."

Beth just hung her head and closed her eyes.

## August 2004

Breathing in the sweet moist air, Liz can't stop the small grin on her face. A Japanese Crape Myrtle tree on the boulevard was still in bloom, and the rare smell of the flowers hung heavily in the air. They were what was causing her every breath to feel so sweet. You could almost taste it. This is exactly why she wanted this job. While other students are indoors fighting summer colds from overly air-conditioned offices or stuck with menial labour at some dead-end retail opportunity—she is free. She is her own boss, in a way. She has complete autonomy over how her work flows and over how her life is lived.

She also has the option of taking days off when she felt she couldn't handle meeting people. The days she felt down. Those days that she referred to as her *blue* days. Fortunately, there hadn't been many of those days lately. Maybe the work she was doing had some positive impact on her mental well-being.

The morning rains had slightly cooled the usually hot August air, and now the day was slowly warming, but only to the point of complete comfort. *It is exactly how I'd set my climate controls if I was working indoors,* she thought. But indoors, there would be no sunshine. There would be no Myrtle trees. And the moist air even made for a "good hair day." Her shoulder-length black hair formed extra tight curls and bounced as she walked. Perfect.

She had brought along the iPod her father had given her at Christmas, but it was turned off now. She didn't want to hear Maroon 5 or Alicia Keys. She was enjoying the natural sounds around her. A small group of chickadees was ushering her along, keeping a few feet in front of her and taking small flights forward to each successive tree that lined the sidewalk. They seemed to be heralding her approach to some unseen audience, their constant chattering adding an air of excitement to an otherwise quiet environment. Even the traffic noise was unusually subdued. Traffic was what kept Vancouver from being as silent as the woods that ran beside the university's campus. Liz spent a lot of time on the trails in those woods. Surrounded by ferns and towering evergreens, with subdued lighting and perfect calmness, Liz would walk for hours and let her mind escape from any stresses in her life. Her studies, the loneliness of living in residence by herself, the distance from her family and friends, all those things that made her both a little sad and a little anxious. The woods calmed her and helped her cope.

As she neared the sidewalk to the next house on her assigned route, she thought about Professor Gilby. Steve. He had asked her to stop calling him professor and just call him Steve. He was a bright spot on her curriculum, a grind of advanced linear algebra, statistics, and abstract calculus. His sociology course, "The Advancing Age of Our Society," was not only more interesting than the other courses, but Professor Gilby—Steve—added so much character to the daily lectures that she eagerly anticipated attending every class. He always had personal stories or anecdotes that added depth to the course material, and he made sure that he got to know every student by name. You didn't feel like a number in his class. You were made to feel important. He was the reason why she had chosen to switch from the sciences to the arts going forward.

He seemed to recognize her enthusiasm. That's probably why she had been approached to help gather data for his research project and why she was doing her current job. He had hired three students, all from the same sociology class. There was herself, Caroline Bottier, and Tiffany Rainchild. She had gotten to know Caroline quite well during the study group they both attended, but Tiffany was almost unknown to her. The Faculty of Arts was very large and sociology courses were popular, making the class size quite large as well. The fact that Tiffany was basically a stranger wasn't unusual. The three students had also been given their separate list of streets and sent out on their own, so there was no chance to get to know each other through the summer work they were doing either.

Thinking of Steve changed her small grin to a full-blown smile. She didn't feel happy very often, but somehow he brought out that feeling in her, and she didn't know why. She really had liked him as a prof. The fact that he was her youngest and best-looking prof might have helped make his classes more enjoyable, with his well-trimmed beard and coiffed hair, but there was something more than that. Something that made her feel like she had never felt before. It was a wonderful feeling. A feeling of complete comfort. It was like taking a class from a peer rather than a prof.

As she turned to walk up the assigned house's sidewalk, she made note of the address at the top of the page on her clipboard: 3230 Evenson Drive. Much like most of the other homes on this street, it was best described as an elegant old two-storey Tudor house with lawns and gardens that revealed the care the owners were providing. A trimmed cedar hedge separated the public sidewalk from the front lawn. There was a beautiful Arbutus tree centered in the yard, surrounded by manicured grass. Two flower gardens were positioned against the front of the house itself. The flower gardens were brilliantly coloured and coordinated with the colour of the house's trim. The house was obviously loved by the owners. Or the owner. Or the tenant. Liz was about to find out which.

Ringing the doorbell, she mentally rehearsed the opening lines. Lines that she had used time and time again since the beginning of that summer. Lines that rang through her mind like a memorized poem from grade school. As the door opened and an elderly woman stood before her in the house's the entrance, she flashed a toothy smile and started her pitch.

"Good afternoon, ma'am. My name is Liz, and I'm hoping you can help me with my university job. I'm conducting a survey—it's very short, with only three questions. Depending on your three answers there may also be an additional set of questions, but is it OK if I just start with the first three?" She held her smiling pose and waited for the answer.

"Of course I can help. How could I say no to a pretty girl like you?" came the reply. The elderly woman actually seemed to be enjoying the interruption of her possibly all-too-quiet morning.

"The research is about our health care system and is being conducted through the university along with a grant from the Aldbrecht Foundation."

"I'm okay with the questions. I already said that, but what's the Old Brick Foundation?"

"The Aldbrecht Foundation. Umm, sorry, I actually don't really know. It's just on my script to mention that." Liz had never been asked that question before. Three plus months of daily knocking on door after door and nobody had brought this up. She became curious herself: *what is this foundation all about?*

"Well, in any case" continued the elderly woman, "what are your survey questions? Let's get on with it."

"Great! First question: Is anyone in this household over sixty years of age?" Liz asked.

"Are you in need of glasses? How old do you think I am?" came the reply, accompanied by a smile that betrayed the false teeth held within. "I'm probably older than your grandparents, for goodness' sake!"

"Sorry," Liz continued, "but I have to ask. I didn't want to assume anything about your age. That would be rude of me. Second question: Does the person or people who are over sixty, ah, I guess that means you. Sorry. Do you have immediate family living with you or near you who will care for you should you become in need of eldercare? For this question, immediate family means siblings or children only."

The older woman leaned back. "I can take care of myself, thank you very much. I have no problems living on my own. I do my own shopping, cooking, cleaning, well you can just take a look at my yard. I do that myself too, you know."

"I'm sorry, I think your yard looks wonderful. And your house seems to be very well looked after. The survey is just trying to determine that if—*if*—you were to become in need of help then who—"

"I don't now and won't ever need help from anyone. Not now, not ever. And why do you keep apologizing. You've said 'sorry' three times now. What are you so sorry about?"

"I'm sor— " Liz cut herself short, catching the offending utterance before it fully left her lips. "What I mean is, I meant no harm. I wasn't insinuating you couldn't care for yourself or won't be able to at any point. It's just asking if you have family that will step forward to help when—I mean *if*—you need help. Do you?"

"Goodness girl! That won't happen. Like I said, not now, not ever. I never married, and both of my sisters are now passed away. Martha had a husband, but he was a real loser who took off as soon as she was diagnosed with Parkinson's. That's what having a husband will get you—leech off you while they're around and then exit as soon as they don't like the music! I'm independent. I am now and I always have been. Life's better that way. When I think . . . "

"Okay," Liz cut in, "this third question is a little more personal, and I don't need details—but just generally speaking—if you were to become in need of support, would you be able to afford your own help, or would you rely on what the government provides for you to be taken care of?" The glare from the homeowner was almost an assault. Liz knew she had to change the course of the conversation. "I'm sorry. I've been rude. I didn't even ask: what's your name?"

"Well," came the reply. "That's the first time you've said you're sorry and probably needed to. I'm Grace Butler. People call me Gracie. You said your name was Liz, right? Is that short for Elizabeth?"

"Yes, it is, Elizabeth Grant. But I only get called Elizabeth when I'm in trouble for doing something wrong at home. Even my parents usually call me Liz. Well, that is, it's what my dad calls me. My mother passed away. Liz is the only name I usually go by." Liz took a moment to write Grace's name at the appropriate spot on the survey sheet.

Gracie unfolded her arms and Liz noticed her own shoulders drop a little. The tension that had been building just abated slightly.

"No." said Gracie.

"No?" repeated Liz, unsure of what message was being conveyed. *Was Gracie not happy with the name Elizabeth being changed to Liz? Was she no longer willing to answer questions?*

The confusion on Liz's face must have been obvious, as Gracie chimed in: "No, I won't need government support. I'm quite capable of looking after myself physically, and quite capable of looking after myself financially as well. There'll be no need to run a tag day for the likes of me."

"Tag day?" Liz asked, slowly shaking her head.

"Tag day. Surely, you've heard the expression! That means they won't have to have a public fundraising to gather money to help me. Tag day. You've probably never been part of one, but please don't tell me you've never heard of them?"

"I've heard the expression before" Liz lied, hoping Gracie couldn't tell. She added "I'm just not one hundred percent clear on what they are. Or were. Also, your combination of answers qualifies you for the long survey. It is optional, and I should warn you it gets more personal. Would you like to take part in these additional questions? As I said, it is optional, and it should only take about ten to fifteen minutes."

"Young woman, you've got some living to experience. Everybody's heard of tag days! I tell you what—I'll put on the kettle for tea, and we can go over those extra questions over a cup of Earl Grey. How does that sound?"

"Great!" exclaimed Liz. This offer came frequently from people who reached this stage in the questions, sometimes even earlier, and Liz loved the tea-visits. She knew the next list of questions were more involved—more intimate—and she wanted Gracie to feel at ease while she asked them. She entered the spacious foyer, and slipped off her light sweater, placing it carefully over the coatrack hook. She followed Gracie into the living room, then Gracie went down a hallway and into a bathroom and washed her hands. Liz noticed the meticulous care that the home had received. The floors were shining hardwood and the artwork had framing to match the trim on the doors and baseboards. The artwork itself was all original oils or acrylics, and there wasn't a reproduction print to be seen. Liz silently thanked her mother for teaching her the difference between fine artwork and decorative reproductions.

The furniture in the room was older, but the upholstery was either recently replaced or Gracie never actually sat in any of the chairs. They were all in perfect condition. The oak and leather ottoman had two large artbooks carefully displayed. Two more were on the oak coffee table. There wasn't a speck of dust to be seen. She could hear classical music coming from the kitchen, though she didn't know the work or the artist. She thought *did they call them artists back then, or what?* Her reverie was broken by Gracie entering the room.

"I was just doing some baking and I had a little flour on my hands. Have a seat Liz, and I'll put on the kettle. Won't be more than a moment. Do you take sugar or milk?"

"No, just clear tea thanks"

"Perfect. That's the way tea should be enjoyed. I'll get out some sugar biscuits and a spot of sherry to go with the tea."

"Sherry? It's pretty early!"

"It's never too early if the sherry is of high enough quality! And it's the perfect ending to tea. Just you wait." And with that, Gracie disappeared around the corner into the kitchen. Gracie's attitude seemed to have changed from having a very defensive stance to one of open arms very quickly. Liz wondered what she had done to promote that, if anything at all.

While she was left alone, Liz didn't choose a seat immediately. Rather than commit to a single location, she slowly wandered around the living room. She noticed the fine works of art, and it made her wish she knew more about art in general. She had been to a few local artists' shows and had learned some basics, but never really took the time to study or grow her knowledge about art in any way.

Her mom had liked art. Their house had a few works by local artists, rather than prints of famous works or generic items from a furniture store. If she had lived longer Liz might have grown a deeper appreciation for art herself, but her mother had passed away when Liz was only nine years old, and her father wasn't into art at all. She had a strange thought: *Is missing my mom why I like visits like this so much?* She didn't want to delve too deeply into that thought. Thinking of her mother always made her emotional. Sad, angry, frustrated—she thought: *no time for that while I'm supposed to be doing my work here! I spend enough time feeling sad as it is.*

She walked up to the mantlepiece above the fireplace and lightly touched the black alabaster sculpture centered there. It was a figure of a bear, seated and looking to one side. She picked it up. It was warm to the touch. *Shouldn't stone be cold?* The bear's stance made her think of her father. Strong, powerful, but reserved. Quiet even. Pensive. She carefully placed the bear back on the mantlepiece.

Moving on to the bookshelves that lined the wall beside the fireplace, she ran her fingers slowly across the leatherbound spines of the collection. The smell of old paper and leather gently tickled her nostrils, and she sneezed.

"God bless you!" Gracie cheerfully offered as she entered the room, tray in hand covered with teacups, cookies, and half-filled sherry glasses. "The tea will be a minute or two. They're mostly first editions." She placed the tray on the coffee table, carefully sliding the artbooks to one end of the table.

"First editions?"

"The books—first editions."

"I . . . I don't know what that means." Liz could feel herself blush a little. It seemed Gracie knew about a lot of things that she herself was ignorant about.

"You said you were in university. Just what are they teaching you?"

"Mostly about statistics, calculus, logic. And I take Modern English. And the sociology course that led me to this summer job. The Advancing Age of Our Society. It's the one I find most interesting. That's why—"

"Advancing age? Is *that* why you are knocking on my door?"

"Not at all! I'm knocking on every door on this street. I had no idea who would answer or how old you'd be!"

"And now you're surprised at just how old I am?"

"I'm not saying that! I…"

"Young woman, I'm just pulling your leg. I know how these survey things work. You've got to relax and enjoy life and not take what old people say to you so seriously. We have a sense of humour too you know. Like in that old movie: 'I'm not dead!'"

"'Not dead'?"

"The old *Holy Grail* film". Gracie hunched over and with a raspy voice quipped "'Bring out your dead!'"

"'Holy Grail'?"

"What year were you born, Liz? Ah, never mind. Let's just say people much older than you aren't necessarily addle-minded. A quick wit isn't the exclusive domain of young people. We can be clever too!"

"Nineteen eighty-four. I'll be twenty next month. I've just finished my second year of a four-year degree. But I'm not sure I'm following—"

"Let me check on the tea. I'll be right back." And with that, Gracie disappeared around the corner into the kitchen again. Liz was confused. Her head was spinning. *Was Gracie deliberately being difficult or was this just her nature?* She usually enjoyed herself when the people she was surveying invited her into their homes, but this lady was different. Liz wasn't sure if she liked it or if she was being made fun of and should resent this treatment. Reaching for a sugar cookie from the tray that Gracie had set on the coffee table, she sat in the armchair beside the couch. She didn't want Gracie to have the option of sitting right beside her, but she wasn't sure why.

"Alright then. Here we go, it will just take two minutes to steep and then we can pour the tea." Gracie placed the stoneware teapot on the coffee table, using a coaster she had brought with her. "Now, what about those questions you have for me?" Gracie chose the end of the couch closest to Liz and helped herself to a cookie and a napkin. "And before I forget, 'first edition' means the book came from the first typesetting for that book. Collectors always pay more for a first edition. Further editions may have corrections that make the book better in some ways, but first editions are the most cherished. That red one on the shelf you were looking at is Jane Austen's *Pride and Prejudice*. It's probably worth several thousand dollars now, but I bought it many years ago for only a few hundred dollars. I like to think of them as my retirement fund. I end up spending a lot of my income on them."

"You work?" Liz tried to not look shocked.

"Of course not! I don't think many companies would find value in investing their resources in a woman of my age. I'm not sure I would want to be held accountable to some manager either. I'm too independently minded to accommodate my taking direction from somebody else these days." Gracie bit into her cookie, holding the napkin chest high to catch any dropping crumbs. "I did work at one time, but I still refer to my retirement fund as if it's something needed for the distant future." Gracie gazed into an unknown spot some distance away and seemed to want to drift away in her latest thought to some unknown time or place.

Liz realized she hadn't also taken a napkin, so she leaned forward to help herself to one. Before she bit into her cookie, she added " 'Holy Grail'?", hoping to bring Gracie back to the present.

"Ah, yes. Monty Python and the *Holy Grail*. There was also a stage play called *Spamalot*. They came from an old British TV show called—"

"Yes! *Monty Python's Flying Circus*! My dad used to go on and on about that show. I've never seen it, but he thought it was hilarious!" Liz seemed buoyed at her awareness of this reference. It might have been the only thing mentioned so far that she knew anything about.

Gracie continued "Well, one of my favourite scenes from the *Holy Grail* movie was John Cleese—he was one of the actors—John came out carrying what was supposed to be a dead person that he wanted to throw on the cart filled with dead people."

"And this was comedy?" Liz was once again puzzled.

"Well, the scene was from the time of the black plague."

"Again: comedy?"

"I think you'd have to see it. It's hard to translate into words. Let's just leave it at that. Anyway, the person over John Cleese's shoulder pipes up and says 'I'm not dead' or something like that. My friends have gotten into the habit of saying that when we greet each other these days. It is a bit of black humour, but it makes light of our pending doom." Gracie got back to the issue at hand: "So, what were these extra questions you had?"

Liz had just bitten into her cookie, and carefully placed the remainder of the cookie gently on her napkin and set them both down on the wide arm of her chair. "Well," she started, quickly swallowing the sugary mouthful and licking her lips clean, "the rest of these questions get quite personal, so I want to assure you that they will never be shared with anyone. They are only counted for data purposes, and then the general data is what is shared with the government. You have one-hundred percent confidentiality, so please be as open and honest as you can."

"There's you," replied Gracie, "and there's whomever you hand these survey papers to. Both of you will know my answers. That appears to be less than one-hundred percent confidential to me."

"But I'm—"

"Relax Liz. I'm not worried. I know what you are trying to say, and I'll be open and honest. What's the first question?"

As Gracie leaned forward to pour tea, Liz asked: "Do you currently own the home you are living in, or do you rent?"

And with that start, the questions kept coming:

"Do you have a mortgage or any other debts?"

"Do you have a pension income?"

"Do you have any royalty income and, if so, from where?"

"Have you any other savings for your retirement years?"

About halfway through the questions, Gracie turned to Liz and looked straight into her eyes. She asked, very calmly, "How old were you when your mother passed away?"

Liz was taken aback a little, but Gracie's approach disarmed her, and she replied, "I was nine years old." She suddenly realized why Gracie's whole attitude about the survey had changed. She cared about the fact that Liz had lost her mother. She actually cared.

"I was eleven. Almost the same as you. My mom had cancer, and back then there wasn't a lot that could be done about it. She stayed in a bed in our living room and lasted about a month and a half before she finally let go and passed away. How did your mom die, Liz?"

"She had cancer too. It was the second time that she had cancer. Before I was born, she had breast cancer, but they treated it and she managed to come out of it OK. At least as far as I knew she was fully recovered. But the second time it was pancreatic cancer, and they haven't found a cure for that yet. The survival rate is very low."

"Oh, you poor dear. Your father has raised you alone since then? Or did he re-marry?"

"No, he has stayed single. He has never even dated. At least, not that I'm aware of." Liz sat in silence for a full minute. Gracie stopped asking questions.

When Liz finally got back to the survey the questions moved into more relationship-based information such as: "Who would you consider to be your closest relative?" and "Who is your closest friend?", followed by "Would either of those people care for you if the need arose?". Liz had felt awkward asking some of these questions when she first started this job in early summer, but after the past few months the questions had become more routine for her, and she had to constantly remind herself that as comfortable as she had become with them, the person she was surveying was hearing them for the first time and might not be as comfortable. She tried to add comments or questions between the formal survey questions that she hoped would keep the atmosphere more casual and relaxed.

And on and on they went. Thirty-two questions in all. Gracie was open and friendly with the answers, and by the time they were completed she was also open to the idea of having a sherry. Reaching for the two glasses and handing one to Liz, she asked: "Who did you say was funding this research?" The small half-full sherry glasses were then filled nearly to the brim. It seemed that Gracie had decided that this visit was going to be a long one.

"Well, both the federal government and the Aldbrecht Foundation. Steve, I mean professor Gilby, was the person who put the survey together. It's his research project, and he has hired three of us students to gather the information. He randomly selected streets in the city, and then he assigned us each a series of streets to survey. He hopes the research will help establish both government policy and government funding for what will become a growing need in society."

Gracie smiled. "It's those darn Baby Boomers again, isn't it? They're all aging, and they want my generation to blaze the trail for better elder care. I'll bet they're saying it's for their parents, but really, I think they're doing this for themselves. For their future. You would think the government should somehow reward me for not allowing my body to contribute to the expense of this issue. Instead, they tax me through the teeth. What do you think will become of this survey and Professor Steve's research? I suppose I should be thankful that this research is looking forward as opposed to all those surveys that ask about the present or try to analyze today's issues by looking at the past."

"What will become of this? Why, I don't really know. Professor Gilby is really the person you should ask. He is a wonderful man and very approachable. It's his research. I'm only gathering the data." Liz noticed Gracie leaning forward to add sherry to both of their glasses. She started to think that this might be the end of a very short workday for her, but she didn't object to Gracie's action.

"Well," said Gracie, "I would guess there is a lot of interest in this kind of research and with the proper application of the information you gather, a lot of good could come of it. Now, I've told you all about me, but what about you? Tell me, who is Liz?"

And at that, the meeting changed from a survey to a friendly visit between two total strangers who found themselves fascinated with each other. Gracie filled in areas of her life that the survey had ignored—her religious beliefs, her parents and her upbringing, her mother's passing, and other personal life stories. She was born in 1925, and shared memories of growing up in the depression years followed by her being a young woman in the war years, and how those experiences had led her to being a career woman without a partner. Liz described in detail who she was and where she came from, and about losing her mother as a young girl. By the end of the third sherry, she was also regaling Gracie with some of the humorous and even some of the embarrassing details of her life.

They both agreed, however, that Gracie's stories had more colour to them. They attributed that to the fact that Gracie was basically four times as old as Liz and had seen a lot more of life. Liz's favourite story that Gracie shared involved her crossing the ocean on a steamship, falling asleep in the deck lounger, and waking to find the chocolate candy bar she had been eating was now melted in her hand and chocolate was also smeared across her face.

Gracie almost couldn't finish the story as she was laughing so hard. As she was trying to discretely get back to her berth to clean herself up, she crossed paths with the ship's captain, giving him a creamy brown smile and chocolaty handshake. He was left gobsmacked!

At one point Liz's eyes came across the black alabaster bear. She mentioned to Gracie how much she liked it. She said it reminded her of her father.

"Well, that bear is very dear to me. It was a retirement gift from my co-workers. My company gave me something as well, but I can't even remember what it was. That bear was in a shop close to the office where I worked, and I mentioned how much I liked it to a friend that I worked with. It sat on that store's shelf for at least a year, and I was going to buy it for myself, but it disappeared from the shelf a few months before I retired. When I did retire and received it as a gift, I realized the staff had chipped in for it many months before I left. It made me realize how much they had prepared for that occasion, and it made me feel very special. I really love that bear. It reminds me of all those dear friends."

It was over two hours before the visit came to an end. As they moved to the front door, Gracie asked Liz to wait one minute. She disappeared into the kitchen, and quickly returned with several sugar biscuits wrapped in a paper napkin and a bag with a freshly baked muffin inside. "You'll need a snack, and this will help your tummy settle." Liz hadn't even noticed that her stomach was unsettled, but it was. She wondered: *How many afternoons had Gracie spent enjoying this much sherry?*

As Liz walked down the front sidewalk, turning to give Gracie one last wave, she decided that this was enough surveying for the day. It was time to return to her residence on campus, and maybe time for a little nap too. This wasn't the first time she had only put in a few hours of work, but she hoped that by working six or seven days each week that Steve would be OK with the volume of surveys she was completing. After all, he had given the three young women doing the surveys the freedom to work whatever hours they wanted and had set no quota on the volume of surveys they must conduct.

As Liz walked to the nearest bus stop to start her way back to her residence, she thought of Steve. She thought about his looks, and about how he dressed. Always very cool clothes, and always with his black leather jacket either on and unzipped or slung over his shoulder, hanging from one finger.

Even the way he walked impressed her; casual, but confident. When he had approached her about this job she was very happy. And it was about more than just the money. It was the chance to keep in touch with Steve.

She hoped all her future employers would be as liberal thinking as he was. And as good looking. That thought made her start blushing. She really did like Professor Gilby. A lot!

# September 2004

The hallway outside of the lecture theatre was electric with activity. Excited first-year students scurried by, anxiously looking for whatever room they should be attending, not having a clue where anything was. Second- and third-year students were a little more organized, but excited to see friends that they had been away from for the four summer months. Seniors were the most grounded and calm, many of them having spent their summer employment working in their respective areas of study and in many cases even with some of their classmates. Their calm couldn't overshadow the earlier years' student energy, however, and Liz could feel it in the air. Or maybe she was feeling this way because of what had just happened.

Professor Steven Gilby had just arrived. Working his way to the theatre's doors, Steve had made eye contact with her, he smiled at her, and he even winked and gave a little nod! He stood outside the doors to the theatre and waited for them to be opened by the current class in attendance.

She had intentionally chosen his lecture slot for one of the most popular third-year courses, Aging With Good Health, and she hadn't seen Steve since she handed in her survey paperwork at the end of August. Steve had sent her an email yesterday and asked for her to stay for a short meeting after class. She didn't think the request was for a bad reason. She had completed almost a thousand surveys over the sixteen weeks of summer and had over forty that were the extended version. She was proud of her efforts. Surely Steve wasn't disappointed in the results. And he had just winked at her as he worked his way to the lecture theatre's door.

As she was lost in thoughts of the pending meeting, Caroline approached her and offered an overly cheery "Hi!" Liz just smiled back. Caroline was one of the happiest people Liz had ever met. She was always full of energy, always in a great mood, and almost always smiling. Perhaps what helped in this was the fact Caroline was positively gorgeous. She had long, straight auburn hair, the kind of auburn that most women would happily pay a stylist lots of money to obtain. Her ivory complexion, perfect figure, and Greek goddess face probably would have suited a career as a runway model. However, Liz was most attracted to Caroline's eyes. They were a hazel brown, but not the heavy brown that was most common of brown-eyed people. Hers were lighter and translucent. The kind of eyes that made you feel you could almost see right into them. Right into that person's very soul. They were haunting, in a very arousing kind of way.

"So," said Caroline, flashing a glowing white smile, "like, did Steve ask you to stay after class too?" Liz was taken aback. She had assumed calling Professor Gilby by his first name had been her exclusive domain. She also thought the invitation to stay after class was for her alone. But then again, why wouldn't Caroline have that privilege too? After all, she had also spent the summer working on the same project, and Liz had previously noticed that Caroline did occasionally stay after class last year to ask questions about the lecture. Now that Liz thought about it, Caroline did stay after class a lot. Quickly gathering herself and hoping her mild shock didn't show, she replied "Yes, he did. I'm wondering what it's about." Liz hoped Caroline had some insight into the reason for this meeting.

"I don't know for sure, but, like, I have a guess. I just saw Tiffany and she was asked to stay after the lecture too. I'm guessing there is either something wrong with the surveys we did, or he needs some clarification of the answers. I think it's something minor. Or, like, maybe he just wants to properly thank us. Who knows." The fact seemed obvious that Caroline had no idea at all, but she was happy to talk about it as if she knew. She definitely wasn't worried about whatever the reason could be. She was just happy, period.

As the doors to the lecture theatre opened and students from the prior lecture started to stream out, Liz looked around for Tiffany. If Tiff had been asked to stay after the class, then she must have been registered for this class, but she was nowhere to be seen.

Steve entered the lecture theatre and all the assembled students streamed in behind him. Liz chose a seat in the third row of the theatre, and Caroline followed her like a puppy and chose the seat right beside her. Liz couldn't help but notice Caroline's perfect figure. She wore a tight-fitting V-neck knit top that revealed every perfect curve of her perfect body. Just perfectly. Liz thought she had never been jealous of another woman's body and felt very confident about her own, but Caroline's was just that much better. That much more perfect. Maybe she was jealous after all.

"Like, where's Tiff?" Caroline asked as she scanned the large room. Liz looked around as well but could only offer a shrug in response. The class had fewer students than the second-year course they had taken together, but Liz did notice a few familiar faces. There were only a handful of guys taking the course, and none of them looked familiar. The lack of men in the classroom didn't bother Liz. She wasn't interested in meeting guys anyway. She liked her alone time and preferred a good book to any guy she had ever met.

The lecture that day had minimal course content, as most time was spent outlining the course material and Professor Gilby's expectations from the students. There were two texts to be read and a project of research with other optional reading and two papers to be written about the research. The marking system was made clear, with the two papers, a mid-term test, and a final exam comprising 90% of the mark and 10% for attendance and involvement in the lectures. Almost all students received that last 10% in full, as it was hard to not get involved due to the way Professor Gilby conducted his time in the lecture theatre. There was no exception to that today…

Professor Gilby ended the class with a participation exercise. "Hands up: Who here knows of an elderly person that is NOT in good health?" About three quarters of the students raised their hands. Both Liz and Caroline knew this process well and raised their hands. This was a typical start to a Professor Gilby course. He continued: "OK, those of you with raised hands can put them down and remain seated while the rest of you please stand up." He waited a minute and then added: "If you didn't raise your hand and you still haven't stood up, you might want to consider joining a support group for self-assurance. In my classes, I'd prefer students who aren't shy about getting involved." Several more students rose. "Now, every person who is seated, take a good look at those who are standing. These are people who will need your help finding a sick old person!" The room filled with suppressed laughter.

"Quite seriously, for the next lecture I am going to ask that each of you return with a written description of one old person that you know quite well.

Students who are standing can sit now." He paused for a moment until the noise of shuffling desks subsided. "The old person can be sick or healthy, but if you know of an elderly person that you consider sick in one form or another, please choose that person. Describe them physically: age, physical appearance, et cetera. Then describe their lifestyle. What are their activities? What are their hobbies? How active are they in their community? You get the idea. There are no specific questions that I want answered. If you've chosen a healthy person, answer the same general questions, what is their lifestyle? Are they generally happy? Take the time to interview these people if you want. This is not a scientific gathering of data, but more of a social exercise in our class getting to know a group of elderly people. We'll be working with them for the rest of this term, so choose your person wisely. You will need to follow up with them. And try to be discrete. Let them know they are needed for your course, but you don't have to insult them by letting them know it is because they are old. Be kind."

"What do you consider as being sick?" came an anonymous question from somewhere in the rear of the lecture theatre.

"First, would whomever asked that question please stand and identify yourself. It is a great question, and you need to be identified, because that is the kind of participation that will get you marks." Professor Gilby waited until a student rose and said her name, then he made a note on a sheet that looked like the class roster. He continued "Great question indeed. Let's get some input into what your peers think about what it means to be sick."

What followed was a respectful group discussion regarding what many students felt about what being sick meant. Was it only physical illness? What about mental illness? Did it have to be life threatening? Were any life-long disability issues to be included? The last point had many students become very animated about the thought of a disability being considered sick. Before the discussion got too out of hand, Professor Gilby raised his voice just enough to be heard above the conversations that had sprouted up in many areas of the room.

"That's enough discussion for today. In my future lectures there will be plenty of time to break into groups and discuss this and other issues that will come up. For this exercise, I will leave each of you to determine for yourselves what is meant by being sick. Write your thoughts on that topic along with the data you gather from your chosen victim. Uhm, I mean elderly person." Chuckles filled the room. "Class dismissed."

And with those last two words the room became a bustle of noise as students gathered their books and note pads and began to leave. A din of voices rose as many of the students continued their interrupted conversations about the definition of sick. Liz remained in her seat. She didn't even notice that Caroline had gone to the front of the theatre and perched herself on the desk beside Professor Gilby. Just as she became aware of Caroline's departure from her seat, Tiffany eased herself into the seat on her other side.

"Hey Tiff. I didn't see where you were sitting in this class, or I would have had you join us." Liz offered.

"I'm not in this class. Well, I'm in this course, but not in this lecture slot. I take it from Professor Wilkinson. She teaches in the last lecture slot of the day."

"I thought Wilkinson was a hard marker. And I thought you liked Professor Gilby after taking last year's course with him."

"I'm not impressed with him at all. I don't find him very professional. He's . . . well, he's just not right for me. Professor Wilkinson is much more suited to my style. I've already taken two other courses from her. She is professional to the core and really pushes me to study harder and learn more. I've no regrets for having taken last year's course with Steve, but I do like Professor Wilkinson much more."

Steve! She referred to him as Steve! *Does everybody?* though Liz. Maybe there was something to be said about him not being very professional. But no, he was good at how he got the class involved and forced participation in class. He was what Liz wanted in a prof.

"What do you think this meeting is about?" Liz changed the topic and hoped for a little enlightenment.

"He told me it was a job offer, but I don't think I'm interested. I already work two shifts at the bookstore on campus and serve tables at The Spotted Gecko on Friday and Saturday nights. Plus, my mom has me helping her at her housecleaning job on weekends. I have enough on my plate, but I thought I'd hear him out at least." Tiffany was bunching up her long black hair and tying it into a ponytail as she spoke. Liz thought of her as being beautiful as well, just not as beautiful as Caroline. "The Gecko pays huge in tips, and the bookstore is minimum wage, but I get a staff discount on my books. With the price of textbooks, that's almost more value than the salary." Tiffany shook her head a little, so the new ponytail was hanging straight behind her.

The Spotted Gecko was the vegan restaurant nearby on Cambie Street. It wasn't the cheapest, so it wasn't a favourite for most of the students, but that meant the patrons had money and tipped well. At least better than students do. Liz also noticed for the first time that Tiffany was always wearing what was referred to as a "tip-top." The kind of top that revealed enough cleavage that men in a restaurant would always tip a little extra. Today was no exception.

Liz became a little jealous at the thought of Tiffany holding down two jobs and wondered if her mom paid her for helping as well. Liz hadn't managed to even find one, and her funds had run out while her student loans were piling up. Her summer job was a huge relief, but Liz was still feeling financial pressure. Her father either couldn't help or didn't want to. He had said that he wanted her to learn about life, not just what they teach you in university. Liz partly respected that, but partly wished she had some support.

"A job offer? Do you know what it is?" Liz asked. She was excited at the thought of any form of income, and the thought of having Steve as her employer again put the excitement into overdrive.

"Don't know a thing" quipped Tiffany. "I bet it's just doing more door-to-door surveys. I bet the three of us didn't get enough done to hit his minimum or something. I'm not going door to door again. I've had enough of the walking, and I am totally tired of all the rejections I got. My ego is bruised enough for the rest of my life!"

*Rejections?* Liz hadn't been rejected very often, and if ever she was it was always in the politest of manners and usually with valid explanations. "I'm putting my kids down for a nap," or "I work from home, and I can't take time for a survey," or other good excuses. Or maybe they were just that—excuses, and Liz hadn't picked up on the fact that she was being rejected. Was she? Or was Tiff being rejected because she was Indigenous? *Were some people really that ignorant?*

"Tiff, I enjoyed the work, and I'd be happy to do it again. I especially liked it when you did find a candidate for the extended version, and they would ask you in for a coffee. I got to know a little bit about each of them, and I really enjoyed those visits."

"The visits? I found most of my long survey people were just old folks that I had no interest in getting to know. I'd rather be with my friends. Hey, Steve's waving us up to the front. Let's go."

As Liz followed Tiffany to where Caroline was perched on the lecture theatre's desk, she thought about what Tiff had just said. Possibly she was enjoying the visits because she didn't have many friends in Vancouver. They were all back in her hometown, and she hadn't kept in contact with any of them. After high school ended, it seemed everyone went their own separate way. Maybe she should try to connect with some of them. She had recently been invited to sign up for the newest free email provider, Gmail, and wondered how she could find out if any of her old classmates had email now and how she could get their email addresses. Her thoughts were redirected when Professor Gilby started to speak.

"Good morning, girls. I haven't had much of a chance to speak to any of you since you've handed in your surveys. I must say, I'm impressed. You three have accomplished a *lot*! So, how's it going?"

"Wonderful!" Caroline chimed in first. "I really enjoyed the chance to work outdoors, and I met a lot of interesting people. So, like, you're happy with the number of surveys we've done?"

"More than happy. And that's why I wanted to talk to you three today. How was your summer, Liz?"

Liz found herself blushing a little. "Fine. Same as what Caroline said." She felt a little stupid that she couldn't add anything more. She knew she found Steve to be very attractive but was becoming uncomfortable about potentially revealing that in front of these classmates.

Tiffany somehow must have sensed the awkwardness and added "My summer was OK too. So, what's this about a job offer?"

*Wow*, thought Liz, *talk about being forward and cutting to the chase!*

"Well, did any of you three know how extensive this survey was?" He continued, and all three heads were slowly shaking a "no" response. "I hired three girls to do surveys in ten different cities. Calgary, Winnipeg, Toronto, Montreal—you get the picture. Now I have collected the thousands of surveys I needed to work with, but I need them entered onto a computer to do the analysis. I've purchased a brand-new Mac and some software to manage the data once it's entered, but first I need it entered. My grant money allows me to pay more than minimum, not much more, but enough to make this a decent job offer. I just want to know if you three would be interested. You did great work this summer, so I wanted to reward your work ethic and give you first dibs on this opportunity."

"Sorry" Tiffany replied, "but I've already got two other jobs, and my schedule just wouldn't allow for adding a third, so I'm out. I also have an upcoming class that I have to get to, so I'm going to bow out and leave, if that's OK Steve. I appreciate the offer though." And with that, Tiff was gone. It was almost as if she couldn't leave the room fast enough.

"How about you two?" Steve alternated eye contact between Liz and Caroline.

"I'd love to!" Caroline spoke next. "Like, gimme the deets!"

"I'd love to as well" Liz hurriedly added. "I'm not working anywhere, and I could sure use the money!" *God*, she thought, *did I sound too desperate?* But she wished she had answered before Caroline. She really wanted Steve to know how much this meant to her. Not only was this providing a job that she dearly needed, but it was also working for her favourite prof. Life seemed to be going in the right direction!

"Well," continued Steve, "There is a lot of data entry work to do, and I am under a bit of pressure to get this done in a timely fashion so I can proceed with my research. I'm hoping to present the first summary of it by the end of March next year. I have one challenge to this job situation: I couldn't manage to get an office for you two to work in, so the only work area is in my office, which can accommodate only one of you at a time. I'll have to be at my desk while this work gets done. I'm not allowed to have unattended students using my office. Do you two think you can work out a schedule to share the work I need done?"

"Sure!" Liz got in her answer first, and Caroline nodded yes as well. "How important is it to have great typing skills? I've never taken a typing course or anything." Liz almost immediately regretted asking this, as she really wanted this opportunity to work out for her.

"Not a problem at all. I've set up the new Mac with a data entry system specific to this survey. I've worked on it for most of the summer. You'll simply have to select the answers from drop-down menus for the three basic questions. The only typing will be the address of the survey and the final comment section, and that is only if the client provided any comments. Typing would help a little, but not that much. OK? Oh, I should add, quite a few of the surveys are the long form. They go into a totally different data file. I have the software set up for that too, but there is considerable typing for those long surveys: names, addresses, and long-form answers. I'm guessing that is less than five percent of the whole pile though. OK?"

"Sure, but, like, what are your office hours? Like, when should we be trying to schedule ourselves to do this?" Caroline asked a much better question, and Liz wished she had thought of it.

"Well, I work every evening until about nine or so, and I'm here in the mornings by no later than ten. I am only lecturing this class you were just in and one first-year class, so that takes away about six or seven daytime hours a week. Quick math tells me there's almost fifty hours available every week, and if we aren't making enough progress in a month or so I will think about coming in on weekends. When the two of you have time to coordinate your schedules just come to my office and use different colour highlighters to mark your work hours on my office-hours schedule. It's posted on the wall right beside my office door. OK?"

"Sure! We could even go now, right Caroline?" once again, Liz regretted how eager she had sounded, but Caroline was smiling and said "sure!" to this option.

"Good!" said Steve as he grabbed his leather jacket and started to retrieve his lecture materials from the desk Caroline was seated on. Liz couldn't avoid noticing that Caroline had positioned herself in such a way that Steve had to nudge her leg off his loose papers that were on the desk. *Was she flirting with the prof? Is that why Caroline had worn such a short skirt?* Liz didn't have long to ponder these thoughts as Caroline slid off the desk and both she and Steve started walking toward the door.

In the hallway and up the four flights of stairs to Steve's office, Caroline managed to keep beside Steve and continued to have a conversation with him. Liz was only a step or two behind them but couldn't hear much of what was being discussed. She did hear part of one question about music but didn't hear enough of either the question or the answer to really understand what was being discussed.

As they approached the schedule posted outside of Steve's office, Caroline turned to Liz and asked, "Do you have, like, headphones or do you want me to leave mine here?"

"What?"

Steve cut in: "Caroline asked if you could listen to music while you entered the data. I said I had no objection, so long as you wore headphones, so it didn't distract me from my work."

"Great!" Liz replied. "I have my own headphones." she lied to Caroline. "There's no need for you to leave yours here." Liz was wondering why she felt the need to lie. *Was it to avoid Caroline making extra trips to Steve's office and using the retrieval of the headphones as an excuse? Or was Caroline just being too nice for Liz's comfort?* Liz also realized this now meant she would have to buy headphones and that was an expense she really didn't need to add to her financial picture.

They approached the door to Steve's office and Steve turned to the hallway wall where his office hours were posted. It was a printout of an Excel spreadsheet, with each row representing a half hour and each of the five columns representing one workday. "Don't highlight the entire space, as I may need to add items myself, but simply put a dot on the left side of each time slot you will be here. Caroline, you take this pink pen, and Liz can be blue."

Now Liz switched from her concern about the headphones to wondering why she didn't get the pink marker. Then she wondered why this even concerned her. *Was it Steve that brought out this strange thought process, or Caroline?* She was flustered and not happy with being flustered. *Why was this happening?*

"I'll go first!" Caroline started toward the calendar.

"Let's take turns." Liz replied. "I'm sure we can agree on who works when." She reached into her purse and retrieved her class schedule, while Caroline did the same. In a manner of minutes the calendar on the wall was populated with dozens of pink and blue dots. Liz noticed that Caroline was taking the later hours on Monday and Wednesday evening, so she added her blue dots on Tuesday and Thursday evenings.

# A NATURAL CAUSE

When the calendar was about half filled, Caroline said "I'd better stop with those hours. Like, I've really got to leave time for studying, and, like, I have a social life to think of too."

"Me too." Added Liz, but then instantly regretted it as she knew she could really use the money that more hours of work would bring. She also knew that she had no social life at all, but she chose to keep that issue to herself.

"Step into my office then, and I'll show you what needs to be done." Steve opened his office door and stepped inside, closely followed by both women.

The office was relatively sparse, with two desks and two chairs. One desk was in front of a wall covered with bookshelves and was facing toward them, with a chair behind it, while the other was turned ninety degrees from it, with a chair that backed to the doorway where they were standing. One large window spanned the entire outside wall of the building, and it looked out onto an open quad where pigeons dodged the students that strolled in different directions. Liz could see that other students had gathered in small groups to chat. She noticed that the flowering cherry trees were no longer covered in pink blossoms but were now beautiful puffs of green leaves. The second desk faced toward that window, giving whoever sat there a great view. Liz's attention returned to the inside of the office. The walls were bare, and bookshelves at one end of the office were almost empty. Even the desktops were clear of any items. A half-dozen moving boxes were stacked against a wall. Liz was staring at them when she asked, "Are you just moving in?"

Steve smiled. "Not at all. This has been my office for two years now. Those boxes are why you're here. They're filled with the surveys that need to be entered onto the computer. There's still a few more boxes to come. The courier hasn't delivered them yet. If you two have the time I could show you what the data entry work will entail. Do you have a few more minutes?"

"Sure!" they both chimed.

Steve started the computer on the first desk, the one facing the window, and wheeled up the chair that was between the further desk and the bookshelf. He had each of them take a seat and stood behind them. "I don't like showing by example. I'd rather you follow my directions and type things in yourselves. You will learn more by doing it this way." He then directed them through passwords for logging on, entering another password for his added security system, and starting the survey software. As he leaned forward to point at items on the screen Liz could feel his hand holding the back of her chair. She intentionally sat more upright and rested the back of her shoulder against his hand. He didn't move his hand away.

After entering one survey as an example of what they were going to be doing, Steve added, "That's about it. This may become very mundane work, but I cannot stress enough how important it is to be one hundred percent accurate. The integrity of my research depends on it."

"We'll do our best. I do have one question though. What is the result you're hoping for with this research? Give us the big picture." Liz was pleased with herself for asking this.

"Well, that is a loaded question. First, anyone doing research should approach any survey work that they do with an open mind. Anticipating a specific result can taint your view of the data that you gather and skew the results in favour of your bias." Steve paused. "With that said, I hope to gather a statistical analysis of what future healthcare spending needs the government may be facing for our aging population. Beyond that, I also want a general feeling for what our wealthier population expects in the way of eldercare. That was the reason for the long version of the survey. I have a feeling that these well-heeled folks won't settle for the current offerings, with tight meal schedules, poor meal selection, minimal planned outings, etc. That part is less scientific in nature and will require follow-up surveys and other work. That is the reason for the general comments section of the survey, and we'll probably go back to a lot of these folks with a second survey next summer. We'll also be starting a whole new batch of initial surveys from new people with questions tailored to clarify this year's results. The whole project may take five or six years to complete."

Caroline swung her chair around to face Steve. "Whatever got you interested in these old people in the first place? Like, was this your focus when you were a student?"

"Not at all. Well, I majored in sociology when I considered myself pre-law. I'm a lawyer. I was called to the bar four years ago."

"What? Then why . . . " Liz was surprised at hearing this.

"Let me explain. I majored in sociology for my arts degree, then went into law. I graduated, was called to the bar, and only lasted a few months. I hated it! I came back and returned to sociology, and I'm currently working on my

PhD. I get paid a whole lot less, but I can look in the mirror and like who's looking back at me. Law wouldn't have allowed me to do that. I tell the class I'm Professor Gilby, but really, I'm an instructor, not a professor. I hope to be a full professor someday though."

Liz realized she was still holding the back of her shoulder against Steve's hand. She leaned forward and spun her chair to face him as well. "Why did you hate law so much? That's a lot of studying for just a few months' work."

"Well, I was in criminal law. My first case involved defending somebody that was as guilty as sin, and I just couldn't do it. I asked to switch to family law and had another ugly experience with a family's estate. The children of the deceased were about to inherit several million dollars each, and everything was hung up because they couldn't agree on some petty things. Stupid things really. A piece of artwork, some silverware, a teak dining set. Petty things. And the firm I was with was happy to have them continue the squabble rather than solve the issue because they could continue to bill the estate for all the time that their fighting was wasting. I brought this up to a senior partner, and the decision was made that I didn't fit the qualifications that the firm needed. I didn't argue. I thought that they were scum, and I was glad to not fit that profile. When I investigated a few other firms, they mostly operated in the same manner. Being a scummy lawyer wasn't for me. I took a month or two to decide what to do next, and here I am: Professor Gilby. I mean, instructor Gilby."

"That's amazing!" Caroline was looking surprised. "So, like, you're still a lawyer?"

"Yes. But a non-practicing one. I have kept the option open to return to law, but I can't see myself doing that. I've found my happy place right here. I think I've found my niche in life."

"This research is your niche? What reward is there in it for you? You're way too young to be concerned about eldercare. Or is it, like, something to do with the Aldbrecht Foundation? What is that anyway?" Caroline was full of questions.

"I'm feeling much better about helping to solve a problem that society will be facing and that's my reward. I feel good about what I'm doing."

"The Aldbrecht Foundation?"

"That is a longer story and for another time. I want to get to my work now. I'll see each of you when you come back for your work shifts. I'll also need you to fill out all the necessary employment forms at that time too. Employment contract, tax deductions, that kind of stuff. Why don't we go for lunch some day and you can continue to grill me with questions then, OK?"

"I have one important question: how much are you paying us?" Liz felt a little awkward, but needed to know what she could expect for income. She had bills to pay.

"I'm sorry, I should have mentioned. I'm budgeting for three dollars an hour above minimum wage. We can review that after a couple of months and see if I can afford more, but I'm limited to the government grant money I have and I can't tell exactly how that will work out just yet. OK?"

Both Liz and Caroline agreed to the terms and stood up to leave the office. As they said their good-byes and exited the office Steve added "One more thing I should mention. I am getting a second computer too. When it arrives, I may be able to have both of you do this work at the same time, but I still have to find a big enough space. I'll keep you both posted."

As they started down the hallway Liz turned to Caroline, "Who knew? Steve is a lawyer!"

"Yeah, like, once he mentioned it to me after class at the end of last year, but I didn't ask any questions and I thought he wasn't a lawyer now. There's more to him than meets the eye. Like, I've gotta run to my next class. See you at Steve's next class. Or, like, when we switch off shifts at this job. I'm looking forward to this!"

Liz started to realize how often Caroline said "like," probably without realizing it. It was getting on her nerves a little. She thought it made Caroline sound stupid, and Liz knew she wasn't stupid. She was brilliant. It was probably just a bad habit, but it was annoying.

At the top of the staircase, Liz asked Caroline "Don't you find him way too young to be a professor?"

"You mean instructor. Like, way too young. And way too hot! I could ride that guy all night long, no hesitation. Like, I wonder if he's married?"

Liz bristled a bit at Caroline's interest in Steve. "I don't think so. He doesn't wear a ring."

"So, you looked! Obviously, you're into him too. What's not to like. He's super smart, seems really kind, and, like, movie star looks. And a lawyer too. Like, you didn't know about that at all, did you?"

"No" was all Liz could reply, embarrassed that the ring comment had the impact that it did. *Why let Caroline know who I'm interested in, especially if she is interested in him too?*

Heading down the steps, Liz excused herself by the third floor, saying she had to be somewhere, but really, she just wanted to be alone with her thoughts. And she didn't want to hear Caroline say "like" one more time. It had been an unusual day. A good day. But unusual.

# November 2004

Liz sat at the desk entering survey data. She had noticed on her first visit to Steve's office that her desk faced the window, but the angle from her seat meant the only things she could see outside were the sky and the top of a couple of the buildings on campus. Steve's desk was at a ninety-degree angle from hers and faced where she sat, with his chair on the far side of it, between the desk and his bookshelves. His view was, well, her. She often felt awkward knowing that he might be staring at her, but she would have to turn to her side to confirm that notion and she didn't want him to think she was checking in on him. She had to work at trying to ignore that uncomfortable feeling.

Liz stroked a red pen across the completed survey she had just entered into the database. Dropping it on top of the other completed surveys that were piled high in the box beside the desk, she retrieved a new one from the box on the opposite side and placed it into the clip board mounted on the side of the computer screen. It was a long version of the survey, and her shoulders dropped a little in disappointment. This particular Toronto student doing the surveys had horrible handwriting, and while the short survey consisted mostly of tick marks that were only a few clicks on the computer, the long survey involved many comment boxes. The amount of typing needed to enter the data from a long survey was quite extensive, and this stack of surveys was almost impossible to read. She sighed.

"What's up?" Steve had been reading at his desk, but obviously he had heard her sigh.

"Nothing really. It's just this person's handwriting. It's almost illegible, and she's not very good at writing. Her sentences are more point form notes. I'm having to restructure what she wrote, assuming I can read it in the first place. It is really slowing down my progress."

Steve walked around his desk and came to her chair and placed his hand on her shoulder. "Look, I'm really impressed with how things are going, and I also have two things to share with you. First, what is the code number at the top of the page? That will identify the person who did this survey work, and I can make sure they don't get hired next summer." Liz pointed to the code on the page. She hadn't noticed the letters and numbers at the top of the page before. She wondered what her own code was. Steve continued: "Second, I have some good news. At least I think it's good news. The second computer arrived and soon you and Caroline won't have to share this one computer."

"Great! I've only crossed paths with Caroline when we have your class together and a couple of times when we were changing our shifts here, but we both have said we'd like to work together on this. Data entry is pretty boring, and just having someone with you will make it less tedious."

"So, I'm chopped liver? I'm not good enough company?" Steve removed his hand from Liz's shoulder and was smiling as he poked fun at Liz.

"Oh no. Not at all. That's not what I meant!" Liz could feel the blood rushing to her cheeks. She was a little embarrassed by what she had said, but she also was afraid she would somehow let it be known just how much she was enjoying being in the same room with Steve. They had spoken very little, as she wanted to impress him with how dedicated she was to the work he was paying her to do, but the few conversations they had were her favourite part of the job. Caroline was right. He was hot!

She also noticed something else. Since she had started working on this data entry project and spending more time with Steve, she didn't have as many "blue" days. Those days when she felt she could barely get out of bed. The thoughts of spending time doing this work while Steve was near her made her happy.

"Relax. I'm just yanking your chain. I have one other thing…"

Just as Steve was about to add to the conversation, Caroline appeared in the doorway of the office. "Hey! You two are crowding my space. Like, It's my shift now."

Liz hadn't noticed the time. "Sorry!"

"You say that too much Liz. Hey Steve, like, how's your day going?" Caroline gave the back of Steve's arm a light squeeze.

"Good! Actually, I'm glad you're both here. I was just sharing some info with Liz that I want you to be in on too. I just got a second computer. It'll take me a day or two to set it up but then both of you won't have to alternate shifts. You can both work at the same time."

"Great!" Caroline cheerfully chimed, and at the same time gave Steve's arm another gentle squeeze.

"But" continued Steve, "I don't have an office space for this to be set up. I considered two computers on this one desk, but the space just won't allow for it. So, with Christmas break starting on Monday, I was wondering, how would both of you feel about working over the break from my condo. It's a two bedroom, and one bedroom is set up as an office space with plenty of room for two desks. It is a thirty-minute commute to campus, so I'd recommend longer shifts, or you'll spend way too much time commuting. What do you two think?"

"Your wife agrees with this setup? We won't be in her way?" Caroline took a small step away from Steve as she asked.

"I don't have a wife. Studying for law doesn't leave much time for dating, and since I've come back to campus to be an instructor my life hasn't had much free time either. I'm guilty of being single."

"That's great!" Liz added, and immediately realized what she had said. "I mean, it's great that there's nobody to be disturbed if we work in your condo. I'm happy to do that."

"Again, chopped liver?" Steve smiled widely.

Caroline faced Steve. "Like, I'd be good with working over the break too, Steve. But . . . uh . . . chopped liver?"

"It's an inside joke. Liz was pointing out what poor company I provided while she worked here all alone."

"Ouch." Liz turned to Caroline. "I just meant I'd prefer if you and I could work together. I don't have a vehicle. Do you?"

"I take the bus. Like, I know you live on campus and will have to commute both ways, but I'm, like, staying in a place close to Main, on Broadway. Where is your condo, Steve?"

"Not far from your home then, I think. I'm in the area where they're planning the new Olympic Village. Listen, it's almost my usual lunch time.

Are either of you available to have lunch with me? We could grab something at the food court and discuss the logistics. OK?"

"I missed breakfast, I'd love to grab lunch." Caroline said. "I can walk to the new Olympic Village area from my house, so like, that's perfect!"

I'm available too." added Liz: "Available for lunch I mean." She was getting frustrated with how awkward she always was, and how often she made herself blush from this awkwardness.

Steve must have sensed her feelings at that moment and came to her rescue by getting the conversation back to be about lunch. "Great, let's just walk over to the food court. I'm vegan, but you two can choose whatever you want and join me at one of the outdoor tables. It's too beautiful a day to be indoors."

Liz had grown up in the country, and she was relatively unfamiliar with what being vegan meant. She had tried being a vegetarian, but when she went back home for a visit her "vegetarian diet" had not gone over well with her father, so she went back to eating meat. She did most of the cooking for her dad when she went home, but he always wanted some form of meat with his meals, so she just cooked the same dinners for them both.

Having some income from this job with Steve meant she could afford lunches out now, and when they got to the food court she treated herself to a Japanese-style stir fry with chicken and mushrooms on rice. As she approached Steve and Caroline, who were already seated and into a conversation of some sort, she noticed they both had salads that were in identical bowls and had obviously come from the same vendor. She regretted not staying with them.

As she took a seat she offered: "I hope you don't mind if I eat meat in front of you." She was unsure of what to do if either one of them objected.

"Not at all," said Steve. "I've only been vegan since my travels to India. I discovered so many vegan options and amazing flavours when I was there, I decided to try sticking with it."

"I'm not vegan," Caroline added, "but, like, I've got dairy and gluten issues, so, like, salads are the easiest option when I'm not cooking for myself."

"So, what were you two talking about?" Liz asked as she tried to avoid the chicken while she picked away at the stir fry.

"I was just explaining to Caroline what the situation with the Aldbrecht Foundation was all about. I receive funding from it to do this research, and because I get some funding from them, then the government is much more prone to also provide funding. If it wasn't for that foundation, you two might have been stuck with jobs at McDonalds for the summer."

Both Liz and Caroline looked a little confused.

"It's like this" added Steve. "When you apply for government grants, the likelihood of receiving a grant is greatly reduced if they realize that they alone are the one source of funding. If you have at least one other source, the chances of getting a government grant are greatly improved. It's like getting a loan from a bank—they're way more likely to approve you for a loan if you can prove to them that you are financially sound and don't really need the loan. If you go to them hat in hand, saying that you are completely reliant on getting a loan from them, you will likely be denied. It's one of life's paradoxes. So, getting the Aldbrecht Foundation money meant I could get the government funding, and getting funding is what really causes the university to employ me. Employment at the university is heavily based on what funding you can bring to the table. Without funding, we'd all be out of a job."

Both women sat and pondered this issue. More questions came up about the funding that Steve answered, but then Liz asked about something of a more personal nature about Steve: "What ever made you focus on this specific area? Why eldercare?" She spent more time pushing the food around in her bowl than she spent eating it.

"Well, I guess it started with my grandmother. The one on my maternal side. My mother's mother. She was getting frail in her later years, and before she passed away the health care system had her panelled. That's when they get people in the medical world to assess her needs and her abilities. They determined it was necessary to provide care for her twenty-four hours a day, but they had no spaces available for that level of care in any facility. She was going to be put on a very long waiting list. They then said she qualified for full time home care, but they could only provide somebody to check on her every morning for about an hour or so. They had no staff available to provide anything more. My mom was my grandmother's only child. That meant my mom and dad had to step in. They took turns living with her, but that also meant missing work. After their allowed sick time from work and their holidays were all used up, my mother quit her job and lived with her mother. Because my mom had quit her job she didn't even qualify for Employment

Insurance, even after thirty-some years of being on the job and paying for it. All this happened while I was studying law and articling.

"After four long years of this caregiving, my grandmother passed away. She was still living at home but was incapable of even feeding or toileting herself. She finally got approved for a care facility about two weeks after she died. After my grandma had passed, my mother had real trouble finding a job again. She was in her mid-fifties, had quit her previous job, and hadn't worked for four years, so most places didn't want to hire her. Overall, the whole process almost put my parents into financial ruin. Fortunately, they were frugal people and have managed to get by, and my grandmother did leave them half of her estate, which did amount to quite a few dollars once they sold her home. But I know there's a lot of folks who wouldn't have been so lucky. That got me interested in this area of eldercare. I was the beneficiary of the other half of my grandmother's estate, which allowed me to leave the law industry and return to campus as an instructor. Here I am now. End of story."

"Wow! Like, how are your parents doing now?" Caroline asked.

Liz cringed at the "like". She realized it was probably very noticeable. She bent her head down to face the rice bowl in front of her.

"Well, my father has since passed away just two years ago, around when I started working at the university. My mother calls herself retired. She couldn't find a job anywhere, and now has my dad's pension to support her, plus she will soon get her government pension. She couldn't maintain their home, so she sold their house and lives in an apartment now, and I'm looking after her finances. She'll be just fine."

Liz looked up. "What about the Aldbrecht Foundation? How did you discover them?"

"You know, that's a story for another time. I'm thinking we should get back to the office. There's still work to be done. I also have to give you the condo information. Address, codes to get in, and a little information about keeping this secret from the neighbours. They wouldn't appreciate a business being run from the condo. The strata board would probably shut this down. All right?"

"Sure, and we need, like, the hours you want us to go there."

Liz cringed again, and this time she was sure Caroline saw it.

"The hours are all up to you. I'm OK with you two working in the one room while I'm working in the condo, or asleep in the other bedroom even. It's totally your call. Let's go back to the office and set up a time when I can have you both there and I'll give you the grand tour. OK?"

As Liz got up to leave, she put the lid back on her stir-fry bowl. She hadn't eaten more than a bite or two and didn't want to waste good food. "I'm available this whole weekend. What about you, Caroline?"

"Same. I've got nothing on. Well, except Saturday night. Oh, and I do have something Friday night too. So, like, Saturday afternoon?"

Liz felt envious of Caroline's active weekend. *Why couldn't mine be busy too?* She did relish her alone time but felt she would like to get out occasionally.

"Well, I'm home until four on Saturday. Can you two make it sometime before that?"

Both Liz & Caroline agreed to come to his condo at one o'clock, and the three of them headed back to Steve's office. Liz gathered her items from the desk to make room for Caroline to get herself set up to work, and as she excused herself to leave the room she couldn't help but notice Steve place his arm around Caroline's shoulder and lean in to quietly say something to her. Half wanting to linger in the doorway to watch more of this interaction, she forced herself to turn away and leave. She didn't like what she was seeing. She wanted Steve to be close with her, not with Caroline!

## December 2004

Liz leaned back from the computer screen and stretched her arms and neck. She had been at the data entry task for over six hours, and she was getting physically sore from lack of movement. She looked out of the window at False Creek. It was cold, and there was almost no activity on the water. Although the view of the bay was quite panoramic, she could only see one boat moving. She wondered how this part of the ocean, a relatively short bay, became named False Creek. Did somebody think there was a creek at the end of the bay and when they found out there wasn't they declared it false? Or was False actually somebody's name. But Creek? Strange name for a body of salt water.

The sky had been grey for a few days in a row. The occasional breeze caused brown leaves to skitter along the sidewalk that surrounded False Creek. She thought they looked like nervous mice, scurrying to find shelter. The smell of decaying foliage mixed with the salt air and created a mildly rich aroma. She had always liked the smells of late autumn. It made her think of her dad, and of being home. She wished he hadn't gone away this Christmas. She'd rather be with him right now.

Just as she was about to start entering the data from another survey, she heard the lock on the front door being opened. Excitedly, she stood up and walked into the living area. Her shoulders fell when she realized it was Caroline.

"Hey girl! Happy Saturday!" Caroline beamed. "I didn't expect to see you here. I thought you'd, like, be done by now!"

For the past three weeks the two of them had been working from Steve's condo, and Liz had become much closer with Caroline. The bedroom office they shared was the larger of the two bedrooms in the condo. Steve had mentioned that the smaller one suited his needs, and the larger one was more fitted to being an office. There was enough room for two desks with chairs, and a small loveseat also graced one wall. The bookshelves were filled to overflowing, mostly with law books, and a four-drawer file cabinet stood at one end of the shelves. Opposite the bedroom's doorway was a huge window, facing out to a view of False Creek. They could see Science World's geodesic dome on the right, and across the water were the office towers of downtown Vancouver.

"I think I'm done. I'm exhausted. I've been here since eleven this morning."

"Well, I'm starving and, like, about to make dinner. Care to join?" Caroline dropped a large paper bag on the kitchen counter. Green produce was protruding from the bag, and Liz noticed a smaller container from the market on Granville in Caroline's other hand.

Liz held herself back from cringing at the word "like." "Sure! I'd love to. What's on the menu?"

"I'm making 'Pasta a-la-Caroline.' It's my own recipe. It's vegan. Steve's probably going to join us too. He's just parking his car." She placed the small container on the counter and started to unpack the groceries.

Steve's pending arrival wasn't a surprise to Liz. He was usually around when they were working, and it was only rarely that she got to work alone like she had today. "Were you two shopping together?"

"No. Not today. I was just coming up the sidewalk when I noticed him driving down the ramp to the underground parking. I don't think he even saw me. Want some wine?"

Before Liz could answer, the front door was being opened again, and Steve walked in. Caroline automatically got down three wine glasses, uncorked the wine, and started to pour.

"Well, this is a wonderful sight to come home to! When are you two going to stop playing house and get down to doing some data entry?"

"I was!" Liz reacted. "I've been here since eleven this morning doing nothing but!"

"Whoa there! I'm just kidding. You know, I came by around two o'clock and you were so focussed on the job that I don't think you even notice me coming or going. I know. You've been working. *Relax!*"

Liz was a little shocked to realize she had missed his earlier visit. She always tried to pay attention to him. She enjoyed his company, and always took a little time to chat when he was around. *Had she entirely missed his stopping by earlier?* She was disappointed with herself for that.

Caroline was handing out the glasses of wine.

"What am I enjoying" Steve asked as he took a sip.

"It's that Argentinian wine you bought for us last week. The Malbec. I really enjoyed it, and I'm thinking it will be perfect with the ravioli I just bought at the market on Granville. It's vegan, a mushroom filling, and I'm making the sauce from scratch. It should only take about twenty minutes. Why don't you two head to the living room and sit while I, like, put this together. Go! Go!" And with the hand motions to match, Caroline shooed the other two out of the kitchen.

"That's one!" Steve smiled as he said that.

"One?" Liz asked.

Caroline quickly flashed a stuck-out tongue at Steve. "He wants me to stop saying 'like.' He thinks it sounds stupid and makes me come across as stupid. I'm trying, but he always seems to catch me. He counts them each time we're together. It's very annoying."

"And you've improved immensely! C'mon Liz, let's, like, leave her, like, now." Caroline flashed another tongue at Steve, but he ignored the gesture while he grabbed Liz's elbow and guided her out of the kitchen. He paused by his sound system to put on a CD and soon both kitchen and living room were filled with sounds of hits of the eighties. "I'm old school!" he quipped as they each took a spot on the living room couch.

As Liz sat down, she shrugged her shoulders and tilted her head from side to side. She reached up with her free hand and tried to squeeze the back of her neck. Steve noticed Liz's discomfort and, without saying a word, eased her a little forward on the couch and angled himself behind her and started to massage her neck and shoulders. "That feels great" Liz almost inaudibly whispered.

Sitting there, they were still in full view of Caroline. They both watched as she filled a pot with water and got out a pan for the sauce. As she started slicing vegetables, Steve stopped massaging Liz and asked: "Are you going home to be with your dad for Christmas?"

"No. I had hoped to, but we both decided that I should stay in Vancouver instead. It will be my first Christmas away from home. Now that my dad's on his own, he's taken to travelling a bit. He's in Mexico right now. I guess he felt stuck with having to raise me alone all those years, and now he's spreading his wings a little. I don't blame him, but I will miss spending Christmas at home."

"Small world" Steve added. "My mom is travelling too. Costa Rica. I don't have a family to have Christmas with either. Maybe we should spend it here together. I do make a great veggie loaf. Probably not the turkey dinner you're used to, but better than eating a TV dinner alone!"

Liz could hear Caroline coughing a little in the kitchen. "You two are lucky. I'm stuck with the regular family routine, and I hate it." She was dicing a tomato, and as she scraped it from the cutting board into the frying pan she added: "I think this is the first time we've all had a dinner together. It's usually just two of us. Me and you, Steve. Or me and Liz. But never all three. Maybe I could convince my family that you two are my new family and I could just join you for Christmas too."

Liz wasn't sure if Caroline was serious or not and hoped she wasn't. She was very keen on the idea of a dinner with Steve. And Christmas at that! She had shared a couple of dinners at the condo with Caroline, but she wasn't even sure if Steve was aware of that.

"If you're serious, I'd like to come for Christmas dinner. What can I bring?" Liz had been fearing she would be spending this Christmas having dinner on campus, where various residences would gather the remaining students in one location to dine together. She would be surrounded by total strangers, many of whom would be from out of the country and would possibly be holding discussions in various languages that Liz couldn't understand. Visiting her father had saved her from that issue last year. Now Steve was coming to her rescue. Liz was getting warm at the thought of this time with Steve. Or was it the wine that was making her warm?

"Just bring yourself. I'll look after everything. Caroline, you can come afterward for leftovers." Steve was smiling broadly at the fact his comment was not sitting well with Caroline. It earned him another flash of her tongue. The aroma of Caroline's sauce was starting to fill the room, and Liz was sure she could pick out at least three different spices and lots of garlic.

The early evening continued with light conversation and Caroline's wonderful pasta dinner. She served the ravioli with a delicious vegetable sauce, a leafy salad, and garlic toast. She let Steve know the toast didn't have butter; she used olive oil instead. It was delicious! Both Caroline and Liz had started to learn about Steve's vegan diet, and both had become accustomed to similar diets themselves, although neither one of them strictly adhered to it when they weren't with Steve.

After dinner they sat at the table and talked for hours. The conversation went through several topics, but the majority of it consisted of sharing stories of their lives prior to knowing each other. Liz was enjoying the depth of information being shared by both of her dinner companions. Caroline had spent summers doing some amazing things, most of which included life-risking adventures on mountains or in the deep woods. Steve talked about his travels to Laos, Cambodia, India, Italy, and France. She especially liked the stories Steve shared about life after his recent loss of his father. The experience had shattered Steve, and Liz felt a whole new connection with him as his challenges very closely reflected her own struggles from her childhood when her mother had passed away.

Suddenly Caroline looked at her watch and gasped: "Oh my god! I'm late! I was supposed to meet Gerry over twenty minutes ago! He'll be mad as hell at me!" Gerry was somebody Caroline had been dating for about a month.

"Want a lift there?" Steve offered, jingling his car keys above his plate. "And by the way, we only got to four. You're getting much better!"

"No, he's meeting me a few blocks away at their band's practice studio. I'll just call and let him know I'm on my way. And saying 'like' four times in this many hours is a record for me. I hope you're proud! You two are on dish duty. I did all the cooking." And with a quick grab at her jacket and purse, Caroline slipped on her shoes and was out the door.

"I can clean this up." Liz offered.

"Just leave it. I can get this in the morning. There's still over half a bottle of wine left. Let's fill our glasses and head to the living room. I need to put on more music. I'll go get the sound started, you pour the wine." Liz didn't have time to respond before Steve left the table to put on another CD. "I hope you like jazz, Liz. I've got a new favorite I want you to hear. The artist is Madeleine Peyroux. Her voice is simply amazing."

Liz topped up the two wine glasses and started toward the living room. Soft jazz music filled the room. Steve accepted the glass that Liz offered and followed her to the couch, choosing to sit close to her in the middle of the couch.

"So, Caroline and I did most of the talking. I noticed you were pretty much silent during dinner. Tell me about yourself. What is Liz all about?"

Liz only now became aware of how little she had participated in the conversation. "Well, there's not much to tell." She was also becoming aware of how the wine was affecting her. She felt a little dizzy. Madeleine was crooning: "Don't wait too long".

"Nonsense," smiled Steve. "Everybody has a story. What's yours? And don't be shy. I've pretty much bared my soul to you. I even shared about how much I cried, and that's not something a man should share."

"Well, I cried a lot too. I was nine when my mom died. Looking back, I don't think I really understood how permanent that would be. She was gone forever, and I think I didn't get my head around that until I was much older. I did a lot of crying, but not the healing kind of crying. Just the sad kind."

"I'm so sorry to hear that" Steve said, as he put his arm around Liz and held her far shoulder. "You must still miss her a lot." With his free arm he reached for his wine and took a long sip.

Liz, without thinking about it, moved toward him a little. She also took a sip of her wine and leaned forward to place the glass on the coffee table in front of her. When she leaned back, she was snuggled into Steve's side. She placed her head onto his shoulder. "Yeah, I do. I miss her pretty much every day. The hard days are times like Mother's Day or her birthday, but every day hurts a little." On her cheek she could feel Steve's heartbeat. "I miss her holding me, hugging me, kissing my forehead ..." and as she spoke, she tilted her head back to look up at Steve. He tilted his head down toward her, and Liz almost instinctively moved forward and kissed Steve. A warm, slow, lingering kiss.

What happened next became a blur in Liz's memory. Kisses continued, clothing was shed, and their intertwined bodies found the way into Steve's bedroom. What followed could only be described as Liz's most ecstatic experience in her life. Steve was everything she had dreamed of him being, and definitely more experienced than those couple of high school boys that she had gone all the way with. He spent the time caressing her, causing her to not only be ready for him but to crave his next move. And there were many. It all seemed to last forever and yet be over in a breath. She didn't have time to think, only enjoy. It was exciting. It was electric. It was sheer bliss.

Afterward, Steve simply held her in his arms. She felt safe. Comfortable. Satisfied. She drifted off to sleep.

The next morning could have been awkward, but it wasn't. She woke up to the smells of breakfast coming from the kitchen, and the sounds of Sheryl Crow coming from Steve's sound system. Her eyes were still adjusting to the daylight when Steve came into the room and placed a coffee on the night table beside her. He picked her bra up from the floor and dropped it on to the bed. "Good morning, Liz. I hope you like chow mein for breakfast."

Steve returned to the kitchen and Liz groped under the sheets until she found her panties. She put her bra on, then her panties. The only other item she could find to put on was Steve's shirt, laying on the floor from the night before. All the buttons were missing, and the front hung open, but Liz didn't mind. She was confidently proud of her body. She walked into the kitchen. The previous day's dishes were all cleared, and the table was set for two.

"How long have you been up?"

"Just a half-hour or so. Time enough to make my favourite breakfast and some coffee. How'd you sleep?"

"Like a princess! Um, about last night…" Liz didn't know what to say next.

"Hey, I think we both enjoyed each other's company. We had fun. And we both got what we really wanted. At least I think you did, right? I know I was happy!"

"Oh god yes. That was, well, really good. But how does this go forward. I mean, you're my prof, and my employer, and…"

Steve started to spoon the chow mein onto the two plates. "Well, I can't see this making any difference at all. You were always going to get an A-plus, because that is the kind of student you are, and as for work, I still need you to complete the data entry." As she took a seat he leaned down and kissed her forehead. "I think 'really good' wasn't the review I was hoping for. Let's try again after breakfast. OK?"

Liz was a little shocked at his response. She thought Steve seemed way too casual about what had happened the night before. Steve could sense her reaction.

"Look, Liz, I've always admired you from afar. I think you're one of the most beautiful young women I know. And I think you've also been a little attracted to me. We're both adults. What happened last night was perfectly natural. It's not a big deal, really. Unless you want it to be a big deal. But I was hoping that we could carry on as before, and just see what comes up naturally. Mimosa?"

Liz could only reply "Mimosa?"

"It's my Sunday morning routine. OJ and sparkling wine. Helps get the day started." Without waiting for an answer, he poured two fluted glasses half full of orange juice and then topped them off with a bubbling wine. "This is a white frizzante that I first tried when I was in Italy. One of my faves."

Liz took a sip and looked up at him. "So, this is routine for you?"

"I like wine. Sue me!"

"No, I mean having sex with students from your class. You seem to think this is no big deal." Liz felt she was possibly being a little too forward with this line of questioning, but she wanted to know where she stood.

"Definitely not. Liz, you are very special. This doesn't happen often. I mean, I'm human. I have my urges. But Liz, the issue here is you. I find you incredibly attractive and very mature. I know I'm a little older than you, but I think of you as my equal. Liz, this has been very special for me."

"OK. But really, where does this go next?"

"Look, I'll say again, let's take this one step at a time and see where it leads. I was kidding about trying again after breakfast, but I'm not kidding when I say this: breakfast is getting cold. Let's eat."

Liz relaxed a little and smiled at Steve. "OK" was all she could add. She reached for the chopsticks and tried a taste of the chow mein. The flavour surprised her. "This is amazing! Where did you learn to cook like this?"

"Wow. At least something I do is amazing. That helps a lot. Thanks." Steve gave his best sarcastic smile.

"Steve, I said the sex was really good. I should have said amazing. It's just…"

"I'm kidding! I don't need a rave review. My ego is intact. Listen, let's just enjoy breakfast and then maybe we can go for a walk, OK?"

"Sure. OK." And with that they ate, mostly in silence. When it came time to leave, Liz went to the couch to retrieve her blouse. There was a small rip in the seam where one sleeve joined the body of the blouse, and the top three buttons were also missing. Parts of the previous night were slowly coming back to Liz. "Um, I don't have anything else here to wear."

"I'll get you another one of my shirts. It looks a little chilly. Is a flannel shirt OK?"

"Sure." Liz put on the shirt that Steve got from the bedroom and stuffed her blouse into her handbag. Slipping on her pants and jacket, she went to the door to retrieve her shoes.

Steve put on his leather jacket and the two of them left the condo. That morning they walked for over two hours, and Liz really opened up to Steve. She hadn't spoken much the night before, or even at breakfast, but now she felt comfortable sharing many stories of her teenage years. When they got to Granville Island, Steve paid for a water taxi to cross to downtown Vancouver, and they soon found themselves in Stanley Park. Walking with Steve was the best Sunday Liz had experienced since she moved to Vancouver. But she was getting tired of walking. It started to rain. Just as Liz was ready to excuse herself and head back to campus, Steve asked "Why don't we head back to my place for coffee. I'm ready for a rest."

Liz couldn't say no. Steve flagged a taxi and minutes later they were back at the condo. "Liz, why don't you relax and I'll put on the coffee and get us a snack. Or have a shower if you want. There are towels in the linen cupboard in the bathroom." Liz just smiled and nodded as her reply and headed into the bathroom.

Standing under the hot shower, Liz reflected on everything that had just occurred. The dinner, the night together, the sex. Even the breakfast and walk— everything started to feel perfect to her. Leaving the shower was when she saw it, and her blood suddenly ran cold. There, hanging on a hook on the back of the bathroom door, was a woman's blouse. Another woman's blouse. She hadn't noticed it when she closed the door. She hadn't noticed it the night before. She hadn't noticed it when she used the bathroom that morning. As she stood there, dripping and starting to shiver, she heard a woman's voice. It was Caroline. She was in the condo too!

Liz quickly towelled off and started to dress. She stopped in her tracks when she realized that the only thing she had to wear on her top was Steve's shirt! How on earth was she going to explain this to Caroline? What to do? Suddenly there was a knock on the bathroom door. "Hey girl, like, I need to pee!" It was Caroline all right. She heard Steve call from the kitchen "That's one!" She threw on Steve's shirt and opened the door.

"Thanks" gasped Caroline. "Sorry, urgent!" And with a little shove, Liz found herself outside the bathroom with the door being quickly shut in her face. Had Caroline not noticed that she was wearing Steve's shirt?

When the bathroom door opened again, Caroline emerged with a cheery "Thanks. That was close! I was entering surveys when you two came in, and I probably should have gone before you showered." She was holding the blouse from the hanger on the door. She casually walked over to the bedroom they were using for an office and hung it on a hanger. As she opened the closet to hang it up Liz noticed all the other clothes in the closet. They were all Caroline's.

"Are you moving in?" Liz asked.

"No, silly, I just have some things here for those times I don't make it home before I start to work here. I spent the night at Gerry's and needed a fresh outfit after, you know, the night before." She smiled. "I also needed a shower when I first got here. I got rained on. By the way, nice shirt choice." Caroline smiled. It was a knowing kind of smile.

Before Liz could think of a reply, Steve called from the kitchen. "Coffee's ready. And I found some muffins in the fridge." As they approached the kitchen, he added "I don't think they're one hundred percent fresh, but they're still edible."

The three sat and drank coffee and ate muffins. The conversation was redirected toward their work project, and Liz was happy for the distraction from the attention Caroline had paid to the fact she was wearing Steve's shirt. Caroline asked "How do you feel about the progress we're making, Steve? Are we going to meet your deadline?"

"Well," Steve wiped his mouth with a napkin. "I think we're on track. Maybe even a little ahead of schedule. But I have been looking at this coming summer and I think I'm going to need help getting ready for the next round of surveys. Would you two be interested in carrying on with the job even

# A NATURAL CAUSE

if the work changes a bit? And how are you with travelling? After exams, of course."

"Travelling?" Liz asked. She hadn't had much time to travel, and the only holidays she took when she was younger were always in the province. Her dad didn't like to stray far from home. Back then, at least. Now he was in Mexico. She suddenly found herself thinking *what changed?* Of course! She had moved out of the house.

"Well, nothing exotic. I did all the set-up and travelling myself last spring, when I got the first survey established. It meant hiring a lot of people, and that took some time. I gave preference to girls in second year, hoping that this year a lot of them would return. I mostly need to quickly review with them some of what we're changing as far as the survey is concerned, and possibly fill a position or two if some of the girls don't come back."

"Girls? Aren't there any men doing this job? In any city?" Caroline seemed a little peeved at this.

"Actually, no. I looked into the research that has been done about how survey data was collected, and a few studies revealed that young women were much less likely to be rejected by prospective survey candidates than young men were. I didn't prevent any guys from applying, and I even interviewed a couple, but they weren't the best candidates, so I didn't hire them." Steve came across as very offhanded, treating this whole issue in a matter-of-fact manner.

He continued "As far as the surveys are concerned, there will now be two separate kinds of surveys. Most work will be the same as last year, with some fine tuning to the questions. There will be another survey, however, where last summer's participants will be encouraged to add a few details to their answers. You two are OK with going back to a few of the homes you've already been to, aren't you?"

Liz nodded yes, but Caroline asked "Where do you want us to travel to, and for how long? Where would we be staying? Are we going to have to pay for any of this?"

"Well, I mentioned this survey was done in ten cities. I'm going to go back to some myself, but I need some cities covered by someone else. I simply can't do it all again. I found that too exhausting. I've received more funding from the Aldbrecht Foundation, and my federal funding was for the first three years of this research. I'm hoping they'll add more years to that funding.

But for this year, I'm financially sound. I'll cover all your costs: flights, hotels, meals. And I'll make sure you're fully informed and trained so you'll feel comfortable doing the job. Plus, I'll make all the travel arrangements. OK?"

Caroline wasn't fully satisfied with the answer. "How long do we spend in each place. And where will you be sending us?"

"Well, I'll cover Vancouver, because Tiffany said she won't be back and I need to hire someone else for her and one more person to cover for the work I'll be taking you two away from. That leaves nine other cities that need handling, and I want to do three of them myself for sure. Possibly four. So that would leave only five or six that I need help with. Each city you visit should be just for a day, two at the most. It is really a quick task that I need handled in each city, as most of the girls already know what they're doing. I know I want to cover Toronto, Quebec City, and Montreal. Possibly Winnipeg. That leaves Edmonton, Calgary, Saskatoon, Hamilton, London, and possibly Winnipeg. I'll know about Winnipeg in a week or so."

"Well," Caroline hesitated for a long moment. "What would you think about sending us together. I don't know if I'd feel safe going to some of these places on my own. And Liz and I could share a hotel room, so it shouldn't be that much more expensive. Does that work?"

Liz stared at Caroline. *She really has her shit together*, she thought. *I would never have thought about asking all these details, or about working together.*

"It'll add expense, because I wasn't flying both of you to every city, but I'm sure I can handle that in the budget. April is still a cheap time to fly. The summer holiday rates haven't kicked in by then. So, Liz, you in?"

Something that had never occurred to Liz suddenly came to mind: She had earned six thousand dollars last summer. If there are three surveyors in ten cities all earning what she had earned, then each summer was costing Steve about $180,000! He said the feds were funding him for three years. *How big were these grants he was receiving?!*

Liz had already nodded but added a verbal "Yes." Things seemed to be happening too fast for her. "I should get going back to my dorm. I'll be here again tomorrow. Excuse me."

As she stood to leave the table Steve also got up. "You're here for an evening shift on Monday, tomorrow, right? Why don't you come early?

Caroline is here for the whole day, and I feel it's my turn to cook a dinner for you two. OK?"

"Sounds great to me!" She tried to avoid Caroline hearing her as she tugged at the flannel shirt and whispered "I'll give it back tomorrow?"

Steve smiled and winked an OK. As she was putting on her shoes, Caroline asked "Are there still a lot of students at res this time of year?"

"Naw. It's a bit of a ghost town. But anyone still in res seems to feel it's party time, so the place can be very noisy. I'm not getting much studying in at all."

"Studying? You should be taking a break! Why not check out of res and spend nights here? The love seat in our office area is a pull-out bed, you know." Caroline seemed to know way more about the condo than Liz had ever noticed.

"It is quiet for your studying, Liz, and it would save commute time. The welcome mat is out. Totally your call though." Steve seemed almost like he was prepared for the offer Caroline had just made.

"I'll give it some thought, I'll let you know tomorrow. I think that might work." Liz replied and with that she stepped out the front door. She could only manage a few steps before she stopped in her tracks. *What on earth is going on?* she thought. It was almost too much to process. *Christmas dinner with Steve? Travel? With Caroline? Move into the condo with Steve? After what had transpired last night?* Her mind reeled.

# January 2005

Caroline quietly slipped out of the cot in the basement of Sister Rose's church, grabbed the backpack that she had stuffed under her cot, and left from the side door leading to the back lane. The overnight guests were supposed to stay until coffee was served and morning prayers had been said, but she preferred to start her mornings her own way, without saying thanks, either *to* anybody or *for* anything.

She knew that this part of her life had to be kept very secret, and that anyone she knew could never catch her sleeping with other homeless people. There were too many stigmas that went along with being homeless, and she didn't want to spend time explaining her situation to everyone she met. She was OK. This was just a temporary inconvenience. She'd find a better arrangement very soon.

When her father had left the family home—he'd been ordered by the court to stay away—she was left caring for her mother. While her father's drinking had always led him to be angry and violent, her mother's drinking simply left her comatose. Caroline had tried to get both of them to seek help with their addictions, but neither one seemed interested in changing their ways. As an only child, and with parents that were incapable of behaving like parents, she learned from a very early age to depend on herself alone. It was in grade twelve, when her mother had finally drunk herself into the serenity of an early death, that Caroline started to live on her own. She never did see her father again.

Trying to handle the affairs of her mother's estate helped Caroline realize how important it was to have money. The bank quickly foreclosed on the family home, as the mortgage and other combined debts exceeded the value of the house. Because Caroline had just turned eighteen, there was no support available for her. She needed to be a minor to receive any government help. The thing that bothered Caroline the most, however, was the treatment of her mother after her death.

Caroline's mother passed away intestate. Because there seemed to be no way to locate her husband, and because the courts knew of the restraining order against him, there was little time spent to extend any effort above the required minimum. Her body was cremated, and the ashes were interred in a plot that the province maintained for such cases. The minimal death benefits that were to come to the estate were taken by the provincially appointed executor to help cover the costs of the cremation and burial, and there was nothing left over. There was no money for a service of any kind. Caroline was the only person to attend the interment. As she left the cemetery, she vowed that she would find a way to become successful, possibly even rich, so that when the time came for her own funeral, she would not go unnoticed.

To this day, Caroline had no idea what had become of her father, and she had lost the need to even care about that. She was going to be OK on her own and she felt freed of the baggage that comes with having a family, especially a dysfunctional one. Whenever the topic of parents came up, Caroline just pretended that her parents were a loving, normal couple and that she visited them regularly, especially on special occasions. At times she even said she lived with them. It prevented her having to disclose the actual background she came from and why some nights were spent in shelters.

As she walked down the lane behind the church, she noticed Walter sleeping on some cardboard he had laid down in the back doorway of an adjacent office building. He was using a newspaper as a blanket. Apparently, he didn't have the four dollars it took to get a cot at Sister Rose's. The church had insisted on a minimum charge, saying it was important for people using the basement for the night to feel they were not getting a handout and were paying their way. It supposedly was to help instill a sense of pride in them. The reality of the decision meant that many people were left sleeping outdoors, even in these cold winter months.

Caroline took out a five-dollar bill and tucked it under Walter's hand. He didn't even stir. About two years earlier, at the end of a day when he had spent the whole day collecting whatever money he could, Caroline let him touch her breasts while he masturbated. He was left happy, and she was left with all his money. Maybe this handout she was leaving was to relieve a little of the guilt she felt. He would have had to go through that night without food, without drugs or alcohol, and without a place to sleep. She thought it must have been a long, cold night for him, but back then she had needed the money for herself. That was the first night that she had purchased enough crank that she could repackage and sell small amounts of it and turn a profit. She never took the drug herself but had helped a few other homeless people access it. Selling it at a profit was a start for her.

Caroline rarely needed to sleep at Sister Rose's now, not like when she first started sleeping there. Right after she had received her bursary money for attending university and had paid tuition and bought the required texts, she was left with just over two-hundred dollars. That was all the money she had to live on for her first semester, and she knew she needed to stretch it out as much as possible. She also knew she needed to find a job, but having just finished high school and competing with university students who had a two-month lead on finding summer employment, she had no luck in getting a job. The money from selling drugs was an easy alternative. She convinced herself that because she only sold small amounts and only to users who would have bought from another person if she didn't supply them, then she wasn't doing any harm. She was just providing a service.

Initially, sleeping at Sister Rose's had been a financial necessity. Now that she could afford an occasional hotel stay, she still preferred Sister Rose's. There were two reasons; she wanted to keep the cash she had to buy drugs for dealing, and many of her buyers were right here at Sister Rose's. It was very convenient.

At the end of the lane she turned right and went to the bus stop at the corner of the block. It was early enough that no other commuters were waiting, and when the bus arrived she found she was accompanied by only two other riders, both of whom were in work uniforms. One looked like a security guard, while the other seemed to have a nurse's outfit on. Or maybe it was a cafeteria worker's uniform.

She got off in front of the Vancouver General Hospital and went in to use the washrooms to freshen up. She knew that if you walked in with an air of confidence the security at the reception desk would assume you were coming on shift and let you pass without questions. The washrooms located close to the entrance were single-user rooms, with doors that locked. She could change and give herself a sponge-bath without anyone interrupting her. She put on a clean top and stuffed her dirty clothes into her backpack, left the hospital, and headed toward Steve's condo.

Recently, she spent most nights at Gerry's. She hoped that she would be able to do that again, and soon. She didn't like having to sleep at Sister Rose's. But Gerry had become very angry with her, and she felt that he was about to get violent, so she had left his condo. He had accused her of taking over his territory, selling drugs to the people who had been his customers and pocketing profits that should have been his. While a little of what he was complaining about was true, it was mostly due to the fact that he was unavailable at certain times, and she was just minding the shop. She had told him that if he had spent less time with his band and more time at the bar, then she wouldn't have stepped into his territory. She hoped he would be open to the idea of a partnership approach and that she could get back to staying at his condo again.

A few months earlier, when she had just met Gerry, her supplier, Zach, had come after her trying to collect money for drugs he said she still hadn't paid for. She argued with him, insisting that the money had been paid. He had given her forty-eight hours to come up with the cash, and now she took extra care trying to avoid Zach by not going to the areas that she knew he would frequent. She was thankful that Gerry had a different supplier, and she simply switched her purchases to him.

As she approached Steve's condo, she thought about what had transpired between Steve and Liz. While she was happy to see Liz living with Steve, she also knew that she resented the happy little home that this created. She still saw Steve on a regular basis, and they still had a very active sex life, but the resentment was over how little it provided her in the way of a normal life, if such a thing even existed. She was lost in thought about what a normal life could look like when a hand roughly grabbed her shoulder and spun her around.

It was Zach. He wasn't alone.

"Caroline, have you been avoiding me? Little Bobby here says you've met a new dealer. Is that true?"

While Zach was a well-built and well-groomed man, Little Bobby was a greasy little guy with thin hair that was slicked down and combed to the back of his head. He was missing both eyeteeth but that didn't stop him from having a perpetual smile on his face. Caroline was creeped out by him.

"Jesus Zach! You scared the shit out of me. What the hell?"

"What the hell is right, Caroline. Or better still, *where* the hell, as in where the hell is my money?"

"I told you Zach. I pay all my bills. That money was paid, I swear!"

"Little Bobby here does the books, and he says you owe. You're not calling Little Bobby here a liar now, are you?"

Caroline heard a metallic clicking sound and looked down to see Little Bobby had opened his switchblade and was holding it diagonally across his chest. She could feel herself start to sweat. It made the January air feel a bit colder. "I can get the money. Five G, right?"

"Today it's still five. Six by tomorrow. And we know where you hang out." Zach nodded his head toward Steve's condo.

"Give me until noon today. I'll be right here. I swear."

"So will we, so you'd better be here." Zach turned to leave. Little Bobby covered one nostril with this thumb and blew snot out of the other, then slowly licked the blade of the knife before tucking it back into the handle and returning it to his pocket. He blew Caroline a kiss before turning away to join Zach. Caroline felt her skin crawling.

She continued toward Steve's condo, trying to figure out how she could get Steve to help her out of this situation. She knew Gerry wouldn't help. It was going to be up to Steve. What story could she possibly come up with to convince him to help?

# April 2005

Liz tucked the sheets into the folding mattress and closed the hide-a-bed back into a love seat. She had felt uncomfortable sleeping in Steve's bed while he was in Montreal. Or was it Quebec City? She was having trouble keeping up with his comings and goings now that all classes had ended and exams were over.

Over the past four months she had been Steve's partner. She had continued to work from his condo and had moved out of res and slept here full time as well. Slept—that didn't really cover it all. She and Steve had regular sex. His desire for it was insatiable. She had gone along with his directions too: wearing costumes, getting tied up, and every different location and position you could imagine. He seemed to be able to convince her into doing his every desire. She was starting to wonder if this was normal behaviour.

She was also aware that she wasn't having any blue days.

She buttoned up the front of her housecoat and walked into Steve's bedroom to return the pillow to his closet. She was surprised at what she discovered: Caroline was sleeping in the bed! Steve's bed!

Caroline stirred from her sleep, obviously woken from the noise Liz had made, and offered a weak "G'mornin."

"Sorry." Liz tiptoed to the closet and whispered: "I wasn't aware you were in here."

"Yeah. You were sound asleep when I came in, and I didn't want to wake you. Have you made coffee?"

"Uh . . . I just woke up too. I'll go put some on." Liz quietly closed the door as she left the room, but it reopened almost immediately as Caroline came out. She was completely naked.

"Why don't you let me treat you out for breakfast. We've both got a lot of work to do today. I don't know about you, but I could use the escape before we settle into the day's work. Brekkie?"

"Sounds good to me too, but you don't have to treat. We can go Dutch, OK?" Liz had been feeling a lot less stressed financially since she had moved into Steve's condo. She was getting paid for lots more hours of work, and living here was saving her thousands on res fees. Steve usually drove her to campus so her bus costs were way down, and she was sure he was paying for the vast majority of the groceries. And for *all* the wine!

"OK. Want to hit the Gecko? I hear they're doing breakfast now, and Steve will be happy to hear we did the vegan thing."

"Sounds great! Are we walking or grabbing a bus?"

"Just finish getting dressed and come downstairs to the parking lot. I have a surprise." Caroline flashed a curious smile at Liz and disappeared into Steve's bedroom to get dressed herself.

When Liz got to the underground parking lot she saw Caroline was waiting beside Steve's car. *Did Steve approve of this?* she thought. As she came closer, however, Caroline tossed a helmet at her. "Put this on" she said. "Hopefully we don't need it, but it is the law these days."

On the other side of Caroline was a brand-new Yamaha motorcycle. And it looked massive! Liz just stared. She had never been on a motorcycle before, let alone one with a woman like Caroline behind the wheel. Or do you still say "behind the wheel" for a motorcycle? Liz looked at Caroline, who was enjoying the shock value of the scene.

"You wanna drive, or should I?" Caroline smiled broadly. "Just kidding. I've been riding since I turned sixteen. Before that even if you include off-road. I got my first dirt bike for my twelfth birthday. This is the Yammy Road Star Midnight. She's a gift from my dad. She's the best ride I've ever owned, but she needs to be handled. She's not built for a newbie. Hop on!" Caroline would never share how she could afford this new purchase with Liz. She had recently bypassed Gerry's contact for drugs and was now buying straight from his supplier. This new guy seemed to be high up the chain and was very liberal with his financing. She had convinced him that she needed the bike, and he just gave her the cash. Well, lent it to her. She had no idea about when he would want to be repaid.

Liz put on the helmet and sat behind Caroline. The helmet smelled of new leather and motor oil. When the bike started and revved up, Liz felt like her heart was racing faster than the engine. Caroline cruised up the exit ramp with confidence and turned to the right on the front street with a quick glance to the left but without slowing down. The rest of the ride was a combination of trying to hold on to Caroline, trying to stay centred, and trying to lean her head out enough to hear whatever Caroline was saying, but the latter was to no avail. The entire time Liz had squeezed her knees into Caroline's hips, trying to secure her hold on the bike.

After she had parked right in front of The Spotted Gecko, Liz said "Did you say anything important? I couldn't hear a word!"

Caroline laughed and reached over to Liz's helmet. "See this switch? It's for the mike and earphones. I was wondering why you weren't answering me. Try it next time!"

Liz blushed. Sometimes Caroline made her feel so naive. She was from a small town, but she didn't like to think of herself as a backward country bumpkin! "Let's eat." She turned and walked into the Gecko. The sounds of Norah Jones filled her ears, and as the aromas coming from the kitchen wrapped around her like a warm blanket she instantly became very hungry.

The hostess seated them at a table beside the window. Caroline had wanted to keep her eye on the bike. It was only two days old. Just as the hostess walked away, their server appeared. "Hey you two! Long time!"

It was Tiffany. And she was wearing another tip top. It was almost hard to look at her. "Hey Tiff. How're things going? I didn't realize you still worked here. How long has it been?" Liz was having trouble trying to find anything else to say. She hadn't seen Tiffany for months now, and really didn't get to know her too well before that. Apart from the previous summer's work, they had almost nothing in common that Liz could think of.

"Things are great! I'm done with exams, and totally into summer mode. You two still writing?"

"Nope! I'm done with exams too. And glad that pressure is off. We have new pressure now, at work." Liz was about to boast about their summer jobs that was going to include some travel, but suddenly remembered how cold Tiff had been to the job offer at the beginning of the school year.

"Yeah . . . " There was an extended pause before Tiffany added "Listen, the chef is trying a new item out for the summer menu. It is a vegan version of Eggs Benny: chickpea-based and it has carrot-lox that are to die for. I tried it this morning before I started and wow—it is great. Want to try it?"

"Sure. Make us two." Liz wasn't sure if she liked how Caroline had just answered for them both but shrugged it off and nodded a yes to Tiff. She did want to try this new menu idea. As Tiffany walked back toward the staff counter, Caroline called out "And two coffees. Please." She turned to face Liz again. "You'd think that she just started this serving gig. Christ!"

"Do you come here often?" Liz sensed Caroline had a level of comfort with the restaurant that she didn't have. This was Liz's first time. For that matter, it was the first time she felt she could afford a luxury like this.

"A bit. Yeah. But I like Trendz better. Better food. And definitely better service." She nodded her head in Tiffany's direction. "Listen, we should talk about what's coming up. We travel in two days, and I think we should go into this with our eyes wide open. I want this summer together to be completely smooth. No bumps. K?"

"Sure. I'm prepped for the work though. What bumps could there be?"

"Well, you should know this: I'm not seeing Gerry anymore. He didn't like the idea of me travelling for this job and, well, that meant I didn't really like the idea of him being part of my life. So, I dumped him. He was getting on my nerves anyway. Fun guy at first, but he grew stale very quickly. Spent way too much time with his stupid garage band. They'll never get anywhere with their obnoxious sound. Total waste of time"

"OK, but how does that create bumps?" Liz wrinkled her forehead.

"Well, there may be others. We're on the road, new cities every day or two. It's like we're on tour with a rock band. For a little while at least. What if one of us should meet someone?"

Liz's forehead remained wrinkled.

Caroline continued "We need a code or something. Something that would allow the other person to know to go to the bar and have a drink. Y'know, while the room is occupied." She signed a couple of air quotes with the last word.

"Ah, I see." Liz hadn't thought in that direction at all. With her and Steve it was, well, settled. And convenient. And comfortable. And kinky. And erotic. They always were together, except for when Steve was super late at his office working on his research. Then she chose the hide-a-bed, and he didn't disturb her when he got home. "What kind of code were you thinking of?" Liz returned the air quotes with the word "code".

"I don't know. We can figure that out. Listen, you and Steve are getting along OK, aren't you?"

Liz found herself blushing. "Yeah . . . OK. Why?" As comfortable as she was becoming with her living arrangement with Steve, she still felt awkward about discussing it with anyone. She didn't want to have people looking at her differently or accusing her of sleeping her way to good marks. It was better kept a secret. Mostly. But Caroline had become very aware of the arrangement. This was not what Liz wanted to discuss right now.

"No reason, just being curious. Think you'll marry him?"

Liz was shocked at the question. "*What?!*"

"I mean, you're keeping it real, right. It's a great fling you're having, but don't put too much stock into it. You should know a few things."

"Like what, for instance?"

"Well, for instance, you're not his only one. Why do you think he wanted to take on Montreal and Quebec City himself? And please don't say for the language. I speak French fluently, and Steve knows that."

Liz sat back in her chair. She was about to speak when Tiffany arrived with their coffees. "Breakfast will be right out." Tiffany smiled at Liz and then gave Caroline a very curious look.

"What's with that look?" Liz stared at Caroline. "And what do you know about Montreal or Quebec City?"

"Calm down girl. It's no biggie. You know Steve and I are still having sex, right? That's obvious. Or were you not aware? Oh, and as for Tiff, let's just say we don't see eye-to-eye on some things."

"What?!" Liz had taken a small sip of coffee but couldn't swallow. But then she thought she didn't want to seem stupid in front of Caroline. She forced the coffee down her throat. "Well, I figured you and Steve had been intimate at times." She couldn't find it in herself to use the word sex. "But . . . "

"The issue with Tiff? Long story, OK."

Liz happily changed her focus to the issue with Tiff. She couldn't get her head around the other item Caroline had just brought up. She needed time to think. "You'll have to fill me in on that long story sometime."

The breakfasts arrived, and Liz focused on the plate that was set in front of her. She took a small bite. It was delicious, but she could still barely swallow. Her stomach was churning now. She didn't want to make eye contact with Caroline. She was wondering how long Caroline had been having sex with Steve, and how often. The thought scared her a little.

"Say," Caroline broke the silence. "Since I'm not staying at Gerry's place these days, I think I'm gonna crash with you at Steve's, OK? At least until he gets back from out east. I just can't deal with moving back to my parent's place. Not now, anyway. I'll figure out something else soon though. OK?"

"Sure." Was all Liz could manage to reply.

"Listen, I hope I haven't said anything to upset you, Liz. I assumed you were aware. You seemed comfortable with your current lifestyle. You've seemed to be getting very casual about a lot of things. You're my best friend now. Easily the best friend I've ever had. I feel very attached to you, and I want you to know that. I respect you, and I just love you. This thing with Steve, it's like, for now. Not forever. Right?"

"I guess so. I just haven't ever put our current situation into proper context, I guess. When, ah, when did you and Steve—"

"When were Steve and I, um, 'intimate', as you called it?" Caroline's voice was sarcastic with the word intimate, and she chuckled and rolled her eyes. "Well, let's just say he doesn't always work late at his office. And yeah, Gerry did catch us at his place. I brought Steve up to show him the view and, you know, things got away on us. Gerry was supposed to be practicing! Maybe that's why his band sounds so shitty. Yeah, and maybe that's why he wasn't so keen on my travelling around the country too. What a dickhead. Anyway, we've also used Steve's office. That second desk has been useful for something."

*Show him the view? Of what exactly?* Liz thought. She just sat in silence again.

"Listen, after we've finished here, can you swing by Gerry's place with me? I need to get my things, and I really don't want to see him, you know, alone. Hey, you're not eating. You're not enjoying this?"

Liz couldn't believe Caroline had switched subjects so casually. *Was* she putting too much stock in her relationship with Steve? She looked at her plate. "It's good. I'll get it to go and eat later. I'm just not that hungry right now. Where does Gerry live?"

"Squamish. He has a great little place looking out at the ocean. I'm gonna miss going there."

The thought of being on the back of a motorcycle and driving to Squamish made Liz both nervous and excited at the same time. It was a beautiful drive and a sunny day. But on a motorcycle? Caroline had pushed her half-eaten breakfast away and she motioned to Tiffany to bring the cheque. When Tiff arrived, she also had two take-out containers and placed them on the table. As Liz scooped her breakfast into one of the containers, Caroline grabbed the bill and said "My treat. Consider it a thank-you for the help you're going to give me moving out of Gerry's." She didn't put any of her breakfast into a to-go box, like Liz did.

The ride to Squamish was as exciting as Liz thought it would be. Caroline didn't take the shortest route, but instead, chose to ride through Burnaby and Coquitlam first, then head up the 7A to the #1 highway. The winding highways weren't too busy and were dry, which was a rare occurrence that spring. Caroline weaved the bike through the light traffic like the expert rider that she was. The scenery was always amazing when it wasn't raining, but on a motorcycle Liz could enjoy it like she never had before. The whole trip was exhilarating. When they finally pulled up to Gerry's condo, Caroline happily bounced off the bike, but Liz fumbled a little as she tried to follow suit. Digging her knees into Caroline's hips had made her thighs sore and cramping.

"Easy does it girl! You're not used to having your legs wrapped around something like this, are you?" Caroline winked at Liz as she reached around her to hold her and steady her dismount. Caroline held on to her a little longer. "You OK now?"

"Sure, thanks." But Liz almost fell when she tried to take her first step. Her legs felt like rubber. "Will Gerry be home?"

"Yeah. They play into the wee hours most nights, so he won't wake up 'til late afternoon. We've got a few hours before that, and this should only take ten minutes, so no worries."

They entered the condo. It was dark, dead silent, and smelled like dirty laundry. Liz could hear loud snores coming from the bedroom. Caroline walked right over and opened the bedroom door. Gerry didn't move a muscle. Caroline entered the bedroom, opened a dresser drawer and started to pile up a few things on the floor. She then tossed a small box onto the pile. It made a metallic jingling sound. "The crown jewels" Caroline whispered as she crossed the room to the closet. She added a few more items to the pile, and then stepped back to survey the room. "I think that's about it." She picked up a small suitcase from the closet floor and started pushing everything from the pile into it. Liz knelt down to help.

"You sure this is everything?" Liz was surprised at how little the suitcase was, and how little the pile of clothing was as well.

"Yeah. I've only been here six months. I guess I knew early on that this wouldn't work out for the long haul."

"What'd you say?" Gerry was sitting up in the bed and rubbing his eyes. "You just getting in?" Then he noticed Liz. "Hey, you joinin' us?"

"No, you fucking moron. She's not joining anything. And I'm not just getting in. I'm so outta here. This is good-bye, asshole!"

Gerry groggily mumbled "Oh. OK." He ran his fingers through his hair, stared at Caroline for twenty seconds, and returned to lying down.

Liz was dumbfounded. This scene was like something she'd see in a movie, but not something she would ever take part in.

Caroline closed the suitcase and nodded her head toward the front door. They both headed in that direction, but as they passed the galley-style kitchen Caroline quickly turned into it and opened a cupboard. She took out a small container and stuffed it into her pocket. Then, without a word, she led Liz out the door and into the street. She strapped the small suitcase onto the back of the bike with a couple of bungee cords she retrieved from a side compartment that Liz hadn't noticed before. They both got onto the motorcycle. Within a few seconds they were off. Liz barely had time to fasten her helmet.

Instead of heading south toward Vancouver, Caroline turned left and headed through downtown Squamish. Liz reached under the helmet and clicked the switch on for her headset. "Where are we going now?" Liz hoped it wasn't too far. Her legs were still cramping from the ride up here.

"Whistler. I've got one last thing to do."

If the ride to Squamish was exciting, the way to Whistler was like a fairground thrill ride. Liz just hung on tightly and tried to enjoy the experience despite her fears. That was hard to do. But the scenery was stunning, and it made Liz aware of how much she missed being home. She missed seeing the mountains that surrounded her small town. She missed her high school friends. She missed her dad.

They arrived at Whistler and Caroline stopped in front of a bar and got off the bike. "Wait here" was all she said, and then she entered the bar. As the bar's front door opened Liz could hear loud hard rock music blaring, and soon the smell of stale beer overtook the leather-and-oil smell from the helmet, even though she was fifteen feet away from the door. It wasn't even noon yet. *Did some people really live like this?* she wondered.

When Caroline returned, she was holding a thick brown envelope wrapped in tape. She put it in the side compartment where the bungee cords had been, and without a word she got on the bike and pulled away. Liz didn't ask any questions.

Caroline chose a direct route back to Steve's, which Liz was very happy to see. It still took almost three hours, as the traffic was backed up on the Lions Gate bridge. Her legs were cramping and becoming more painful by the minute. When they pulled into the underground parking Caroline had to practically lift her off the motorcycle, and then had to help her walk up to the condo.

"Take a load off. I've got something that will help those legs." Caroline motioned toward the bed in Steve' room. It was still unmade from the morning. Without giving it much thought, Liz kicked off her shoes and lay on the bed, face down. It was more of a crash landing than a laying down.

"Don't move. Just relax" Caroline whispered into Liz's ear as she reached under her and undid the buttons on her jeans. Liz just lay there as Caroline went to the foot of the bed and pulled her jeans off. She poured some liquid into her hand and then rubbed it on the inside and the back of Liz's legs. Exactly where the cramping felt the worst. Liz reasoned that Caroline must have experienced this pain herself at some point, because she seemed to know exactly where to massage.

Within a minute, Liz could feel heat from the liquid that Caroline was using. Even the scent was helping her feel better. "What is that?"

"It's just called Heat. I added the lavender myself. Does this feel good?"

"Hmmmm . . . " was all Liz could reply. The massage slowly softened to a gentle rub, and Liz drifted off to sleep.

When she awoke, she found herself neatly tucked under the bed covers. She could hear the shower running, and one of Steve's jazz cds was playing in the living room. The scent of lavender hung heavily in the room. She slowly got out of the bed. Her legs were feeling much better, but still a bit tender. She slipped on her jeans and walked into the living room just as the shower water turned off. She knocked on the door. "I need to pee."

"Have at 'er." came the answer. "It's unlocked. I don't mind." Caroline never failed to shock Liz. Today was no exception. She entered the bathroom and sat on the toilet. Caroline was towelling off in the shower stall. "Man, you crashed hard after that ride."

After Caroline was finished with the bathroom, Liz took her turn in the shower. When she stepped back into the living room, Caroline had set the table with a dinner for two.

"I know you didn't have much for breakfast, and it's almost dinner time, so I thought you'd be hungry. It's not totally vegan, so don't tell Steve I brought butter into his lair. The recipe requires it, in my mind at least. Dig in!" Caroline was already seated, and Liz slid out the second chair and joined her.

She took her first bite and instantly made a guttural "mmm" sound. "What is this? It's delicious!"

"Another recipe of my own making. I haven't named it yet, but the flavour you're getting is mostly from the nutritional yeast and the curry combining. The noodles are flavoured too. I find this blend very tasty if I must say so myself."

"It's delicious!" Liz repeated.

"Steve really likes it too, but for him I have to use vegan butter. I don't think it's quite as good."

Liz felt her stomach churn a little, and it wasn't from the food. All day she had struggled to avoid thinking of what Caroline had told her about Steve. His sexual meandering. His unfaithfulness. Mentioning his name suddenly brought it all back. She chose to quickly change topics. "So, what was in the envelope that was so important? Can I ask?"

"You just did ask, but no, you shouldn't. Can I just say that it was something that was mine that I didn't want to give away?"

"Fair enough. I'll not pry. Then what was that thing you got from Gerry's kitchen cupboard?"

"My god you're in a curious mood, aren't you. OK, that one I can show you. But later, OK? Let's eat."

After their early dinner, they both took time to review their travel arrangements and schedule for the coming days. *Finally*, thought Liz. It was after five and she felt she hadn't accomplished anything work-related this entire day. She was almost expecting it when Caroline left the room and returned with two glasses of wine. Some of Caroline's crazy behaviour's shock value was starting to fade, thought Liz. But not all of it.

Several hours passed, and a couple more glasses of wine were drunk, when Caroline got up and stood behind Liz's chair. She held Liz's shoulders and started to gently rub them, then leaned forward and softly said "Want to see what I got from Gerry's cupboard?"

"Sure" said Liz, expecting it to be some kind of fancy kitchen gadget. Caroline was quite the cook, and what else do you keep in kitchen cupboards?

Still leaning down from behind Liz's chair, Caroline gave Liz's cheek an ever-so-gentle kiss and whispered into her ear, "Wait here." Liz felt herself blushing from the kiss, but she liked the feeling it gave her.

When Caroline returned, she was holding what looked like a small silver flask, less than a quarter of the size of the whiskey flask she had seen her dad use. It had a larger lid too. While Liz sat with a puzzled look on her face, Caroline unscrewed the top and tipped it sideways to let a little of its contents pour into the palm of her hand. It wasn't liquid. It was a white powder.

"Is that what I think it is?" Liz asked. Caroline sure knew how to regain her shock value in a heartbeat.

"Uh-huh. It is. Ever try it?"

"Uh, no." Liz felt this was a time to be honest. She hadn't tried any drugs at all, and the thought of doing drugs scared her a little. Well, it scared her a lot.

"Want to?" Caroline asked. "I can show you how. Just a little. Just to see. OK?"

Liz stared wide-eyed at Caroline. Why did she feel she couldn't say no? She slowly nodded a yes but repeated: "Just a little. Just to see."

Caroline lightly licked one finger and dipped it into the cocaine. "Smile and show me your teeth." As Liz smiled Caroline gently placed her finger into Liz's mouth and stated to rub the powdered finger on her gums. She repeated the move a few more times, rubbing different places inside Liz's mouth, and then Caroline took a small metal tube from her pocked and sniffed the powder that remained in her palm into her own nostrils.

"Putting this in your mouth works? I've only ever heard of people snorting coke."

"Taking it orally is easier at first. And the kick in time is a little slower. It's a little gentler. I thought I'd be gentle with you. This may help. Here . . . " And Caroline guided Liz up from her chair. In a single move, she had her arms around Liz and then gave her a passionate kiss on the lips. Her tongue explored Liz in ways she had never experienced before, even from Steve.

Liz felt her head explode. Not explode really, just open up. Completely. Her chest was heaving with excitement. She reached up and put her arms around Caroline's neck. The kissing continued as Caroline started to undo Liz's top. Liz helped. Then it was Caroline's top, and within moments they were embracing each other, completely naked. Caroline took Liz by the hand and led her to the bedroom.

Liz felt that every sensation she had ever experienced before was just a muted imposter of what she was feeling now. Every place that Caroline touched gave her a euphoric thrill. And Caroline knew exactly where to touch. She knew how to touch. Her kisses, her touches, everything she did caused Liz to become more aroused, more excited. She even guided Liz's hands to show her where to touch back, and Liz found she enjoyed doing that even more than being touched herself.

They lasted well over an hour, constantly exploring new ways to please each other, until both women separated from each other and laid back, completely spent. They slept.

The next morning Liz woke up to an empty bed. Caroline was nowhere to be found. There was just a note on the dining room table. It simply said: "I'm really looking forward to travelling with you! C."

## July 2005

Summer was speeding by in a flash. Steve had hired a replacement for Tiff and a fourth student to help with the Vancouver workload, because he knew Liz and Caroline needed more of their time to cover some of the supervisory related tasks he had assigned to them. That left Liz with a few available days, like today, where she could take some time off and shop for a new outfit or two. Just walking downtown had a different feel than the other days had. These days were rare.

Liz had already visited several of the people she had surveyed the previous year, and also added quite a few new long surveys to the pile from the additional people she had met with. She was pretty sure the job would last throughout her fourth year of studies. She had even started debating doing a master's degree after she graduated. She could afford that option now.

While each of the people she had resurveyed were great to talk to and visit with, by far her favourite was Gracie Butler. This year's visit involved even more sherry, and Gracie had asked her back for dinner that night. Liz had accepted, and after dinner they promised to see each other and visit again, whenever Liz's studies allowed for it.

Steve also sent Liz and Caroline on a second round of trips to various cities where he felt some follow-up work was needed. Just like the first trips they had taken earlier that summer, there was no need to come up with a code for Caroline and Liz to use. They enjoyed each other. Liz had started to enjoy her relationship with Caroline even more than the one she had with Steve.

Liz walked out of the clothing store she was in and noticed across the street was the Axe 'n' Hammer, a bar that was popular with many students. Most people just called it the Axe. She had heard of it before, but never really knew where it was. Spending some time in a commercial area like this as opposed to the residential areas where they were doing surveys did make for some pleasant surprises. Liz also noticed the neon OPEN sign was flashing. She wondered if they offered anything for lunch.

Crossing the street, she looked at the menu posted in the window beside the door. There were some good-looking options. *Why not?* she thought, and walked in. Janis Joplin assaulted her ears and the stench of stale beer did the same thing to her nostrils, but the overall vibe suited her mood this particular afternoon.

Sitting alone in a booth she ordered her lunch from the lone bartender working that day, then looked around the bar. There were gawdy pictures of leather-clad ladies, beer ads with similar images, and some graffiti-like canvases with tags attached showing the prices the artist wanted for them. Then she saw something that made her smile: a poster about a band that was going to appear that Friday, for one night only: The Bangers. No cover-charge. First set 10:00 p.m.

She was pretty sure that The Bangers was the band that Caroline's previous boyfriend was in. Caroline herself had moved on to another boyfriend, ironically with the same first name. Liz and Steve had taken great joy in referring to the new boyfriend as "Gerry version 2.0" or "The Sequel." It bugged Caroline a little, but she laughed it off and just said "2.0 was better than that old Beta release I had!"

Liz had become comfortable with Caroline's ability to have a physical relationship with both her and her new boyfriend at the same time. Caroline had moved into Steve's condo since she parted ways with Gerry. The first Gerry. But now she spent most nights at Gerry 2.0's apartment, which was only a few blocks from Steve's place. There were nights when Caroline stayed at Steve's, but that was usually when Steve was away. Liz shared her hide-a-bed with Caroline most of those nights. When Steve was home, Liz maintained the same relationship with him as she had before, but she never got over what Caroline had disclosed. She wondered if they still met at Steve's office but had decided to just go with the flow and not think too much about that. She was enjoying the lifestyle, especially the sex, and really enjoying the financial situation it left her in.

When her lunch arrived, she pointed at the poster and asked the server, "Will that night be heavily attended? Are they a big draw?"

"No" was all he said, and he laughed as he walked away.

As she slowly worked her way through the french-fries on her plate, she thought back to something Caroline had done when they were in Winnipeg together. Somehow, no matter what city they were in, Caroline seemed to always find a source for her drugs. Usually, it was coke. When they were in Winnipeg, Caroline had left Liz in the room and went down to the bar. Within minutes, she had convinced some middle-aged guy to come to the room where Liz was, knock heavily on the door, and demand entry. He even flashed what looked like a badge as Liz opened the door. Within seconds he grabbed the small bag of coke from under a pillow and started accusing Liz of being an out-of-town dealer. Liz was crapping herself! The episode went on for almost ten minutes before Caroline came through the door and started rolling on the bed with laughter. Liz was shaking and crying, partially from relief, but partially from anger. "How could you do that to me?" she screamed. It took her a long time to calm down. The badge had been a beer label stuck to the inside of the guy's wallet. Even Liz herself found the humour in that.

"I just regret I couldn't get this on video!" Caroline kept repeating between laughing fits.

The episode ended with the three of them doing some coke and heading to the bar together. Apparently, the coke hit was this old guy's payoff. Caroline had then found a way to dump him and head back to the room with Liz. The make-up sex they had that night was extremely good. Liz smiled now as she thought back to that night. But she wanted revenge. This might be her chance!

Liz finished her lunch and did a little more shopping, then headed back to the condo, a little earlier than on most days. Steve was there when she arrived, and Caroline wasn't. Perfect!

"Hey Steve, how'd you like to help me get even with Caroline? She played a trick on me when we were travelling. It's payback time."

"Sure!" Steve said. "What trick did she play on you?"

Liz hesitated. She was pretty sure that Steve was totally unaware of the fact that she and Caroline did cocaine. Or that they slept together. "Well," she stalled for time to think. "Can I just say she scared the hell out of me? I want to share my revenge idea before she walks through the door. I'll fill you in on her prank another time, but here's what I want to do now." Liz was relieved that Steve didn't press for details on Caroline's prank.

She went on to describe where she had eaten lunch, what she had seen on the poster, and then explained her prank idea: "Why don't we convince Caroline to get Gerry 2.0 to join us at the Axe. Gerry's band—the old Gerry—his band, well, they're playing this Friday at the Axe. We arrive before the band goes on. Order something that will keep us there for quite a while, pizza or something. Then watch the fireworks. I'd just love to watch Caroline squirm when she's stuck with the two Gerrys in one room! Whad'ya think?"

"Ha! I'd love to see that! I haven't been to the Axe since I was a student myself. It used to be the place to be seen. Is it still?"

"Not really. At least I don't think so. I don't really go to a lot of bars or places like that. I don't like to dance, and I really don't like loud music. But for this, yeah, I'll go!" Liz wondered if Steve was much of a dancer. Or if he liked this kind of music. They hadn't been seen together in public at all. Their time together was spent mostly at the condo. Except for a couple of restaurant visits they weren't out much, and Liz thought that was for the better. She really didn't want any classmates to see them together.

Steve's face lit up. "I've got an idea. I can ask Caroline to join us with The Sequel as a double date with you and me. I know she'll go for it because she's brought the idea up with me before. We don't even have to say exactly where we're going until later, just tell her it's a night out. You said Friday, right? This is perfect. I owe her for a nasty prank she pulled on me too. Listen, I've got to get back to campus right away, but let's get this plan in motion. I'll do the initial invite—she'll be less suspicious that way. OK?"

"OK." And with that, Liz just watched as Steve slipped on his shoes and went out the door. She wondered if he really was going to his office, or . . . ? Then she reminded herself, she wasn't supposed to be taking him too seriously. But it was still hard to do. She still really liked Steve. Maybe even loved him. But she wasn't sure.

Friday arrived quickly that week. Steve had arranged for the night out, and the three of them had decided to have a late lunch so that they could last a little longer and enjoy a late bite that night once Gerry joined them. All three of them were having drinks by three in the afternoon. Later, Steve said he need to "take the edge off" before their night out and headed to his

# A NATURAL CAUSE

bedroom for a short nap. Caroline and Liz went to their office-cum-bedroom and Liz picked up some paperwork and started to file it in the cabinet. Caroline closed the bedroom door and took the paperwork from Liz's hand, placing it back on the desk. "I've got a better way to kill a few hours" she said, as she reached into her pocket and pulled out her miniature silver flask.

There was something about Caroline's way of approaching things that Liz couldn't say no to. They took turns sharing her little silver straw, and what followed had almost become routine. The love seat became a bed in one swift motion, and they took turns unbuttoning and removing each other's clothes. They didn't bother with climbing under the sheets, and the silk duvet cover felt wonderful as it slid against Liz's skin. While in the throes of their caressing each other, Caroline suddenly stopped and stood up. "Come here, stand up for a minute." Liz instinctively stood up from the bed. "Follow me."

What happened next was the most surreal moment in Liz's life. Caroline held her wrist and led her into the hall between the two bedrooms, then gently opened Steve's bedroom door. Steve was sleeping soundly. She led Liz to one side of the bed and moved around to position herself on the other side, and then motioned for Liz to crawl into the bed, while at the same time crawling in herself. She reached across Steve to pull Liz toward Steve's side. Steve woke up. All he could utter was half a word: "Wha?"

For the next hour, the three of them enjoyed each other's bodies in ways Liz had never dreamt possible. Caroline seemed to know every move to make, and Steve was a more than willing partner. When they finally were completely spent the three bodies collapsed on the bed, exhausted. Steve was the first to get up. Without saying a word, he grabbed some clothes and went into the bathroom. They could hear the shower come on. Caroline leaned over and gave Liz one more long, lingering kiss. Then she whispered: "We can shower next."

The drive to the Axe went in complete silence. Steve seemed to be lost in his thoughts. A little earlier Caroline had left on her bike to get Gerry version 2.0 while Steve drove Liz to the Axe. They arrived at the bar before Caroline and selected a table very close to the stage. They chose the seats with their backs to the stage for themselves, so Caroline and Gerry would be facing it. Liz made sure that any posters announcing the evening's entertainment were not in sight. She walked up to one that she saw and took it off the wall. The bartender gave her a strange look. "Memento." She said as she walked past him. He just shook his head and sniggered.

They ordered a drink each while they waited for Caroline and Gerry. They glanced backward and watched as two roadies arranged the amps and speakers. The roadies were huge, with tattoos covering their muscled arms. Beer bellies hung out from under each of their t-shirts. Liz was glad that she didn't have friends that looked like that. They scared her a little.

Only a handful of other patrons had come into the bar, definitely for drinks but not necessarily for the entertainment. Then Caroline and Gerry arrived. They took their seats and ordered drinks, and then the four of them agreed to ordering a couple of pizzas to share. Before her drink arrived, Caroline motioned to Liz to follow her to the bathroom. They were barely through the entrance to the bathroom before Caroline got out her flask of coke. For the first time in her life, Liz was doing a second hit of coke in one day. This was a day of firsts, she thought, and the double-Gerry card had yet to be played!

When they returned to the table, Gerry & Steve were awkwardly trying to find common ground to have a conversation about. The band took the stage. Liz kept her eyes fixed on Caroline to see her reaction. As expected, Caroline's face froze in shock. Liz was grinning at her achievement.

The band kicked into their first tune. Caroline switched her gaze toward Liz. "You bitch!" she silently mouthed, although the music was so loud that the words could have been yelled and nobody would have heard them. Liz smiled broadly and mouthed back "Got ya!"

Caroline couldn't just leave without some kind of explanation to her current boyfriend, and she didn't want to get into that so early in their relationship. She just tried to avoid looking up at the stage, and when the pizzas arrived, she stared at the slice on her plate without having a single bite. Liz enjoyed the prank, but as the band's set dragged on, she started to feel the whole thing had carried past the point of enjoyment. She was almost relieved when the set ended and Caroline announced that she wasn't feeling great and wanted to leave. Steve insisted that he pay for the whole bill, and once that task was done the four headed out of the bar together.

They had barely made it out of the bar and onto the front sidewalk when they were surrounded by the band—and those two huge roadies. "You think

I didn't see you, you little bitch! You stole my fucking drugs, and you stole my fucking money! I want them back!" Gerry's eyes had that kind of look that let you know he was serious. There was a fire coming from them. "Cal told me you showed up at his bar the same day that you left me and you gave him some bullshit story about you bringing the money to me. I want my fucking money back!" He glared at Caroline.

"Look, Gerry, I'm sorry. And half of that money was mine. I earned it. You know that!" Caroline was completely aghast. She had no idea of what to do next.

Gerry 2.0 looked at Caroline. "You just called him—" He was cut off from completing the sentence.

"Look, I know you've already snorted that coke into that hollow little head of yours, but I want my cash. And I want it fucking now!"

Steve stepped in. "Look, I can get some money. Right now. I can get you your money. Just relax!"

Gerry didn't move his glare away from Caroline. "This old guy your new boyfriend? Ain't he the guy you were fucking at my place? He looks like he'd be your type, old and feeble. He looks like he'd be easy to break too." One of the roadies had positioned himself behind Steve.

"He's not my boyfriend. He's my boss. And he has money. Lots of money." She turned to Steve. "Steve, I'll pay you back, I promise!"

"How much are we talking here. I've got my bank card and can deal with this right now!" Steve was trying to take some control of the situation.

"It was almost twenty grand. And given the coke you stole, I figure an even ten should be mine" Gerry didn't move his glare from Caroline.

"Ten grand! Hey, I can't get that much from a machine. But I'll get it to you. I can get it for you by tomorrow. I promise!" Steve was starting to get nervous.

Gerry glanced away from Caroline for a moment, making a head motion to the other roadie. Liz didn't even notice him move up behind her. Before she knew it, he had a large tattooed arm around her and a knife was held up to her throat. Gerry turned to Steve. "Maybe I should keep this little pussy as collateral until you pay me. What would you say to that?"

Steve reached toward his pocket to get his wallet, and before he knew it a gun was being pointed at him by the roadie, who move from behind Steve to his side. He could feel the muzzle in his ribs. "Hold it! You don't need that!" He nodded his head at the gun. "I'm just getting my wallet out!"

At the edge of her vision Liz noticed two people on the sidewalk approaching the scene. They must have seen what was going on, because they suddenly turned around and hurried off in the opposite direction. Steve continued: "I'm going to give you my business card. If I don't pay you, you'll know where to find me, and I sure as hell wouldn't risk my career and my reputation by having you show up on campus to collect. My bank has a branch open on Saturdays. I can get you your cash tomorrow and this whole thing will be done, OK?"

Gerry seemed to relax a little. He took the business card Steve offered him and squinted to read it. He looked back at Steve. "Ten grand. Tomorrow. No bullshit stories or excuses, or I show up at your shitty little job and get you fired. Right?"

"Sure. Ten grand. You've got it. As soon as my bank opens tomorrow. My cell phone number is on the card. Call me and I can bring it to wherever you want." Steve nodded toward Liz, who was still having a knife held to her throat. "No need for that to happen."

Gerry thought for a little while, then said "Deal". The gun was tucked back into the roadie's jeans, and Liz felt knife move away from her throat and the arm around her ease up and let her go. She almost dropped to the pavement in relief. She was shaking.

The band and the roadies disappeared around the corner and entered the bar's back door. The four of them stood still, the shock of what had just happened hung heavily in the air.

Caroline spoke first. "Steve, I'm so sorry. I had no idea—"

"Not another word!" Steve cut her off. He was livid. "That's twice now. Here's what will happen next. You 'll come to my condo tomorrow. Between ten and noon. While I'm at the bank. You'll get your things out of there, and I won't ever see you again. Ever. You got that?"

Gerry 2.0 had stood with his mouth gaping through this entire episode and now was looking at each of them in complete amazement. "Um, look, I'm good taking a bus home." He started to step back. Nobody paid notice. He turned and quickly walked away.

Liz was still shaken to the core. "Steve, take me back to your place. Please."

Caroline stared at Steve for a moment, then walked to her motorcycle and started it. She revved the engine and was on her way.

Steve walked up to Liz and put his arm around her shoulder as he said, "C'mere. You look rattled. Let's get you home."

On the silent drive back to Steve's, Liz thought about everything that had happened that entire day. Despite the insane events of the day, the thing that stuck out the most in her mind was a difference in words. She had asked Steve to take her to "your place." Steve had called it "home." She knew it wasn't "home." Not to her, at least. And at that moment she knew what she had to do.

The next morning Caroline arrived shortly after ten. Steve had already left for the bank. Liz was filling her own suitcase.

"What's going on Liz? Did something happen after I left last night?"

A very cold "no" was all Liz offered in response. They both packed their things in silence. Caroline left first.

As Liz started toward the door to leave, she got out the envelope with the note she had written the night before. She felt Steve deserved an explanation: that she had decided to focus on herself, and what she needed. She needed a change. The sex, the drugs, and the job. She was through with all of it. Everything was going to change. Starting now.

# April 2018

The glass roof to the atrium looked like it was crying. The steady drizzle of rain that was falling cast a gloomy mood over the entire lunchroom. It had been raining steady for five days now. Beth was getting tired of it. She looked back down at the lunch on her plate. The sandwich looked just as sad as the day, with stale hummus and limp lettuce. The lettuce looked days old. In actuality, it was, and Beth should know. She had made the sandwich herself. The soup from the cafeteria kitchen was beef barley, and the smell of beef lessened her appetite even more. She put the sandwich back in the plastic container and placed it in her lunch bag.

Donna joined her at the table. It was their usual table. Everyone in the lunchroom sat at their usual table. It seemed funny to Beth, but all these government workers around her seemed to really like routine, and they were seriously challenged when anything changed too much. About three years earlier, when the lunchroom closed for a week for some minor renovations and a new coat of paint, you'd have thought people were going to take up arms against the man! She had even recently heard a co-worker complain about it, and the renovation had happened years ago. They wouldn't let go.

Donna smiled and gave Beth a cheery "Hi!" as she took the seat across from her.

Beth just gave Donna a weak smile back. Donna was the perfect lunch partner. She understood Beth's illness, how it could affect her ability to be personable, and how it came in cycles. She seemed to know when to talk, and when to just eat in silence. She seemed to instinctively know that today there was a need for silence.

Above the sound of the rain Beth could faintly hear instrumental music. They were popular tunes but instrumental versions that were best suited for an elevator. Or a government office. Beth had grown to enjoy them a little.

As they shared their lunch hour in silence, Beth thought about the advice her counsellor had given her years earlier, when she had first sought help dealing with everything in her life. She had just finished university and had landed a government job that included health benefits. Counselling was one of the benefits, so Beth thought: *why not? What harm could there be in this?*

Within the first few sessions, the counsellor had been the one to suggest a name change. "It will help you identify with a whole new life and a whole new lifestyle" were her words to Beth. So she did. Elizabeth changed from Liz to Beth. Every person she had met since that day referred to her as Beth. Everyone she knew did. Except her dad. And Tiffany. She thought of them as the hangover group. The counsellor's advice had helped her stop dwelling on the things she did during those two years at university, and Beth appreciated that.

She remembered sharing with the counsellor all the events that had led her to seek help. Her mother's passing. The sex with her prof. The sex with Caroline. Her using drugs. Everything that made her feel confused. She told stories about the entire fourth year of school, always trying to avoid seeing Steve, and trying to look for Caroline, to make amends. It had been hard, but she was mostly successful at avoiding Steve. She never did see Caroline that final year. She talked about her change of jobs for that last year of university: waiting tables at the Gecko. Tiffany had helped her land the job, and they had become good friends over that final year. Beth still kept in contact with Tiffany to this day, but it always bugged her a bit when Tiff occasionally called her Liz, an old habit that Tiff found hard to break. And Beth also told her counsellor the hardest thing she was still dealing with: she never saw Caroline again. Not at school, not out in public, nowhere. It was like Caroline had never existed. And that hurt. She wished she had said something the last time they were together, when they both were packing to leaving Steve's condo, but she hadn't said a thing.

Liz also shared with the counsellor how often she felt blue. The counsellor had recommended seeing a doctor and possibly getting a prescription to address the feelings she had at those times, but Liz had decided to not consult her doctor. She didn't like the idea of taking drugs, even ones prescribed by a doctor. She wondered if her foray into using cocaine had tainted her view of drugs in general. In any case, she simply struggled through those blue times unaided.

"A penny for your thoughts." Donna offered.

"Oh, sorry. I'm not very good company today. Sorry, Donna."

"No apology needed, Beth. You look lost in thought. Anything I can help with?"

That was Donna. Like a crutch. Or a lifeguard. Beth loved her time with Donna and really appreciated her as a friend. "I'm OK. I'm just tired, I think. I'm hating this rain, and I don't think I'm getting a very good sleep these past few nights."

"Have you tried that lamp I bought for you? This is the kind of weather it's meant to help you with. Did you give it a go?"

"Not yet Donna, but I will. Tonight. For sure. Thanks." Beth was always getting gifts from Donna, and they were always very thoughtful gifts. Beth could never figure out how to return the favour. Donna seemed to have so much more than her: a husband, two great kids, a house with a yard. Beth thought *how could I add to that lifestyle with anything material?* Then Beth had another thought: *Did Donna feel sorry for me?*

After lunch they walked to the elevator together. As the elevator took them to their eleventh-floor office space Beth noticed the music in the elevator was the same as it was in the lunchroom. She smiled. Two totally separate sound systems, one sound. The elevator doors opened on eleven, and they both got out. "Want to come over for dinner? Greg's off with the guys on a fishing weekend. It's just me and the rug rats." Donna offered. Now Beth thought it really was out of pity.

"Thanks, but I'm putting in a little overtime tonight. You know they're going digital with all records, and I've raised my hand to help scan all the estate files. And there's a million of them! Well, really, about fourteen thousand. All probated estates between the year 2000 and last year when they started entering the information using the new online process directly. That's our department's portion to scan. It'll keep me here after-hours for months. And I could use the OT money. Rain check, OK?"

# A NATURAL CAUSE

"OT on a Friday night—I've gotta get you a life!" Donna turned away and headed toward her own office area, calling back "Let's make that rain check happen soon!"

Beth entered her cubicle and stared down at the stack of estate files that had been placed there. Between that stack of files and the new scanner that had been added to her desk there was hardly room for her computer and keyboard. She wished she had a bigger space. She felt so cramped here. Taking her seat and picking up the first file, she started to go through the very mundane task of scanning pages and adding them to the online records system the government now employed. She was unaware that in the next few hours her interest in this task was about to take a drastic turn. She was just running on auto pilot, barely aware of what was on the pages she was scanning.

Hours passed. Most of her co-workers said good night to each other and worked their way to the elevator. Only Donna paid some notice to Beth as she waved good-bye and called out "night" on her way past Beth's cubicle. Beth settled herself into a routine evening of scanning and digitally filing away people's estate paperwork. The footprints that they left behind.

That's how Beth thought of these records. They were the only lasting records most of these people would leave behind. Hundreds of years from now there would be some obscure reason to look up one of these records, and for a very brief moment that person would be remembered again. Briefly, but tangibly. And then they would become nobody again. This was their footprint.

Several more hours passed. Occasionally, quite rarely actually, Beth noticed an item that didn't fit in with the more common bequests in the scans she was doing. She came across one now.

This person who had passed left her entire estate to a charity. Not just her money, not just a piece of property, but everything. The house, the car, the bank assets, their insurance proceeds. When Beth flipped to the next page the hair on the back of her neck stood up. There was the name, plain as day. She hadn't thought about it in years, but it was undeniably the same one she had known before: the Aldbrecht Foundation!

Beth flipped back to the first page. The name of the deceased was Harriet Tiegwell. Not a name she recognized at all. She looked at the address of the deceased but didn't recognize the street name. Then she noticed why: it wasn't a Vancouver address. It was in White Rock. Beth had never been there. Not even thinking of why she did what she did, she wrote the address on a small notepad she had retrieved from the single drawer in her desk. She placed the note pad back and continued to scan, suddenly aware her supervisor was approaching her cubicle. Her name was Elaine, but everyone called her The Supe. Nobody else in the department was very fond of her, but Beth thought she was a nice person and a good manager. However, after almost twelve years of working together, Beth didn't feel very close to her. This wasn't unusual. Beth wasn't close to most of the people she knew. Only Donna.

"Beth, it's a Friday night and it's late. I'd like to go home now. OK?"

"Sorry." Beth replied. She hadn't realized that she was the only one still working in her entire office area, and she knew The Supe couldn't leave without everyone else leaving before her. She gathered her purse and raincoat, and then grabbed the notepad from her desk and shoved it in her pocket. "I'll see you next week," and she got a smile back from Elaine, who was standing with her purse in hand and her raincoat already draped over her arms. They rode the elevator to the lobby together, but when the elevator doors opened, Beth hesitated and let Elaine leave first. As soon as Beth could determine which direction Elaine was going to take, Beth went in the other direction. That meant a longer walk to a bus stop, but Beth didn't like being forced into a conversation with someone she barely knew, although she had no reason to avoid her. Elaine had always treated Beth fairly. However, she was happy with Donna being her only friend at work. She didn't need anyone else.

Seated on the half-empty bus, she took out the note pad and stared at the address. North Bluff Road. White Rock. She wasn't sure why, but she decided then and there that she was going to White Rock tomorrow. She hadn't thought of the Aldbrecht Foundation in years, and never did find out what it was all about back when she worked for Steve. Her old curiosities about it were coming back to her now. She felt she had to go.

Saturday morning came, and for the first time in a long while the sun was shining on the streets of Vancouver. She placed some dry food in Sneakers' dish and added a scoop of canned, then cleaned the water dish and added fresh water. Sneakers was a great companion. He was another suggestion that the councillor had given her. Someone to come home to. Sneakers was grey

A NATURAL CAUSE

and had four white paws, which led to his name. He purred as loud as a chainsaw every time he was fed, and this morning was no exception.

Beth got out her phone to try and book a car-share vehicle. Two were parked within a block of her home, so she decided to get one right away and have breakfast on the road. She still wasn't sure why, but she could feel her excitement build as she made these arrangements. Within ten minutes she was on the way to White Rock. She forgot to stop for breakfast.

An hour later, when she turned onto North Bluff Road, she pulled the car on to the shoulder and looked up the house number on her notepad. Then she looked at the number of the house she was parked in front of. She figured she was only a block or two away, and the sun was still shining, so she decided to walk the rest of the way. She exited the car-share and locked the doors, which stopped the billing to her account and freed the car for the next driver to use.

When, according to the house numbers at least, she was still two houses away from the address she was looking for, she noticed something that led her to believe which house it probably was. It had a large sign in the front yard. She stopped in front of the house and read the sign: "Harriet's House" was in big bold letters. Below it in smaller letters was more: "Dignified End-Of-Life Care." In even smaller type were the words: Funded by the Aldbrecht Foundation. Engraved in relief was an image of Harriet herself, slightly smiling at the viewer and looking very dignified. Her name and her birth date and the date she passed were also inscribed below her image. Wow.

Beth thought Harriet had done something very classy. She found a great cause, and her life will be remembered for a long time to come. What a wonderful legacy to leave behind. Dignified end-of-life care seemed to be a natural cause for an elderly person to relate to and for them to support. Her stomach broke her silent reverie by giving out a loud growl.

Beth kept walking past the house and noticed that there was a hospital a little further ahead. *They must have a cafeteria* she thought and walked into the main entrance. The receptionist directed her to the basement and Beth soon found herself seated and enjoying a healthy vegan breakfast of oatmeal and fruit. The room smelled of cinnamon, and Beth noticed that the aroma was coming from her oatmeal. She also noticed that the music in the background was identical to what they played every day in the lunchroom of her office building. And in her elevator. She wondered if it was some major government decision, as in "the official sound of your government at work".

She contemplated the discovery she had just made about Harriet's House. *What would move a person to donate everything to one cause like that?* It was a fabulous cause, no doubt, and a natural cause for an older person to support, but *what had happened in Harriet's life that helped her make this decision?* And, more importantly, *what on earth was this Aldbrecht Foundation all about? How was it involved with this issue of palliative care?* She resolved to investigate these questions more deeply.

Picking up her phone, she touched the app to book her vehicle for the trip back home. "Crap!" Beth looked around to see if anyone had heard her, but her voice had gone unnoticed. She looked back at her phone. The closest vehicle was in Vancouver! Someone else had driven off with the previous car she had used. What was she going to do? She couldn't just wait for another car-share vehicle to be dropped off in White Rock. That may be hours. Or days!

She walked up the stairs to the main floor and asked the receptionist what her options were. "Take the bus" came the quick reply. Beth felt embarrassed. She had never been to White Rock and had no idea that the bus service came out this far from Vancouver. She left the hospital's lobby, and instead of heading directly to the bus stop, she decided to take one last look at Harriet's House. She wanted to remember it clearly.

She was standing in front of the house, staring at the sign, when the front door opened. "Can I help you with something?" came the call from the lady standing at the opened door.

"No. I was just admiring the house. And the sign."

"Why not come in and take a look around. The residents are all sleeping right now, so I can't show you their rooms, but come and look at the rest of the place if you want." She seemed happy at the thought of having a visitor.

Beth's body was automatically walking toward the front door before her mind had the chance to decide. She shook hands with the lady, only now aware that she was wearing what looked like a nurse's uniform. "Welcome to Harriet's House. Should I put on the kettle for tea? Or would you prefer coffee? My name's Velma."

"Tea would be nice. Thank you, Velma," came Beth's reply. She knew why she wanted to stay for a visit. She wanted to learn more. "I'm Beth."

Passing by the stairway beside the entrance, Velma pointed up and said "There are four bedrooms up, but we won't go there until one of the ladies are awake." After a quick tour of the kitchen, where Velma put on a kettle, and a brief look into the dining area, they both sat down in the living room. The room was eerily silent. She noticed one wall had a bank of four TV screens, each showing a sleeping patient. Beth noticed that all four were women. "So, is it your mother?" Velma asked.

"What?"

"Are you looking for a place for your mother? That is what most of our guests come here for. Or for their father. Are you looking for a place for a loved one?"

"No, not at all. My mother is dead, she died many years ago, and my father lives in Mexico now. No, I'm here, well, I'm here because of Harriet. I . . . uh . . . I knew a little about her. I wanted to know more." Beth was hesitant to explain the real reason she was here, and her job did require her to be careful about sharing confidential information. She knew probated wills were a matter of public domain, but it was just easier to explain to Velma that this was a personal matter.

Just as the kettle whistled from the kitchen, one of the patients stirred in bed and from the TV screen you could hear her starting to moan loudly.

"Duty calls" Velma said as she rose from her chair. "I'm sorry to hear about your mother. She must have been quite young. How would you like to look after the tea while I get this." She was pointing at the TV screen. "The teabags are in the cupboard right above the kettle, and the teapot and cups are on the counter. I'll be right down." She was heading up the stairs before Beth could offer a reply.

Beth put two teabags into the teapot, filled it with the hot water, and placed the teapot and two cups on a tray to carry back into the living room. As she placed the tray onto the coffee table, she looked at the TV where Velma was tending to one of the patient's needs. She was giving her a needle.

When Velma returned, Beth asked "Are you a nurse?"

"Not a nurse, no, I'm a registered HCA. A Health Care Assistant. I can do some things a nurse can, but no, I'm not a nurse. I was one back in the Philippines, back home, but here in Canada they don't recognize the education that I took."

"Oh. I'm sorry. What were you just doing?" Beth was pointing at the TV screen.

"Pain management. At this stage, that is all we do. These ladies all have DNR orders. Do Not Resuscitate. They want to be left to die naturally, not to be forced to live. They don't want to live any more. They've all made their peace with that. Our job is to try and keep them as comfortable as possible. So, you're not here looking for care for a loved one, but you were hoping to learn more about Harriet?"

"As I said, I knew her a very little bit. She inspired me though. I was hoping to learn more about her life."

"Well," Velma started to pour the tea. "I'm afraid I can't help that much. I'm the only staff member that's been here from the beginning, so I doubt the others would be able to help you either. I just assumed she was a rich old lady with a big heart. That sign out front is all I know about her."

Beth's shoulders dropped a little. Then she perked up. "What do you know about the Aldbrecht Foundation?"

"The Aldbrecht Foundation? Well, not too much more than I know about Harriet. That foundation's name is on my paycheque. Well, it was when we used to get paycheques. Now the money is automatically put into my bank. I think I still see that name when I get my tax slips, but I really haven't paid any attention. Why are you asking about that?"

"Just like with Harriet. I knew a little about it, but I was hoping to learn more. For no reason really, I just was curious."

The rest of the visit was pleasant, but Beth didn't learn anything more about Harriet or the foundation. She never got to visit a bedroom, but that didn't really matter to her. She thanked Velma for the visit and the tea and headed out to catch the bus to Vancouver. She checked the app one more time, but there still wasn't a car-share vehicle to be had. Sitting on the bus for over an hour, Beth made a resolution. She was going to find out more about the Aldbrecht Foundation. After all, at one time they had been her employer too, in a roundabout way.

When Beth woke on Sunday she laid in bed and thought about what the previous night had disclosed. After the trip to White Rock she had spent hours on end at her computer trying to find out more about the Aldbrecht Foundation, all to no avail. The foundation had a very minimal online presence. Now she was exhausted from a lack of sleep.

*Why wouldn't they have a website?* Beth thought. *They cater to a very old audience, maybe there's no need?* She did find a couple of mentions of the foundation, but they were in blogs and neither one revealed much detail at all. The search had been frustrating.

She got up and put two slices of bread in the toaster and started a small pot of coffee brewing. She gently squeezed the handful of avocados to find the ripest one, and mashed it with pepper and a little lime. With her plate of avocado toast and a full cup of coffee, she sat in front of the apartment patio doors and stared at the mountains above the North Shore. Sneakers jumped onto her lap, curled himself into a ball, and purred loudly. She enjoyed her single life. She did have a love interest years ago, shortly after graduation. He was a really great guy, named Cliff, and they had a lot of common interests. He could even handle her mood shifts and was very accommodating to them. He had decided to move to Toronto for a job opportunity, and Beth certainly didn't want to move there. She always thought of Toronto as a great big ugly city with tons of poverty and streets that smelled like urinals. Or was her decision because she really wasn't that attached to Cliff?

Living alone now meant she could take all the time she wanted to do whatever she wanted, whenever she wanted. Having a lazy morning with coffee and avocado toast was a freedom she could enjoy without being judged by another person.

The previous day's trip had left her with more questions than answers. She suddenly had a thought: *What about researching Harriet House! Why didn't I think of that last night?*

She gently ushered Sneakers to the floor, walked up to her desk, and sat in front of her laptop. It was still on from the night before. She entered the words Harriet House on the search engine. Over twenty million results. She added the words White Rock, only to find information about several B&B places, and lots of results where one or two of the keywords were missing. She deleted the words White and Rock, put quotes around the first two words, then added the word hospice. Finally, there it was: Harriet's House, White Rock, Dignified End-Of-Life Care. She clicked on the link that took her to the website.

She was immediately disappointed. The site was very poorly constructed and had nothing more than a picture of the building, a picture of the sign in front of the building, and the address. That was it. No phone number, no links to other pages, no other information. Not even a picture of Harriet. She pushed the laptop to the back of her desk and returned to the coffee she had left on a shelf by the patio doors, cupping it in her hands. She slid one door open and stepped out onto the balcony for some fresh air. It was almost noon, and it was already warm, but that didn't help wake her up at all. She stepped back inside, closed the door, and placed her coffee back on the shelf. She walked back to her bed and laid down. She felt like she was done for the day and drifted back to sleep.

# May 2018

It had been three weeks since Beth had taken the trip to White Rock, and despite keeping an eye out for similar bequests in the estate files she was scanning, she had come up empty handed. It was not a surprise to her, though, as she was one of sixteen people assigned to this scanning project. What were the odds of another estate like Harriet's ending up in the piles of files that she was given to process?

At lunch that day she decided to share the entire story with her lunch buddy. Donna sat in silence while Beth explained about her summer job while on campus, leaving out many of the sordid details. She wasn't ready to share everything with Donna. That was Liz's life, not Beth's. She didn't want to jeopardize the relationship she had with Donna by bringing up Liz's history. She didn't even share the fact that she used to call herself Liz.

Once she had reached the point in her story where she had returned from White Rock and was hoping to find another estate with more information about the foundation, Donna interrupted: "Why didn't you just search the records that were already scanned?"

"What?!" Beth replied, a little shocked.

"Yeah. The Medical Records department I work in does that all the time. We use the same system your department is upgrading to. For our old records that were scanned a few years back, we can just enter keywords and search them. If we want to, say, find out how many people died from prostate cancer in a certain year, we just put in the year and the disease. We can filter out the records that came up in error quite easily, then boom. We have our answer."

"I had no idea we could search these files. I thought the access would rely on searching the deceased's name—that's how we're filing them. You can actually search for words in the scanned pages?"

"You bet. Give it a try after lunch. Maybe you'll find that mystery estate you're looking for. Maybe even two or three of them!"

Beth couldn't finish her lunch quickly enough, and even threw out the last part of her sandwich, which she rarely did. Wasting food was a mental stress for her. She excused herself from Donna and went straight back to her desk.

She sat at her computer screen and looked for some kind of icon that would do what Donna had suggested. There wasn't one to be found. When one of her co-workers returned from her lunch break, Beth asked if she knew of any such function in the system. She received a solemn "no" in reply and the co-worker carried on, zombie-like, to her cubicle. Most of Beth's co-workers were in a bad mood these days. Rumours had spread that there was going to be a downsizing. With any new records now being entered directly online, and the backlog of old records almost completely processed, there was going to be no need for the archive department to have this many clerks. The entire staff in the department had become morbidly quiet, as everyone pondered their future while still completing the final steps in this mundane scanning task. Beth couldn't stand the situation, and finally went to her supervisor's office and knocked on the door.

"Enter" was the businesslike reply. Elaine looked up from her desk at Beth. "What can I do for you?"

"Well, I was just wondering. With all this data being entered, what happens next? What will become of the people who've been doing record-keeping for this department?" Beth was hoping to find out who was going to be accessing the information.

"Close the door and have a seat, Beth." Elaine went to a filing cabinet in the corner of the office and took out a file. It was Beth's personnel file. Beth started to feel a little sorry she had approached Elaine and wished she was back in her cubicle.

"What are your concerns about the future of this department based on, Beth?"

"Well, you must know there are rumours going around about a downsizing. Are those rumours true? And what will happen to all of us?"

"You've been here for, let's see, twelve years. Twelve years later this month. Happy anniversary Beth. You must know this already, but that makes you the most senior person in our crew. Were you aware of that?"

"Yes. I'm the longest serving clerk here. But will that matter? Will there be any of us left after this conversion is finished? Will my seniority help?" Beth had almost forgotten why she came to Elaine's office in the first place and was now focussing on her career.

"Well, the exact situation isn't known just yet. You do know, though, the government does its best to reassign workers rather than simply get rid of people. They have a lot invested in these people already, they all have had training and the track records about their work ethic are a known commodity. They would much prefer to redeploy when needed, as opposed to training brand new people for any openings that come up."

"Will I be redeployed then?"

"Actually, no. That is why I asked you to close the door. I need someone to replace me. I've been thinking of approaching you earlier. A few weeks ago, when we left the building together, I was going to ask you to go for a drink or a coffee so we could discuss this. You had walked in the opposite direction that I was going, and I didn't notice until you were out of earshot. But now seems as good a time as any. I've been admiring your work ethic, and I'd like you to consider applying for my position when it comes up. I'm leaving, and my position will be posted shortly. Would you consider applying?"

"I, um, I'd have to think about that. I haven't even considered it. I assumed you were going to be here forever." Beth felt awkward having made that last comment.

"You didn't think I had ambition? I noticed you've kept your distance from most of your co-workers, and that will come in handy when it comes to being their immediate supervisor. Those that will remain, that is. I've reviewed your work history here, and it is top notch. Combined with my recommendation, I think you'd be a shoo-in for this position. That is, if you would want it."

Beth realized she hadn't asked Elaine why she was leaving. "Are you quitting or going to another position?"

Elaine chuckled. "I'm retiring, Beth. I've got thirty years in with the government, and I turn fifty-five next month. I'm going to spend a whole lot of time doing the travelling I've been meaning to do for the past thirty years, before I'm too old to enjoy it. Now, what about you. Are you interested in my position?"

"I'd never really thought about this before. I think I'd be interested, but I'd really like to think about it a bit more. Um, thanks for thinking of me for this. I'll take that as a compliment. Thank you."

"Beth, you've been a great employee for me. Not only are you the longest tenured person here, you also are usually the first to volunteer for overtime when extra work needs to be done. You always have signed up for any extra training that has been offered. I personally can't think of a better qualified replacement for my position here. And by the way, the posting will go up this Friday, so if I were you, I'd have my resumé ready to go. If you want to apply that is. And please feel free to use me as a reference."

"Thanks" was all Beth could reply, and she hung her head so Elaine wouldn't see her blushing. She could feel her cheeks getting hot.

"Is that all you were wanting to talk to me about—job security? Or is there something else on your mind?"

"I think that's it. And thank you again for thinking of me for this position. Again, I take that as a huge compliment." Beth started to stand up.

"Oh, and by the way, they've just posted job training for the program used for accessing the information that we're all busy trying to put online. You'll need that even if you just stay in your current position, but you'll need it even more if you become the department head. You'll have to help train other staff and be able to provide some initial training to any new employees. If you're interested, I'd recommend signing up for that training right away. As I just said, even if you want to remain in your current position, that training will be critical."

Beth's mind reeled. She knew she was blushing. *That's why I came to your office in the first place* she thought. *I want to access the information!* She quickly excused herself, both to hide any possible redness her cheeks had gained, but also to make sure she didn't say anything that would give away her motive for this visit. On her way back to her cubicle she paused at the bulletin board and took a copy of the upcoming training that was being offered for Data Systems Management Clerk II positions. She had seen the posting before but didn't even relate it to her current department because the position title was so strange. She was pretty sure that she was the first employee to take a copy of the posting.

Sitting back at her desk, she resumed the routine of opening a file, scanning the contents, entering some data in a couple of fields on the computer, and refiling all the original paperwork in the box beside her desk. It was the first time she had felt that this job was beneath her.

That Friday, her resumé and cover letter were submitted before the day was through. Just over three weeks later she was seated in the desk that had been Elaine's for the entire time Beth had worked for the department. And it felt right.

The data systems training followed in the middle of Beth's first week on the new job, and Beth found herself spending that Tuesday and Wednesday in a classroom setting with seven of her co-workers. She felt a little awkward now that she was their supervisor, but even more so knowing that two of them had also applied for her current position. Apparently, Elaine had put in a great reference for her. She had to get used to this new relationship with what was her previous peer group and felt a little happier now knowing that none of them had become great friends.

The new software they were training on had everything Donna had mentioned. They could search the scanned files for almost any items they wished.

Beth did her best to resist using the training period for the new access system to look up anything related to the Aldbrecht Foundation in any of the records, but the first day after training Beth couldn't resist a quick search to see if there were any hits. She was a little shocked at the results. There were fourteen probated estate record hits ranging from the years 2006 until 2018. Just as she was about to open the first record, one of the employees, one of *her* employees, knocked on the door. She quickly shut down the software and looked up. "Yes?"

"Excuse me, Ms. Grant, but there's somebody here to see you. Can I let them in?"

Ms. Grant! She hadn't been called that her entire life. It felt so strange! Beth smiled. "Show them in please."

It was Donna. She quickly closed the door behind her and turned toward Beth, beaming a huge smile. "O—M—G!" She almost hissed so the sound wouldn't carry to the common area outside Beth's office. "Did you hear that? Ms. Grant! You have arrived girl! Congratulations!"

Beth suddenly felt a little awkward. She hadn't spoken to Donna for almost two weeks. She hadn't taken time for their usual lunches together, and she hadn't even called her. They had only exchanged a couple of text messages and emails. And Beth was feeling awkward about that kind of treatment toward her closest friend. Donna deserved more than that. "Oh god, I'm so sorry Donna. I've been so tied up, and I've been—"

"Not another word, girl! You've been tied up with this promotion. I get it. But if it will help you feel less guilty, come for dinner tomorrow. Greg's going to put on a Friday night bar-b-que, and he said he has a wicked new veggie-patty recipe he wants to try out on you. We're going to have some salmon he caught just this past Saturday. You're welcome to try some too, if you'd like, but you'd prefer the veggie option, right?"

Donna was so pumped that there was no way Beth could decline. "What can I bring?"

"Just bring yourself. This is a 'celebrate Beth' night, for the new job. So, how'd you like working in an office? It beats cubicle city, right?"

"Well," Beth was about to answer, but a second knock on the door stopped the conversation. "Come in."

It was the same person that had brought Donna into the room. "Ms. Grant, there's a small problem with the new system. There's an urgent request for a record, and none of us can get it to come up on the new access system. What should we do?"

"I'll be right with you. Sorry Donna—duty calls."

Donna gave a smug smiled and rolled her eyes at Beth. "Aye-aye, Ms. Grant" She gave a sarcastic salute, spun around and left the room, calling back "See you tomorrow!" Beth didn't feel this salute treatment helped her look professional in any way and was glad that the employee had left the doorway and had not seen these actions.

At the end of the workday an email came from Beth's manager. "Please see me on your way out" was all it had said. When she stopped at her office before leaving the building, she was asked to take a seat. "Six" was all her manager said, and then she stared at Beth.

Beth knew what that simple word meant. "Do I go strictly by seniority?"

"I would recommend it, unless you want a lot of grief in the weeks to come. Give me their names on Monday and then let's meet and discuss how to approach each one. And you should be aware, these are severances, not redeployments. We will be dealing with some strong emotions next week.

You and I both know that this will be a huge disruption to their lives. These women have families, mortgages, bills to pay. I know this will be hard for them. I'll be with you for the whole process, as will Marilyn from HR."

Beth started to understand why Elaine had wanted to retire and not be a part of this severance process. Now Beth was stuck with doing the dirty work, and she was still in her first week on the job!

The next evening, having dinner at Donna and Greg's was a needed escape for all three of them. The kids were having a sleepover at Greg's parents, so both parents could let their hair down and relax. Donna grumbled a little about how much grandma and grandpa spoiled the kids, but she was happy for the break. Beth struggled to just act happy and tried hard to not be thinking of work.

Beth had brought a bottle of wine, but it was set aside while Greg produced a bottle of champagne from the fridge. Not just a sparkling wine, but real champagne. Donna announced: "This is a time to celebrate!" and congratulated Beth again as they toasted her new job. Beth tried her best to keep herself in a celebratory mood, but the thought of what she had to do by that Monday lingered over her like dark cloud. A gathering storm. She had to pull out the files for six co-workers and get paperwork ready for them to be let go. No, not co-workers. She had to think of them differently now. Six of her staff.

Beth never made it home that night. After the champagne and then some wine, Greg thought it was a good idea to get out some Scotch. Neither she not Donna were big Scotch fans, but that night they both indulged. Heavily. Beth spent the night on their couch. The next morning the Scotch idea seemed even less appealing.

After coffee and avocado toast, Beth excused herself to go home and shower, but headed straight to the office. She identified the six employees that were about to be let go, and filled out some of the paperwork that would be needed that Monday morning. Then she sat and stared at her computer.

Almost mechanically, she logged on and typed in what she thought was the same search she had entered two days earlier. This time the system replied with sixteen records, not fourteen. She must have altered her search a little, she thought. This new system was going to take some getting used to. She opened the first record and started to read.

Record after record, they all read the same. The sole beneficiary was the Aldbrecht Foundation. In every case, the entire estate was left to just the one beneficiary. Houses, cars, savings accounts, investments, everything. Then she opened the file that startled her the most.

It was the estate of Grace Butler. Gracie. *Her* Gracie. Everything was left to the Aldbrecht Foundation. Beth leaned back in her chair. This was more than she could handle. Her head was starting to pound. Partially from the task of lining up six people that were about to be let go, but mostly from what she was reading now. Well, that and from the Scotch she had drunk the night before. She turned off the computer and started to pack up her things.

She was about to leave the office when she had a sudden thought. She returned to her desk and started her computer again, logging on as quickly as she could. This time she searched for only one record: the estate of Grace Butler. Only one entry appeared on her screen and she quickly opened it. Scrolling through the pages, she came to the will itself. There, on the very last page of the will, was what she was looking for.

The lawyer's name: Steven Gilby.

She turned off the computer and walked out of the office almost in a trance-like state.

That night Beth had trouble falling asleep. She thought back to those summer months, canvassing so many people until she found candidates for the long survey. The follow-up calls to those same people, gathering even more information. Had it all been a set-up for some kind of scam? If so, was *she* implicated in the scam? Could *she* be held liable for having helped set this up?

It was around three a.m. when she realized there were more questions that needed answering. She vowed to go into the office again and dig deeper into this issue. Tomorrow was Sunday, and she'd have the office all to herself. Well, it was already three a.m. Sunday. She just knew she needed more information. And more sleep, but that eluded her for the rest of the night.

Early Sunday morning she fed Sneakers and went straight back to the office and retrieved all sixteen records. The first thing she looked at was the back of each page of every will, and she found that each one had been set up by Steve Gilby. She knew immediately that something was very wrong about this. Then, while confirming Steve's involvement on the sixteenth will, she

# A NATURAL CAUSE

looked at who had witnessed the will. Caroline Bottier. Beth almost jumped back from the computer screen when she saw that name.

She went back to the main screen and searched again to get the list that had all sixteen entries. She opened the top file—the date of death was marked November 7, 2005. Then she looked at the back page of the will. There were those same two names: Steve Gilby and Caroline Bottier. Then she opened the last file on the list. The date of death was January 15, 2018. Just four months earlier. It wasn't a file that needed scanning, as the information had been entered directly into the system. She turned to the back page of the will. Steve Gilby and Caroline Bottier.

She wanted to know if they were all like that, so she got out a note pad and wrote down the names, addresses, and date of death of each one. In every case, the beneficiary was consistent and so were the details of what they were to receive: everything. When she checked the will documents, they all read lawyer: Steve Gilby, witness: Caroline Bottier. She turned off the computer and left the office, not sure of what to make of this entire thing. It confused her.

After she left the office, she didn't head in the direction of her apartment. She knew where she wanted to go next.

She soon found herself standing in front of Gracie's house, 3230 Evenson Drive. Well, the house that used to be Gracie's. There was no sign revealing it to be another hospice. It looked lived-in. There was a bicycle leaning up on the side of the house. There was furniture visible through the windows. The gardens, however, didn't look the same. They looked like they had been unattended since Gracie had passed. And the Arbutus tree was now gone, with only a stump to show where it had been. She got out the notepad and looked at Gracie's date of death. February 6, 2012. Six years ago.

She must have been staring at the house for quite a few minutes, because eventually the front door opened. "Can I help you with something?" the woman called.

"Uh, no. I was just looking. I knew the lady that used to live here. Did you know her?"

"No, but we did buy the house in an estate sale, that must have been her estate we bought it from. It was a Ms. Butler, if I recall. If she was a friend, I'm sorry for your loss. Did you want to see the house one last time?"

"No, that's fine. I'm fine. Thanks." And Beth walked slowly away, not sure of what to make of this information. She just wanted to be home and to get some rest.

When she finally arrived at her apartment, Beth was exhausted. She put a plate of leftovers into the microwave and poured herself a large glass of water. She had barely finished both when she lay on top of her sheets and fell fast asleep. She awoke the next morning in the same place she had lain down, still fully dressed. Her head was still racing with all the information she had gathered over the weekend, but she showered and got ready for work. She had a job to do, and six young women were about to find out they were no longer wanted in her department. She had to focus on that.

## June 2018

By the end of the first two weeks, Beth had settled into her new position. The severances were a difficult task but had gone quite smoothly. It seemed each employee she had to let go wasn't surprised at the news. They were expecting it. *There is a value to the rumour mill*, she thought.

She only managed to get away for lunch one or two times a week and was constantly feeling bad about abandoning Donna at their lunch table. Donna took it all in stride and kept saying "When you get settled into your new routine, we'll get back to ours." She was a brick.

Beth had taken to staying late and mostly had used the time for her actual work, but she did do a little more investigating around the Aldbrecht Foundation, all to very little avail. Internet searches provided millions of hits, with everything from promotion pages for certain charities to provincial government websites that listed charities in each province. There was nothing very informative about the Aldbrecht Foundation that she could find. She was becoming more and more certain that she had come across a case of inappropriate behaviour, possibly even fraud, but who should she turn to with this information?

On the fourth Monday in her new position, when Beth was about to go for lunch with Donna, she had an idea. She picked up her notepad with the information for the estates she had found where the foundation was the sole beneficiary. She grabbed her purse and her sandwich and went down to the lunchroom.

Donna was already waiting for her, and smiled, giving Beth a cheery "Hi!".

"Hi Donna. Listen, I have a favour to ask." And Beth immediately felt embarrassed at blurting that out before exchanging even a token of pleasantries. She could feel herself blush. They had shared minimal time together since Beth started her new position. This was awkward.

"Sure. What is it? I'm glad to help if I can." Donna didn't seem phased by the direct approach Beth had taken.

"Well, here's the thing. I can't really say why, but I was wondering if you could look up the cause of death for some people on your records. Can you?"

"Jeez Beth. I can, but you know I could get fired for that!" Donna had lowered her voice to a hissed whisper and looked around the cafeteria to see if anyone was paying attention to her. "All of the information I can access is strictly confidential. These are medical records, and even for dead people they are considered very private. I could lose my job, and I'd have trouble getting another one if I'm fired with a reasonable cause. You can't ask me that!"

"Oh God Donna. I'm so sorry. I haven't thought this through at all." Beth lowered her eyes to stare at her sandwich.

"What is this all about anyway? Are you in some kind of trouble or something? This isn't like you Beth. Not the Beth that I used to know at least. What's up?"

"No, no trouble. Not at all. I'm just looking into something. It isn't important Donna. Never mind. Forget I even asked. Let's just eat lunch."

Donna exhaled a deep sigh. "Sorry Beth. I didn't mean to get all bitchy with you. It's just I've never been asked to do something like that. You scared me a little."

"I'm sorry too, Donna. It won't happen again. I promise." Beth slid the notepad into her purse and tucked it under her chair.

They spent the rest of the lunch together talking about Donna's kids and about Greg's latest fishing trip. But the conversation was forced. Not casual, like it usually was.

When she returned to her office, Beth closed the door behind her. She swore she wanted to keep an open-door policy, but right now she wanted to have a little privacy. She sat at her computer, and this time she searched something else. She typed "Steve Gilby" and hit enter.

She noticed he wasn't on social media of any kind, No Facebook, no Linked-In, nothing. There was a site from him being Professor Gilby. "He made it to being a professor" she found herself saying aloud to an empty office. The site also gave the date he ended that position. It was in 2010.

Then she found a hit that was more like what she was hoping to find. The site read Gilby LLP, Family Law and had a picture of Steve on the main page. He looked the same as when she had worked for him. *Maybe it was an old picture*, she thought.

She took note that his area was family law, but she had no idea of what that meant. She also saw he had an office in downtown Vancouver. She wrote the address down on her notepad.

After spending a little time reading his biography, which was very generic in nature and didn't mention his work in the field of education at university, Beth found one area of his site that really interested her: Licensed Provinces. She clicked on the link. Every major province was listed, right up to the Quebec/New Brunswick border.

Beth leaned back in her chair. *Oh my god!* She thought. *I've only looked at B.C. What about all the other cities in the other provinces where the healthcare survey work was carried out. This could be way bigger than I thought!*

Before she opened her door and returned to the work she was supposed to be doing, Beth tried one more search. Caroline Bottier. Almost no hits, and those that did come up were nothing to do with Caroline. Her Caroline. She gave up for the day and returned to her work. Later, while on her way home, she decided to not let this entire process interfere with her job. She would only investigate things on her own time, not while she was getting paid.

That evening, while she pondered the approach she had made to Donna, she tried to think of anything else she could investigate that would shed any light on these unusual estates. She knew she couldn't go to Steve himself. She was almost certain he was doing something wrong. She was not going to get him involved at all. Not yet. Possibly not ever.

She was also afraid that some of her feelings toward him might come back too.

Then she thought about Tiffany Rainchild. They hadn't seen each other in a few months, so it would be perfectly natural to get in touch for an evening out together. Tiff had worked with Steve on the same survey project. Maybe she would have some helpful information. She picked up her cell and dialed.

"Hey Tiff! It's been a while. Want to get together for drinks, or even dinner?" She waited for the answer. "Great. How about dinner this coming Friday or Saturday. Does either one work for you?" then: "Great. Friday it is.

Say, want to hit the Gecko? I haven't been there in a long time." Followed by "OK. Is eight OK with you?" And the dinner was set.

For the next few days at work Beth did settle into a routine and had lunch with Donna every day. She wondered if that was out of guilt for what she had asked her to do this past Monday. The topic never came up again. Things were seeming to get back to normal, the "new normal" for Beth's new job at least, but she could not shake those prevailing thoughts about Steve Gilby and the Aldbrecht Foundation. When Friday finally arrived, she left the office the first moment she could. Once home, she sat at her kitchen table before going to meet Tiff. She tried to sort out her thoughts and even wrote down a few questions. She wanted to get some answers.

At the Gecko that night, Beth was anxious to get going with questions but was careful to approach anything she asked in a very casual matter. She didn't want a repeat of her interaction with Donna. "Say Tiff, remember Gilby and that whole survey thing? I wonder whatever happened to all that work we did."

"Who knows, and personally, I don't really care. I thought that guy was an ass. No, not an ass. He was a creep!"

"That's why you quit after the one summer?"

"Yeah. I don't know if I ever shared this with you, but once, when he came to this very place and had me as his server, he tried to hit on me! He was what, probably twice my age? And he thought I'd be into him. What a jerk!"

*Only a few years older, and he was hot*, thought Beth. She was calculated in her response, though she could feel her cheeks getting rosy. "OMG! You're kidding right? What do you mean he hit on you? What did he say?"

"I forget exactly, but then, after he creeped me out, along comes that other girl, Caroline. Remember her? She sits down at his table and joins him for dinner. I bet she was the kind to put out for old geezers like Gilby!"

Beth could feel her awkwardness rising and the blushing getting worse, so she switched the topic to be about the new look at the Gecko. After she felt she was in a little better control of her emotions, she pried a little more: "So, you never saw Gilby after that? I seem to remember you even took courses in other lecture slots just to avoid him, right?"

"I saw him in the halls at U the odd time, but I never took another course from him, and I didn't work for him again. Not after that, for sure. It still makes my skin crawl. Ick! I've also seen him around Van from time to time, but not recently."

"What about that other girl? Caroline?" Beth was trying to play a little dumb.

"Caroline? She was a bit of a bitch you know. I sure she was doing this Gilby guy on the side. I bet that's how she kept that job with him for so long. Say, how long did you work with Gilby?"

"Not much longer after you stopped. I was paying my own way through, you know. Res and all made university really pricey too. So, I needed the part time work, I needed the income, but I didn't do another whole summer with him as my boss." It wasn't a complete lie, she thought. She didn't finish the complete summer after her third year. She had walked off the job in August.

"Well, you're lucky he didn't try and hit on you."

Beth looked down at the table, fairly sure her blushing would let Tiffany know that the last statement wasn't true. "So, Tiff, you said Caroline worked a long time with Gilby? How did you know that?"

"I guess so. At least I think she was working with him. I didn't see her around campus at all, but I saw the two of them together a couple of times for a year or two after I graduated."

"After you graduated? As in, after 2006?"

"Yeah. I graduated with you, same year. Remember?"

"But then, where did you see her? Them?"

"My mom works cleaning houses. She's a smart lady. She does homes on the North Shore. Especially West Van. Those people have more money that brains. It costs her a few bucks to water taxi it across the bay, but she says the extra pay she gets is worth it. After graduation, I helped my mom quite a bit, until I finally got my current job, and I'd see those two at a place right beside where my mom and I cleaned. A real nice place too."

"The one you were cleaning, or the one where you saw them at?"

"Both, really. There are not many dumps over there." She nodded her head toward the north. "So anyway, why all this interest in them all of a sudden?"

Beth felt the sudden need to back off with the questions and change topics. "I dunno. I'm just feeling nostalgic for my university years, I guess. No real reason. So, how are you liking work these days?" And with that, the topic was dropped. But Beth did find out one thing: Caroline had continued seeing Steve in some fashion. Her signatures to witness the wills were already proof of that, but this is what journalists call "corroborative evidence."

As they paid the bill and prepared to leave the Gecko, Beth asked "Does your mother still clean houses these days?"

"Yeah. Why, do you need someone?"

"No. Not at all. I have a tiny apartment. Takes me five minutes to clean. I was just wondering; does she clean the place where you saw Caroline?" Beth was straining to sound casual.

"In West Van? Yeah, she does. Why? Are you trying to connect with Caroline?"

"Well, it's just I was trying to get in touch with her many years ago. Just to contact her and say 'Hi'. But I couldn't find her at all, not even on the 'net."

"Well, you know she changed her name, right? I think she's married now. I forget her last name, but it isn't Butter, or whatever it was. Now it's something else. God, I pity the poor guy she married. I bet she's a handful! I myself am glad to be disassociated with her."

Beth wanted to correct Tiff's pronunciation of Caroline's last name but refrained. She just hugged her friend good-bye and started to walk home. Tiffany went off in the opposite direction. A marriage and a change of her last name. *Why hadn't I thought of that?*

When she got home she tried to think of how to search for Caroline's name change, but the long day had taken its toll on her ability to think straight, and she gave up and went to bed. She fell asleep with the rhythm of Sneakers' purrs vibrating against her chest.

The next morning, she logged on and tried several searches. After a few hours and no success, she decided to get out for some fresh air and coffee. When she got to The Smiling Bean, her favorite coffee shop, the aroma of fresh baked pastries filled the air. She realized she hadn't eaten and ordered a chocolate croissant as well. It was only after she had placed her order that she noticed Donna seated alone at a table. This coffee shop was far from Donna's home. It was a Saturday and Donna didn't have her kids in tow. She took a seat at Donna's table.

"Hey girl! I didn't expect to see you here!"

Donna looked up. "Hey! Great so see you! I have a morning off. I'm kid free —Greg has them at his mom's. They're helping her with her flower gardens, so I expect to see two very muddy rugrats when I go home. Are you just getting up?"

Beth decided to not share what she had been doing up until now. "Yeah. Lazy morning. What are you reading?"

Donna flipped the book over to show Beth the cover. "I think you've read this already. You told me about it at lunch. I think that was last week."

"Oh yeah. I read that a few months ago. I'll not say another thing, I don't want to spoil any of it for you. Especially the ending! Say, want to do some 'shopping therapy' after coffee?"

"OK, so there's something interesting at the ending. I thought it was going nowhere right now. I almost gave up reading it. I'd love to do some shopping. Greg's not back until late afternoon. Where were you thinking?"

"I hate malls. Something about chain stores really doesn't turn my crank. How about we walk down Main and hit the clothing shops there?"

"Sure. And I know of a couple of antique stores I love checking out too. You good with that?"

"Sure." Beth was feeling wonderful that the past month of missing lunches seemed to be forgotten. She really appreciated Donna's friendship. Beth knew that she herself was a difficult person to approach and felt that was why she had so few friends. The two of them finished their coffees and left the shop.

While at a gently used clothing shop, Donna brought up the favour she had been asked to do. "When you were asking for the information about how some people had passed away, what were you trying to find out? What were you really looking for?"

Beth was taken aback a little. "Nothing really. I just noticed there was a common thread in their estates. I was wondering if there was anything else in common. No need to do that though. I think I'm fine with not knowing." She knew that last part was a lie.

"So, you're looking for a common disease or something? I've thought about it a bit more. If that's what you're looking for, I might be able to help. Maybe I can just pass on a generic yes or no, you know, if there is a common disease or something. No details though. Just a yes or a no. I'd also want to get my manager's permission, just to be safe. Would that help?"

Beth was hesitant about getting one more person involved, but she was curious about Donna's thought: a common cause of death. She had no reason to think there would be a connection, though. She wondered why she had asked Donna for the favour in the first place. This conversation had caught her completely off guard. "You know, can I just keep that in mind? At this point, I'm fine with the information I have already. OK?"

"Sure. If that changes, just let me know." Donna smiled at Beth and disappeared into a changing room with several items to try on.

The rest of the shopping trip continued without returning to the subject of medical records. When they parted ways and Beth returned to her apartment, she sat down at her computer and once again tried to find information about Caroline's married name. She failed to find anything. She found the whole process very frustrating.

She left the apartment and walked the two blocks to her local grocery store. She wanted to treat herself to a good homemade veggie lasagna. When she was paying, a small item she purchased was rung through and the cashier's comment about it made her realize there was another step she could take. It was one of those tiny moments in life that appear insignificant but have huge implications. Something like the Chinese proverb, where the beating of a butterfly's wings can be felt on the other side of the world.

She had purchased a set of three new dishcloths, something she had been meaning to do for weeks. When the cashier rang them through, he casually said "That's the only item you have to pay tax on today. That's smart shopping." Tax! Beth hadn't thought of it before, but she knew even nonprofits had to file tax returns. And she was pretty sure that nonprofits had to make their financials available to the public! She paid for her groceries and hurried home to her computer.

It was only a matter of minutes, and she found the government site that posted the financial reports for every nonprofit in the country. She entered the keyword Aldbrecht, and up came the detail page for the charity. Her heart raced. Now she could at least find out what this organization was all about, at least from a financial perspective. Maybe this would give her insight into what had funded the research she took part in, and possibly what Steve Gilby was up to when he was having people direct their entire estate to this one cause.

As she dug deeper, she was amazed at the volume of information that was made available to the public. She spent several hours reading the reports and was madly writing down notes. Some items she didn't fully understand. Most items. But a few really stuck out in her mind:

> The foundation had "total salaries paid" listed as over fourteen million dollars.

*How much of that is going to Steve?*

> Government funding to assist with salaries was fourteen million dollars.

*So, the foundation doesn't pay anything toward salaries?*

> There were over two hundred and fifty-seven million dollars in capital assets.

*Just how big was this organization?*

> Donated assets received in 2016 (the latest of the reports filed) was over twenty-six million dollars.

*How could it be that this charity was not accessible online, but they were getting this much support?*

Then Beth clicked the link that was the biggest shock of the search. Under the page titled Detail Page, she noticed what was called the "effective date"—the date the charity first came into existence. It was January 2004. Four months prior to her first summer working for Gilby. How could a charity fund a summer project, with what seemed like a lot of money, when the charity itself had just been established. That seemed very fishy to her.

She also noticed there was a page titled "Directors." When she clicked on it the page opened and she saw four names. Steven Gilby. No surprise. *Caroline Bottier! Surprise!* Beth noticed there were two other names, Nancy Cho, and Vivian Simmons, but she had already seen the names she wanted to focus on, and almost forgot to add the last two names to the notepad. Just as she was about to close the computer for the night, she wrote them down.

Another sleepless night followed, and Beth struggled to think about the right way to approach this. She had already been in bed for several hours when her stomach rumbled and made her aware that she hadn't eaten. The groceries she had purchased that evening were still in the bag on her kitchen counter, along with her new dishcloths. It was 4:30 a.m. She decided to deal with eating and the groceries in the morning.

What should her next step be? She had noticed that there were options to ask for more information from CRA and also noted there were some records listed as confidential. She had looked up two other charities just to see if having confidential material was common, and it seemed it was. She was afraid to ask for more information from CRA, because that might be revealed to the directors of the charity, and she didn't want that. She thought about going to the police, but still felt a little uneasy about having taken part in the process that this charity seemed to be benefitting from. She also didn't feel she had anything concrete to offer to the police for them to go on. She would feel silly going to them with nothing more than a hunch.

Sleep did eventually come to her, and Sunday morning saw her sleep until almost noon. She never did that.

With a fresh coffee in hand, a slice of avocado toast beside her, and Sneakers doing figure-eights around her legs, she sat in front of the computer and reviewed her notes. What could she try looking into now? Not even sure why, she decided to get a map of Vancouver and mark down the addresses of the donated houses. Maybe a pattern would show up. Or was she becoming delusional?

It took about an hour, but finally she had all properties that were in the greater Vancouver area and marked them with big red dots on the map. There were fourteen, with two properties outside Vancouver, including Harriet's House. She tried to see a pattern, and even held the map sideways and upside down. *This is nuts. I'm going a little crazy* she thought. Then she did notice one thing in particular. There was only one house north of the Burrard Inlet, in West Vancouver. Not even sure why, she decided to pay that address a visit.

She got dressed and reserved a car-share vehicle. As she was walking to where the vehicle was parked, she caught a reflection of herself in a store window. She smiled. *I don't look like a sleuth!* she thought. Wearing a summer skirt, a halter top, and sandals, *It looks more like I'm going to the beach!*

Crossing the Lion's Gate Bridge to the North Shore, Adele playing at full volume, she keyed the address into the GPS on the car. Turning left, towards West Van, she found her way off the busy highway. She liked it when the vehicle she booked had GPS. Not all of them did. The house was on Marine

Drive, which she knew fairly well, but it was a long road, and she wasn't sure where this house number would take her. When she finally got close to the address, she parked the car. It was hard to find a parking spot on Marine as the two-lane road skirted the ocean and frequently had no shoulder, but she found a spot with a view of the house whose address matched what was on her notepad. She felt confident that nobody would need a car-share if they lived in this neighbourhood, so she got out, locked the car, and released the rental.

She walked toward the address, admiring the amazing properties as she passed them. Each had a beautiful home, double or triple garages, well-tended landscaping, and—best of all—a wide-open view to the Burrard Inlet, where massive container ships were all anchored and waiting their turn to unload the stacks of containers that they had on board. Her mind reeled at the thought of how many millions of dollars each one of these homes would cost.

She had another thought: *There is no way a student would have gone door to door gathering survey information on this street! The house lots are all gated!*

A lady walking a massive dog was approaching her from the opposite direction just as she came to the correct address, so she decided to keep walking by. She could turn around and walk back in another minute. When she did turn around, the same lady was also reversing her path, and Beth walked by the address a second time without stopping, but she did try and get a good look at the property. The home was amazing! The main floor was all glass and granite, with parking underneath, and a second floor that seemed to only have windows facing the ocean. A combination of fence and cedar hedge ran along three sides of the property, and a steel gate blocked the driveway.

Beth was still not sure why she wanted to see this home. She got back into her car-share, which this time had been left exactly where she had parked it. As she pulled out, she drove very slowly past the property for one more look. She noticed there wasn't a hospice sign identifying this property, exactly the same as she had found at Gracie's home. It looked like any other multi-million-dollar property on this road. She drove on. Before the next bend in the road, she took one last look in the rear-view mirror. And she hit the brakes!

The gate to the driveway was opening. Very soon a car pulled out and started to drive in the direction Beth had just come from. Beth immediately found a driveway to help her turn around, and then she started to follow the car. It was a fairly new black Mercedes convertible. Typical for the neighbourhood, she thought. They drove one behind the other for only a block when Beth decided to let more space come between them. *Am I turning into a spy?* she wondered.

About three kilometers later, Beth saw the Mercedes turn right, into a grocery store parking lot. She slowly approached the same parking lot, saw that the Mercedes was parked close to the entrance of the grocery store, and chose a spot at the very furthest place away from it. Then she felt her solitary car at this end of the lot stuck out like a sore thumb, but before she could change her location, the driver of the Mercedes got out. Beth shivered at what she saw. It was Caroline!

Unsure of what to do next, she did what every serious spy would do. She panicked! As soon as she saw Caroline enter the store, she put her car back into drive and headed back to her own neighbourhood. It was time to regroup.

# July 2018

It had been a couple of weeks since Beth had spotted Caroline entering the grocery store on Marine Drive. She had taken time to sort out the information she had gathered so far, but still found she couldn't put the pieces together completely. It was Friday and she sat on the bus on the way home from work, wondering if she should really spend yet one more weekend totally focused on this project. It was consuming too much of her time. Too much of her life, really. She thought about the information she had gathered so far, and tried to establish items that could be taken as fact.

The first, and most obvious, was that something underhanded was going on, and Steve Gilby was the main figure behind it all. Had he established a charity to fund the research he was doing when he was working at the university? She recalled him saying the government funds he received were tied to him also getting other funding. Was *that* the entire reason for the charity to begin with?

Second was the use of the survey information. He had said it was for the government, for helping to plan for future healthcare costs. Now the people who were surveyed, the people she was starting to refer to as "the victims," were having all their belongings donated to a charity. To *his* charity. That was definitely wrong. He got government funding and then used the entire project to gain millions in cash and even more in property for his charity. And the salaries the charity was paying out annually were simply outrageously high and totally funded by the government. Surely there was something nefarious about that too.

Third was the charity itself. Beth had checked several other charities and none of them were invisible online. Every one of them had been using an online presence to promote what they did and encourage support through donations and volunteerism. *Why was the Aldbrecht Foundation so secretive?* Not only was that just not normal, but it was also very strange. Extremely strange.

Fourth was the involvement of Caroline. She wasn't sure how that fit in, but she knew it couldn't be good. Why did she have no online presence at all? She recalled the last time she had been with Caroline. Steve had told her to get out of his condo. When he had saved her by repaying the money she had stolen from Gerry, Beth remembered he also had said "That's twice." *What was the first?*

As she sat on the bus she thought: *this weekend was going to be like the past several weekends. It was going to be consumed with trying to solve this puzzle.* She also knew she had to do one more review of what information she had gathered. And she was going to try and see Caroline again and maybe even speak to her. She had gone back and parked close to the Marine Drive address three more times, but didn't see any activity and didn't have the courage to approach the house. Not yet.

When she got to her apartment, she decided to do something she had seen many times on TV. She took the two oil paintings down from her living room wall. She got out a roll of masking tape and her notepad and started to stick pages of information on the newly vacated wall space. After about eight pages were arranged into an order that made no sense to her at all, she stepped back and looked at them. Yeah. No sense at all.

She called out for pizza, poured herself a glass of wine, and sat in the chair that faced the wall and looked again. Still nothing. When she reached for the bottle to top up her glass, she noticed the wine was the same one she and Steve had drunk that first night at his condo. She chuckled at herself. She hadn't noticed this before. Was that her subconscious working when she picked it up? Her phone rang, and she let the pizza delivery girl into the building. When she was handling the payment with her charge card, the girl looked at the wall filled with pages from the notebook and said "Nice artwork!". Beth ushered her out the door.

Seated again, with wine in one hand and pizza in the other, Sneakers purring at her feet, Beth continued to stare at the pages on the wall. Then she placed the wine and pizza down. She approached the wall, ever so slowly. Why hadn't she seen this before? There, on the list of sixteen estate names

# A NATURAL CAUSE

and addresses, was Nancy Cho, died December 20, 2012. There, on the list of directors for the charity, was Nancy Cho. And the address for the estate? It was the house on Marine Drive that she had seen Caroline at. Her mind raced. This raised so many new questions.

She then looked up at the name of the other director, Vivian Simmons. There on the list of estate names: Vivian Simmons. Died June 12, 2013.

Why, and how, could a dead person be on a list of directors? She checked again for the date of death for Nancy—December 20, 2012. Six years later, she was still listed as a director of the foundation. She assumed Vivian Simmons was in similar stead.

Nancy's estate, including her house, was all now foundation property, but Caroline was living there. How can this be justified? Surely this was another one of Steve's ways of financially abusing the people he had surveyed. Those people that Beth herself had surveyed.

Vivian's estate was also the property of the foundation, and now she was listed on the board long after she had passed away.

She picked up her phone and called Tiff. "Hey girl, Happy Friday. Say, remember how you told me your mom cleaned houses on the North Shore and you were helping her when you saw Steve and Caroline?" She didn't worry about being discrete. When Tiff had replied "Yeah," Beth asked the critical question: "Was it on Marine Drive?" When Tiff replied yes, she also asked: "What's this all about?" but Beth said: "I'll get back to you and explain, I've got to deal with something right now, OK?" and she hung up before Tiff could get in a word.

Beth couldn't make a lot of sense about what she was now discovering, but she knew what she had to do next. She had to talk to Caroline! She sat down, finished her pizza, and drank most of the bottle of wine. She spent the night sleeping in the easy chair with Sneakers on her lap. The next morning, she awoke with a horrible hangover and a very stiff neck. She went and showered and got ready for the day.

She was sitting once again in West Vancouver in the car-share vehicle, listening to Drake, volume on low. She stared ahead at Caroline's house. Well, the house where Caroline lived. Nancy Cho's house. No, a house belonging to the Aldbrecht Foundation. She had to find a way to make sense of this whole thing. She was focused on the gate to the driveway for almost two hours when somebody knocked on the driver's window. She almost jumped out of her skin!

It was the lady with the huge dog. Beth rolled the window down a little. The lady spoke first. "Are you OK?"

"Yeah. I'm fine." Beth didn't know what else to say.

The lady bent forward to speak into the slightly opened window. "I was just a little worried. For you that is. I'm not worried about you being a thief or anything. It's just that I've noticed you before, you know, when I'm walking George. That's my dog's name. George. Anyway, I walk by here a lot, and haven't seen you here until three weeks ago. Then, suddenly, I've seen you three times. Maybe even four. I'm not nosy, you know, I was just concerned. I heard once about this lady who committed suicide and people who had passed by her day after day before she, you know, offed herself, well they just kept on going. They didn't stop and talk to her. Then afterward they said they wished they had stopped. And you know how she did it? She sat in a car and took a bunch of pills. So, nobody saw anything weird or anything, but they still felt bad. Anyway, I didn't think you were going to kill yourself or anything, but, you know, if you did and I didn't stop, I'd feel bad. Say, this is one of those car-share cars, isn't it?" When she finally stopped long enough to take a breath, the lady stood straight up and waited for Beth's reply about the car.

"Yeah. It is. Look, I'm just trying to connect with an old friend, and I've lost her phone number, so I'm just hoping to catch her coming home or leaving, so I can say 'hi.'"

The lady looked around. Beth thought she moved a little like Big Bird. Then she bent down and started again: "I'm thinking you're aimed at that house over there" She was pointing. It was the house where Beth had seen Caroline. "Well, you must know Nancy then. I feel sorry for her, you know. With her husband, his name is Huang, or something like that, he's away all the time in Singapore and everything. She must get lonely these days. But I hear he's doing really well with his business, you know. Apparently, the import business is really good. I mean, you know, just look at their house. He must be making good money! Anyway, I've known Nancy for quite a few years now. Not well, you know, but I've talked to her a few times. She always seems to be in such a hurry though. Anyway, she says she likes being alone. Her cleaning lady is quite nice too. A real looker, you know. And always dressed up real nice. Not like a typical cleaning lady. Always dressed really nice."

Beth thought, this poor lady. She doesn't even know Nancy has passed away, and thinks Caroline is a cleaning lady. "You don't happen to know her phone number, do you?"

"Oh goodness no. All the people in this neighbourhood, you know, well they keep that kind of information to themselves. It's too bad, you know, because I'd love to be able to call some of them and visit. Anyway. That cleaning lady. Like I said, a real looker. I got her number because I thought I could use a cleaner myself. But Craig, that's my husband, Craig, he said, you know, we don't need one. He said we should get rid of George, because he sheds so much, and then I wouldn't have to clean so much. So anyway, I didn't call the cleaner. I think Craig doesn't realize just how much I do in a day. He's at work and puts in lots of overtime, you know, and with walking the dog and cleaning the house I'm kept really busy. And I do the grocery shopping too. Thank God they deliver. Could you imagine if I had to fit in-store shopping into my day as well? I just couldn't, you know. Plus, their delivery boy, you know, he's a real sweet kid. I probably tip him more that I should, but he's so sweet. He likes George too. Sometimes I pay him to walk George, you know, when it's my crampy time, or whatever. He's a good kid."

Another breath in allowed Beth to interject with the question that had been on the tip of her tongue since this lady had started her latest tirade. "Do you think you still have that cleaning lady's phone number?"

"So, you might need a cleaner too? Do you live in West Van too? You know, I've—"

Beth cut her off. "I'd be really appreciative if I could get that number, if you still have it."

Big Bird stood straight up again. She looked down at the open window with a bit of a scowl. "Well, how about I go look. I'll see what I can find. If I don't come back, then I didn't find it." And she stiffly strutted away.

Beth regretted how she had cut her conversation short, but within those past few minutes this lady had gotten on Beth's nerves. Possibly amplified because she was feeling a little rough from the red wine the night before, but the non-stop nattering was enough to drive anyone to distraction, she thought. She was relieved when she saw the lady approach the car, holding a scrap of paper. Rather than roll down the window for her, Beth got out of the car and stood to meet her.

"Well, isn't this your lucky day! I found the paper she wrote her number on. I'll tell you, she was a real looker, and dressed to the nines. She drove a cute little car too, and I noticed her shoes matched the colour of her car. Did I tell you about her other neighbour? The house on the far side of Nancy's. She has this older lady doing her cleaning. Been doing it for years, you know. Anyway, she comes from the East Side. Not the really bad area, where all those street people are. Is that what we can call them these days? Street people? Anyway, her cleaner lives where all these artist types have studios and things. Craig and I saw her once when we were there to buy some art for Craig's office. In a way that area's kind of interesting, but I prefer the views you get up here. But, you know, I guess you have to be able to afford it here."

Beth held up one finger and retrieved her cell phone from her pocket. She touched the screen and held it to her ear. "Hello? He did *what*? Oh My God, I'll be there as soon as I can. Yes. I'm in West Van, so I'll be a while getting there, but I'll be there as soon as I can. Just try and keep him calm. If it gets worse, call an ambulance, OK?" and she lowered the phone and touched the screen again before slipping it back into her pocket. She turned toward Big Bird and said "I'm so sorry. It's my dad. He's got heart issues, and I've got to run and look after him. Can I come back sometime and visit? You seem really nice. Can I call you another time?"

"Well, I would love that. I'd already written my number on this sheet too, because, you know, I thought we had a real connection here." She handed the sheet to Beth and continued "My Craig has had some heart issues in the past, you know, and I thought it was his work that caused it. But now, you know, he's working harder than ever and yet his doctor says his heart is better than ever. It's some kind of vibration thing, you know, where his heart doesn't beat quite properly" Beth was easing back into the driver's seat. Big Bird continued. "And he has to go and get these regular check-ups because of it. You might want to get these tests for your dad, you know. Maybe that's what is helping Craig, and, you know, maybe it could help you dad too. Anyway, you've got my number there. Say, maybe you should give me your number too, you know, in case you lose that piece of paper or something."

Beth had to interrupt again with "My dad needs me, I'll call you though, OK?" And she started to pull away. She could see Big Bird in her rear-view mirror, standing as tall as ever and staring at her the entire time her car was in view. Once she went around a curve and was out of sight, she looked at the piece of paper. She had Caroline's number! *Cleaning lady? Not likely.* Beth needed to know the truth about the situation. She smiled, remembering Big Bird's comment about shoes matching the car. *It's pretty easy matching shoes to a black Mercedes* she thought. *What a crazy lady!*

She pulled into the parking lot of the grocery store again. It was the first available area to park at. She got out her cell phone and stared at the number on the paper. Finally, she dialed the number. A woman's voice answered: "Hello?" —the voice seemed different to Beth.

"Hi, um, Caroline?"

"I think you've got the wrong number."

Beth repeated the number to the woman on the phone to confirm she had dialed it correctly.

"That's this number, but I'm not Caroline. Sorry."

Beth thought of a different approach. "Um, do you clean houses?"

"Certainly not!" and the line went dead. Beth sat there, very confused.

Then her phone rang. She answered: "Hello?"

"Hey, are you the woman with that enormous dog?"

Beth didn't know why she said this, but "Yes, yes I am" was her reply.

"Well, then yes. I do clean houses. When would you like me to come over?"

Beth had to think fast. "Can we meet for coffee first? I just want to ask about your fees and what you do and don't do, OK?"

"Rest assured, I do everything. And my price is straightforward. But if you want to have coffee first, sure. How about that place called Theo's? It's just up the street from where we met that day. Right beside the small grocery store called Hanson's. You know it, right? I could be there in five minutes."

Beth was already in the same parking lot where Theo's and Hanson's were located. "OK" she said and hung up the phone. She walked into Theo's, ordered a coffee, and took a seat. The smell of fresh coffee hung rich and thick in the air and helped reduce the nausea brought on by Beth's hangover, but the techno track that was playing way too loud on the sound system was causing her head to throb a little. She recalled a short story from her early school days, where a man overheard a story on a train about a murder case. She didn't remember the details, but did recall the feeling he had of a steel band tightening around his head and tiny hammers tapping on the steel. She had that feeling now.

She was the only customer in the coffee shop at that point. *Not a good sign for the business, especially at this time on a Saturday,* she thought. After about five minutes a woman walked in. She was young looking, about twenty-five. She was beautiful. She was dressed very fashionably. But she wasn't Caroline!

The woman ordered a coffee and was about to sit at a different table when Beth caught her attention and motioned for her to sit at Beth's table. The woman obliged.

"You're not the dog lady" was all she said. Beth knew this was the woman she had called.

"No. I got your number from her though. I hope that wasn't being too assertive." Beth looked down at her coffee, which was almost finished by this time.

"I like assertive. I think this is going to work out just fine, you and me. So, is an afternoon time like this best for you? Saturday afternoon? This works well for me."

Beth started to feel a little puzzled. "I think so." She couldn't think of what else to say or ask.

"Look, is this your first time hiring someone?"

"Yeah" Beth answered. *Why would I need a cleaning lady in my small apartment?*

"Maybe we should lay down some ground rules. Would that help?"

"Yeah," Beth answered again. *What would be the "ground rules" for a cleaning lady?*

"Well, rule number one, it must be your house. No other place."

Beth nodded but was starting to get confused. *How could she—?*

"Second, I get paid up front, not after."

Beth was still nodding.

"Third, everything is on the table. Nothing is too kinky. But if it gets rough, I want no bruises. Nothing visible at least. Got it?"

Beth could feel herself starting to blush. *She wasn't talking about cleaning houses at all! She was a sex-trade worker! What the hell was going on?*

"Last rule, if it's for more than two hours, I add to the price. Five for the first two hours, another two hundred every hour after that. And you pay if any clothes get ripped. Are we clear?"

Five hundred dollars! Beth stumbled around for words. "Look, I, uh—"

"What's your name?"

"Uh, Beh . . . uh, B-Bev. Beverly."

"Listen, Beh-Uh-Beverly, maybe you need to think about this a bit more. You've got my number. I'll wait for your call. And if it goes to voicemail, make sure you leave a number, not just your name. OK?" She got up to leave. She hadn't touched her coffee.

"Wait a minute!" Beth struggled to think of something to say but came up empty.

"What?"

"Reference! Yeah, a reference. How do I know—"

"You're kidding, right? And you need a resumé too, I suppose? Look, if you know doglady then go ask her about the house on Marine where she and I met. The woman living at that house has been a client for years. Her name is Nancy. If you know her too, go ask her. Then call me." And with that, she left the shop. Beth watched as she went to the parking lot and got into her bright red Porsche 911. The last thing she noticed were her shoes. They were bright red too.

Beth sat alone in the coffee shop now, struggling to sort this whole episode out. Nancy was dead, at least according to estate records. She wondered: *How can a dead person be having sex with a hooker? Either Nancy faked her death, or...?* It came to Beth in a flash. Caroline was Nancy. Nancy was Caroline. Nancy was dead—the real Nancy. Caroline was using her name. *But then, what about neighbours who knew the real Nancy. From before this name switch. How could a whole new person step into another person's shoes and NOT get noticed by the neighbours? Caroline becoming Nancy couldn't be right. That made no sense at all. And would Caroline hire a woman for sex?* She picked up the untouched coffee from the far side of the table and started to drink it. She had started out the day thinking she was going to get some answers. All she was getting was more confused. And more hung over.

She drove home in silence. She didn't need music to confuse her thoughts. She needed to figure out exactly what was going on. She parked the car and went up to her apartment. It was early afternoon, and she decided two aspirins and a nap were the best steps to take next. She swallowed the pills and drank the large glass of water. As she was wiping her lips dry, she looked once more at the wall of papers. Pulling the list of sixteen names from the wall, she placed them by her computer. She typed in a search for one name: Nancy Cho.

Thousands of hits came up. She added "Vancouver," and fewer results showed, but none seemed to be the right Nancy Cho. She then added Marine Drive. There were only about thirty hits. She started to browse through them. The one that really caught her eye was a site with information about her house purchase on Marine Drive. It was the original real estate listing. Beth was curious about how much one of those houses would be worth. There was the listing. Purchased in 2013, before the prices of homes really went crazy in Vancouver. Still, the purchase price was just over four million dollars. And that was five years ago, so she figured it would be about seven or eight million now.

Beth thought about the woman who tried to sell her a home not long after she first got the job with the government. The house was priced at two hundred and eighty thousand, but the agent had told her she could probably put in an offer for two seventy and get it. She backed out, not wanting to commit to a mortgage of that size. The agent showed her that the monthly costs would be only a couple hundred more than what she was paying in rent, but Beth was still nervous with the idea. She didn't buy it, and every once in a while, since then, she had looked to see what the value of the house was. About a year ago, a decade after she had backed out of the chance to buy, she saw it was sold again at one point five million dollars. She stopped looking after that.

She decided to go to the office that Sunday. She had stolen time from her work while she looked into the strange activities surrounding the Aldbrecht Foundation, and she felt she should put in a little extra time to get caught up with some tasks that she had fallen behind on. Sitting at her desk, fresh coffee on one side of the keyboard, and a chocolate croissant on the other, she logged on. Without any real reason, and instead of starting to work on an overdue task, she pulled up the estate file for Nancy Cho.

She scanned the estate records for anything she might have missed. She started with the will, and saw again that Steve was the lawyer, and Caroline was the witness. The will also had her place of residence on Marine Drive, and listed her complete assets, the largest of which was a very large deposit at the credit union. Eleven million dollars. *Steve had done quite well with this one*, she thought.

She was just about to close the estate system down and move on to her work when something caught her eye. There, on the page of assets, was the category Real Estate and Other Property. The category was left blank. There was no value listed for a house! Thinking this might have just been in error, she looked through the same listing in several other records that had left their estate to the foundation. All of them seemed to have the value of the house listed. Was this just a simple error?

She went back to Nancy Cho's file and looked at the list again. Real Estate and Other Property was left blank. She stared at the screen. She then switched to the real estate site and looked up the address again. Purchaser: Nancy Cho. Value, four point one million dollars. Date of sale, March first, 2013. She went back to the estate records system. Nancy Cho, date of death, December 20, 2012!

This was it! She had evidence of a clear case of fraud!

Beth didn't get any work done, and after a few minutes she exited the office to head home. The coffee and croissant were left sitting on her desk. She wasn't sure of everything that was going on, but she was sure of two things. First, she was going to the police with this. It was time to get professionals involved. She was in over her head. She was going to let them know what she had found and turn everything over to them. Then she would walk away from it all.

Second, she was going to call her counsellor.

# August 2018

Late one Friday afternoon, Beth found herself outside an office, waiting. She had come to the university on a bus once again. It had been almost a month since Beth decided to get the police involved. The first week she'd spent just deciding who to approach. That was possibly the hardest part.

When she used the 'net to help her to decide which way to turn, she ended up more confused than before. There were options like the Better Business Bureau, that had a fraud department, or the Insurance Bureau, where there was a similar area to report to. She crossed those two off the list very early. Then there was the issue of government departments. Several of them had areas that may have been appropriate. She had stroked the "Cyber Crime Unit" off her list, as well as the "Government of Canada Fraud Reporting System." Both of these seemed to focus on specific areas of interest, and she wasn't convinced her situation fit their criteria.

She felt that she had to go to the police. But which ones? Every bit of evidence she had discovered so far was based out of Vancouver, so it made sense that she should go to the Vancouver police. Then she looked back on the fact Steven Gilby was licensed in six different provinces. *What if the investigation went beyond Vancouver? Would Vancouver police be able to handle that, or would they turn it over to the RCMP? Would they want to cooperate with the RCMP, or were they almost in competition with them?*

Beth finally decided to start at the top and chose the RCMP. Their offices were right on campus. She had walked by them on her way to the woods that she'd spent so much time in as a student. After giving up on finding the appropriate phone number to call, she decided to go to the office herself.

Three weeks earlier she had taken the same bus route to her old campus. It brought back a flood of emotions. It had been a very lonely time in her life. She held onto memories of Steve and Caroline, and how she now felt that they had both taken advantage of her. Her counsellor had walked her through these thoughts years ago and explained to her how she had been groomed and preyed upon. She still struggled with those descriptions. She felt guilty herself, thinking that she had done something wrong, so how could she be the victim?

Walking to the RCMP office that morning, as she passed by her old residence building, she had noticed two young girls sitting on a blanket spread out on the front lawn. They looked so young to her. So innocent. So vulnerable. *Was I like them?*

When she first went to the RCMP office, she had been directed to an officer who had interviewed her. It was only thirty minutes into the interview when he stopped the questions and excused himself from the room. He had returned minutes later, and introduced her to Detective Ken Groemann, from the fraud division. That was three weeks ago, and now, on another Friday, she found herself outside Ken Groemann's office one more time. Waiting.

"Beth, come in. Sorry to keep you waiting. Can I get you a coffee or water?" Detective Groemann stood outside his doorway and motioned Beth inside his office.

"I'd really love a coffee, thanks." Beth walked into the office and took a seat. Detective Groemann didn't have to get a coffee. He simply held up one finger, and a minute later a coffee was brought in by one of the clerks from the front office area. Beth thought she could use this kind of service back at her apartment! Then she took a sip of the coffee, and immediately changed her mind. Its taste was disgusting, and it was cold. Tepid at best.

Detective Groemann went around his desk and sat across from her. "So, Beth, I must say this: You've done a lot of legwork here. You've even documented it all very well. We don't usually get this much detail when we are first brought into a case, and it will help us a lot. Thank you."

"I recopied everything when I decided to turn to the police for help. My original notes are a bit of a mess. Actually, I only discovered some of the details I pointed out in the summary when I did the rewrite. I feel embarrassed that I had missed them until the rewrite."

"Yes, well, the notes are clear and concise now. About that summary you wrote, do you mind if I ask you a few questions about that?"

"OK." Beth shifted nervously in her chair.

"Well, we're going to follow through with an investigation. That means we think that there's enough merit in what you've brought forward to spend our time and resources on. That doesn't happen very often. I'd say, maybe one in twenty times. But that is just a guess. The bottom line is this: we are treating your case as a very serious issue. Do you understand what that means?"

"I think so." Beth continued to shuffle a little in her seat and placed the full coffee cup on the desk. She had lied. She wondered what Detective Groemann had meant. She was relieved when he continued.

"I'll be perfectly clear with this. We may continue to need your involvement. We have access to many systems to clarify the information that you've started out with here, but some things we may need your help with. Are you willing to cooperate with us?"

"Sure." Beth was getting a little more nervous. "What kind of things will you want me to do, Detective Groemann?"

"You can relax a little Beth. It won't be anything dangerous. And you can drop the Detective Groemann thing. If we're going to work together on this, please, you can call me Ken."

Beth didn't feel like she was any more relaxed. "What kind of things?"

"Well, for instance, you have access to estate records, that sort of thing. Even with confidential information, I could get paperwork together and legally access all the kinds of things we need, but if you are OK with it, my having you get some information for me would be a whole lot easier. And quicker."

"Well, if it's estate information you want, that's all on public record. It's available to anyone. Why would you need me?"

"Look, I said there would be nothing dangerous, so this is the kind of thing that I'm referring to. Every government department, even every private business, they all have their own way of doing things. Even doing a search of records that are public takes us way longer than it does for someone who knows their way around that information. I'm not asking you to do anything illegal or sordid. I may just need help, OK? It is more estate information I need. You people are using a whole new system for those records. You know your way around that system. Will you help gather the information that I need? It would help me a lot."

Beth could feel herself start to relax a little. "Sure, what do you need?"

And Detective Groemann—Ken—started to list all the items he needed printed for every one of the estates that she had brought to him. There was a lot of printing to be done. She started to imagine how many hours of work she had just agreed to. But she wasn't having second thoughts. She was happy to still be involved. She wanted to see this whole thing through to some form of resolution.

When he had completed giving her the whole list, he added "Look, it seems you haven't been completely open with me. Can I ask you something?"

Beth sat back, a little in shock. "What?"

"Well, we haven't spent the last three weeks just looking at what you provided us. We did a little digging ourselves. It seems you've kept one fact out of the picture."

Beth was like a deer in the headlights.

"It seems you knew this Gilby guy from before. You didn't tell me that. Do you want to talk about that now?"

Beth could feel the blood rushing to her head. Her cheeks were probably bright red, she thought. She had told the police that she came across this information at work. She didn't say that she was one of the people who had helped Steve gather the information on those people that were about to become his victims! And what about living together. How much did Ken know? How much should she tell him?

"Look, you seem to be flustered. That's OK. Why don't you go home, and while you're doing the favour I asked for, think about how honest you want to be with me. I'd like to think we're on the same team here, Beth. And I hope you don't let me down."

Beth smiled at him and rose from her seat. "I'll cooperate. I'll get this paperwork you need back to you on Monday." With that, she left the office.

Instead of heading home, she called her counsellor once again, and booked a time to meet the following morning. She was going to need help with this. She was thankful that the counsellor kept Saturday hours. She then went to her office. Most co-workers were just packing up for the day. She had taken the day off, and she could hear people whispering to each other as she arrived. Finally, one of them asked her "Don't you ever take time off for real?

We see you here all the time Beth. You need to add balance in your life. We're worried that his new position is taking its toll on you."

She smiled. She had been worried about what her staff thought about her. This question meant that at least one of them cared a little! She said that she was just there for a few minutes and thanked the employee for her concern. She then stood close to the elevator and said good-bye to everyone as they left. She knew she had to do more to connect with staff members. Not make friends, in case, well, you know. But connect.

Beth was about to leave the elevator area and go to her office when Donna showed up.

"Hey Beth! Listen, I've got another child-free day tomorrow. Want to go for coffee and some more shopping therapy?" Donna was beaming with a smile. *How could she be so perpetually happy?* Beth thought.

"Sure. I have a doctor's appointment at nine, so why don't we meet at ten thirty. Is The Smiling Bean a good place to meet?"

"A doctor's appointment? Nothing serious I hope?"

"Not at all. Just a regular check-up." Beth lied.

"I found a better place than the Bean, right on Main too. I'll text you the address, OK? Ten-thirty girl!" And with that Donna hopped through the open doors onto the elevator.

Beth went to her office, settled in at her desk, and started to print. There were about thirty pages of details that Ken had asked for from each of the estate's records. Some of the files were PDF copies of scanned paperwork, and their print copies were very difficult to read. She fought with the print settings, trying hard to make each page as legible as possible. By the time she was done it was almost eleven o'clock. She hadn't eaten yet. She placed the pages of each estate into a separate manila folder and labelled the file with the name of the deceased. She paused and looked a little longer at one of the files: Grace Butler.

She thought about what all these files represented. Each one was a life story. Each one had some untold narrative, containing everything from sorrow to joy, conquest to failure. Stories that will never again be heard. She felt that a great vacuum had been created by their passing. Every one of them. She had to bite her lip to keep from crying.

With the paperwork all stacked neatly on one corner of her desk, she headed home.

On the bus an older man had chosen the seat right beside her. He stunk of booze. There were other seats on the bus where he could have sat alone. Not wanting to offend him by changing seats, Beth chose to get off the bus a few stops early and walk the rest of the way home. The local grocery store was closed, but a small sushi restaurant located right beside it was still open. There were no customers inside. She entered the restaurant.

"Are you just about to close?"

"No no no. Open to midnight. Have a seat." And the man stepped out from behind the counter and pulled out a chair, handing Beth a menu. Softly playing in the background she could hear classical music. It was a familiar sound. Her mind went back to Gracie's living room. The plush chairs, the first edition books, the treasured black alabaster bear sculpture, the classical music, everything. It always amazed her how a smell or a sound could return her to a different place or another time. Sometimes she even felt it took her to a place she'd never been, but it somehow felt familiar anyway. This is exactly what she needed to end her day. She enjoyed her sushi and went home to Sneakers.

The next morning, the session with her counsellor had been more forceful than any session she had previously experienced. Beth had brought up the situation with Detective Groemann. She was always completely open with her counsellor but chose to not call him Ken. She didn't know why. When she got to the part where he had asked about her connection with Steve, the counsellor had insisted that Beth be completely open and honest with him and tell him everything.

"What possible reason could he have for knowing we had sex? Why does he need to know that? Or even that I lived at his place? And the time I had sex with both him and Caroline? How could that possibly help him solve this case? This is personal information about my life. It won't help the case in any way that I can tell!"

"But Beth, he is looking to build trust. He needs to understand the big picture, and he needs to know you will help him discover that. After all, he is a detective, and you aren't. He may have reasons that neither you nor I know about. That is his job. But I do know that he needs to figure out if he can trust you, or if you are one of the bad guys."

"One of the bad guys!?" Beth was taken aback. She hadn't thought of that.

"Yes. You aren't a criminal Beth. I know that. But he doesn't. After all, one of the ways that a criminal will work is to distract from themselves by leading police in other directions. They get involved so they know what is being investigated, and make sure all the fingers are pointing to somebody other than themselves."

"Oh my God. I never even imagined that."

"No, you haven't. That's because you're not a detective. And you're not a criminal. But Detective Groemann doesn't know that does he?"

Beth left the session with a headache coming on, and almost wished she hadn't agreed to meet with Donna. When she saw Donna's beaming smile waiting for her in front of the coffee shop, her attitude changed completely.

"Hey girl! I hope you didn't have breakfast yet. This place makes an amazing veggie crepe. I have no idea how they do that, but it is to die for. Let's eat!" And Donna opened the door.

When Donna placed her order, she asked Beth if she wanted the same as her. Beth agreed, and the two chose to sit in a booth that had a street view. They both liked to people-watch. The coffee shop had an open grill, and the air held a greasy breakfast smell to it. The Guess Who was singing "These Eyes," and Beth noticed that the sound was coming from a turntable located beside the espresso machines. There was something comforting about the sound, and she thought it might be because of the vinyl.

Donna started the conversation. "So, you have seemed more and more distracted over these past couple of months, Beth. I don't want to pry, but is something wrong? You're not sick or anything, are you?"

"No, nothing like that at all. I'm fine. It's just this new job, I guess."

"No, I don't think that's it. Look, we've known each other for almost ten years now. I can tell when something is up, and something is up. It all started that day you came down and asked me for some medical information. You haven't been the same since that day. Beth, we're friends. If you don't want to tell me, I get it. But I want you to know I'm here for you if you need. OK?"

Beth thought for a moment. She was getting tired of going through all this on her own. Her counsellor hadn't acted like a friend today, although she was probably saying the appropriate things and was right about being open with the police. *And if I can't trust Donna, then who can I trust?*

"It's like this, Donna . . ." And Beth spent the next thirty minutes filling Donna in on the story. She left out some parts. Mostly the parts she was hesitant to share with Ken. But she did share about her summer job, about Gracie, about the sixteen files she found, and about Nancy Cho. She didn't talk about her relationships with Steve or Caroline. She also left out the parts about the cocaine. She ended by telling Donna about going to the RCMP.

Donna, who had sat quietly listening the whole time, finally spoke. "So that's why you wanted to know about the cause of death. You were looking for more clues. I am so sorry I came across so hard with you that day. I had no idea."

"Donna, you did the right thing. I don't even know what I was asking for, or why I was asking for it. I don't think the cause of death is relevant to this fraud case. You'll keep this all to yourself, won't you?"

"Yes. Of course. I won't even tell Greg. Listen, I offered this to you once before. If you want, I could look into the medical records of those people, and while I can't give you any specific information, I can at least let you know if I find out something the police should be looking into, OK?"

"You know, why not. That would be great. I'll get you those names on Monday, OK?"

"Beth, I am just so impressed at how brave you are for taking this to the police. I think I'd be too scared to get involved. Good for you, girl!"

Eventually the conversation turned to shopping, but they both decided that today just taking a walk down Main would be better. They parted ways late in the afternoon, and Beth went to her apartment. She picked up the phone and called her father. She usually did this about once a month, but it had probably been almost three months since her last call.

When he answered, the first words out of his mouth were "Long time!" Beth felt a little guilty. She could hear mariachi-style music in the background.

"How are things in Villa del Mar? Still enjoying the Mexican lifestyle?" Beth's father always stayed in a place just south of Puerto Vallarta. It was far away from any tourists, and the cost was ten times cheaper. The locals had gotten to know him, and affectionately called him "El Turista," because there were no other tourists in this tiny village. Beth had never gone to visit him there.

"I am. But funny you should ask. I'm starting to miss home a little. I'm thinking of moving back to Canada someday soon. Maybe I'll even move to Vancouver, so I can keep an eye on you."

"Where are you right now?"

"I'm in a little place called Tacos Teleton. Tacos and cold cerveza. It's got no air conditioning, but there's some shade that has a fighting chance to beat the heat. There's a wonderful breeze coming in off the Pacific right now too. What's the weather like up there right now?"

This was one of his favourite things to ask, even though he could look up "Vancouver Weather" on his cell phone anytime he wanted. "It's just perfect. It has been sunny all week, and blue skies help me. You know that. So, what's this about coming back?"

"Well, I was thinking maybe next spring. One more winter away, and then I'm going to come back. Say, you're not sounding like your usual self. Is everything OK?"

My God. How can he tell this from thousands of kilometers away? "I'm doing fine, dad. I just miss you, that's all."

"I miss you too, sweetie. I'll come home soon though. I promise."

When they hung up the phone, Beth poured herself a large glass of wine and sat staring out at The Lions. At this time of year, they were devoid of snow. She wondered if the north faces of the mountains, shaded from the sun, still had snow. Some people said that with the right lighting these mountain peaks actually looked like lions, but she could never see it.

She thought about what Ken had asked her, and about what her counsellor had advised her. She made the decision. She would open up to Ken. She had done a lot of walking, and without having eaten a supper the wine was going straight to her head. She figured that she either had to go to bed, although it was only dinner time, or she had to do something to keep from falling asleep. She went to her dining room table and opened her computer. It was almost a routine at this point, but she couldn't resist. She entered all the names she had previously entered, hoping to find some missed clue about any one of them. She started with Caroline, then went on to Nancy, then Gracie, and so on. Nothing new came up, but before she knew, it was ten o'clock. Now she could go to bed and expect a reasonable night's sleep. After she laid down, she realized that she still hadn't eaten. She decided to just stay in bed anyway and drifted off to sleep.

Sunday came and went without her finding a need to leave her apartment. She spent the day drinking coffee, eating avocado toast, and snuggling Sneakers. On Monday morning, she went into her office just long enough to gather the paperwork she had printed and place them into a file box, and then let a couple of her staff know that she had to leave the office for a meeting. She took a bus to the RCMP offices and asked for Detective Groemann.

When Ken saw her into his office, he offered the usual: coffee or water, and this time Caroline asked for water. He went to get it himself. While he stepped away, she took out the printed documents and placed them on his desk. When he returned with the water, his focus was on the pile of papers.

"Does this mean you're on our team?"

"Our team? I thought it was just you."

"Believe it or not, I'm just the pretty face. There are three other detectives from this office also working on this with me. Well, this and about two hundred other cases. But each one of those officers will give whatever time slices I need to help with our case, so we're a team, right?"

"I see."

"I will promise you this, though, I will be the only one to know any information that you want me to keep confidential. I won't let any of the others know. I promise. OK?"

"Sure."

"So, do you have anything that you want to share?" He sat upright in his chair and folded his hands together, placing them on his lap. His shoulders were rigid.

There was a minute of complete silence. It looked like Ken was going to speak again when Beth beat him to the punch. "Yes, there is. There's a lot. But all of this is between you and I, OK?"

"OK." Ken settled back in his chair, dropping his shoulders a little, and let Beth take her time. And she did take time. A lot of time.

Beth told him everything. About her dad and about her losing her mom as a child. About her going by the name Liz. About the summer job. The part-time job. The visits with a lot of older people. All about Gracie. And working in Steve's office. She talked about what she knew about the other girls who had helped with the survey. She told him about what Tiffany said had happened between her and Steve. She talked about Caroline doing cocaine, and Caroline's boyfriend Gerry who she had stolen money from. And she told Ken about the sex. About her and Steve. About her and Caroline. About Caroline and Steve. And then, hardest of all for her, about her and Caroline and Steve. She told him about her doing cocaine as well.

When she was done, she felt spent. She sat in her chair and stared at the feet of the desk in front of her. She couldn't pull herself to look at Ken at all. They sat in silence for what seemed like hours, but it was probably about five minutes. Finally, Ken broke the silence.

"So, you've been very honest with me. We knew some of these details already." Beth suddenly looked up at him. "Not all of the details, but we knew that you had lived with Steve, and we figured out it wasn't to learn church hymns. We also knew Caroline was into things she shouldn't have been. You've opened up to me, so now I think I can open up to you." Beth was staring at him, wide-eyed. He continued: "We know she wasn't just doing cocaine herself, but she was a small-time dealer as well. We have old records of that. We figured she might have introduced you to it as well. We weren't sure. But then she stopped, no dealing, no buying for her own use, and we don't know why. After about a two-year stretch, she disappeared from our radar completely. You've helped us figure out how. She's now Nancy Cho. We couldn't have done that without you."

"But how can one person become someone else? That doesn't make sense to me."

"Given the right circumstances, it can be quite easy. In this case, a woman from outside of Canada, Nancy Cho, spends her final years here, and the feds have no records of her at all. No tax filings, no government pension money coming in. In her case, no need for it. She was wealthy. The province knew of her, but only enough to issue her an ID. That was all she needed to open a bank account. That was also all she needed to buy a house. Or, to be more accurate, that is all Steve needed for Caroline to buy a house in her name, with her money, using Steve as her lawyer."

Beth was silent, taking in everything she was being told.

"This is where it gets a little awkward, though." Ken took a long pause. He cleared his throat. "What they did was fraud, one hundred percent. It is a huge crime. They did it inside the charity though. That complicates things a little. The way it may be seen by a judge is that they were a little offside in the use of the foundation's assets, and they may get the foundation shut down because of it, but I doubt that either one of them will serve time for it. They will look at all the good the charity has done, and possibly see this as a minor infraction. Fines, maybe. Shut down the foundation, maybe. But jail time? Probably not."

"You said 'all the good.' What did you mean?"

"Well, the Aldbrecht Foundation is probably way bigger than you thought. Karen and Tim—those are two of the team members—well, they investigated things in other provinces as well as here in Vancouver. There are a total of twenty-two hospices being run in six provinces, and there are a total of over seventy patients getting end-of-life care from this one foundation. There are over a hundred and sixty employees getting good salaries for providing, from what I understand, is a well-above-average level of care to those patients. That is what this fraud charge will be facing, and that is what shutting down this foundation could put an end to. The courts will think very seriously before letting that happen."

"Then what happens now?"

"We continue. I told you on Friday that we don't approach most of the cases brought forward with the same amount of seriousness that we are giving this one. We think there's more to it than what we know so far. And what's more, I need to know you are willing to be part of this team. Not just for getting files we need, but for help carrying this investigation further. You proved yourself today by all that you told me, but I need to know this; if I call on you to do more, are you willing?"

"More?"

"As I said Friday, nothing dangerous. We just may need you to help get more information. Can we count on you?"

"I guess so. Sure. What do you want me to do?"

"We don't know just yet. I'll contact you when we do know. One thing though, have you had any contact with Nancy in the past few years? The one you knew as Caroline."

"No, I haven't. I saw her leaving that house on Marine Drive, but I didn't talk to her or anything like that. I'm very certain that she didn't see me."

"Well, don't contact her. Same goes for Steve. From now on I want you to stay a long way away from them both unless I ask you to do otherwise, you hear. This is very important."

"OK." And Beth got up to leave.

"I want to make sure you've heard me. I said stay away from both of them."

"OK. I heard you. I haven't connected with either of them in a long time. That isn't an issue."

"One last thing." She turned and looked at Ken as he spoke. "Thank you." Ken leaned back in his chair. "You probably haven't had anyone thank you for all you've done. I wanted to be the first. You've done a lot of great work here." He smiled at her. She smiled back and walked out of his office, feeling a load had been taken off her shoulders. Before she left the building, Ken caught up with her. "One more thing I should mention: the next steps we take are going to take quite a bit of time. You might not hear from me for a long while. Months probably. But I promise, when we are ready to make moves on this, or if we need your help again, I'll call. You have my word on that. Just try and put all of this out of your mind in the meantime. It's our job now."

Beth smiled at him again. Once again, "OK" was all she could say. As she left the building his voice saying to "put all of this out of your mind" rang in her ears. That would be nice, she thought, but she also knew that it would be impossible.

## January 2019

Beth hugged her coffee mug to warm her hands. The outside temperature had fallen below zero again, and there was snow on the ground from the previous night. Sneakers refused to leave the warm bed that morning, forgoing his chance at eating. The apartment was warm, but just looking at all the snow outside made her feel cold. She was glad it was a Saturday and that she didn't have to go out in the cold if she didn't want to. She watched out the windows as street crews blocked off the streets below. Vancouver didn't clear the snow from all of the streets. They just declared many of them closed until the snow melted. She guessed it was for some kind of liability issue, and wondered what would happen if the snow stayed for several days. Weeks even.

She hadn't waited for Detective Groemann to call her. She called him in early October, and again in late December, saying that last time it was just to wish him Happy Holidays. But it wasn't. Her not knowing about any progress that was being made was driving her crazy. Ken hadn't given her one hint, and just kept repeating that they were on the case and that she should put it out of her thoughts. "Relax!" he kept saying, but she couldn't push this whole affair out of her thoughts, and she certainly couldn't relax.

The other consequence of being left out of the loop was the frequency of Beth's blue days. Usually the winter months were a little worse than the rest of the year, but this year the winter months had become unbearable. For the first time in her life, Beth had taken sick time away from work. She didn't have a flu or anything, she just couldn't pull herself together enough to go to the office. Some days she hadn't been able to get out of bed. She felt guilty about that, which fed even more into her sad feelings and created a downward spiral that she seemed incapable of stopping.

She showered, threw her housecoat back on, and poured a second mug of coffee. She was just settling into her easy chair when her phone rang. It wasn't a number she knew, so she was almost positive this was Ken calling with the update she had so anxiously been waiting for. She touched the green icon and held the phone to her ear. "Hello?"

"Hello Liz. It's been a long time."

She froze. She could feel a tingling sensation go down her back. She started to shake. He didn't have to say who he was. She could recognize Steve's voice anywhere!

"Steve! How are you. It *has* been a long time. What have you been up to?" She instantly regretted asking that question. *What the hell was I thinking!* "Hey, can you hold on for a sec. I left some water running. I'll just be a sec." She congratulated herself on the quick thinking for this stall tactic and put the phone on the table. She needed time to think.

She couldn't call Ken, as her phone was in use with Steve on the other end. Ken had said no contact. Obviously, he didn't give those same instructions to Steve. He probably hadn't even been in Steve's presence yet, for all she knew. What the hell was she going to do here? She picked up the phone again and hoped for the best.

"Sorry Steve, I can talk now. How have you been keeping?"

"Just fine. Keeping busy with my work. I'm no longer at the university either. Just keeping busy with my own small law practice. Liz, how have you been?"

Beth hated the fact he was calling her Liz. "I've been OK. I'm with the province now, working in record keeping." She intentionally kept it vague but regretted telling him anything. "So, what gave you this sudden urge to call? I haven't heard from you in years."

"Listen, I'm sorry to do this to you, but I need to see you. I need to ask you to do me a small favour, and it's hard to discuss over the phone. Can we get together for a few minutes so I can fill you in?"

My God! What was she supposed to do? Ken had said absolutely no contact, and he had said it twice. She needed him to give her advice, and right now. *Why has he taken so long to update me on the case?*

"Liz, are you still there?"

"Yes. Sorry Steve, I'm still here. This just caught me a little off guard. I don't know if seeing you is such a good idea. I think maybe—"

Steve cut her off: "Listen, this will just be for a few minutes. And I promise: I'll behave! This is more or less a professional visit, and just a short one, OK?"

"I guess, yeah, I can see you. How does tomorrow work for you?" She could call Ken and get instructions about whether or not to show up for the meeting. Then she added "How about meeting at The Smiling Bean. It's a little place on Main close to Broadway. Does that work?" The Bean was a public place, so Steve couldn't make a huge scene if he knew she was giving the police information about his activity.

"Well, no. Sorry. I'm leaving tonight on a flight to Toronto. I know where that Smiling Bean place is, but could you meet me there today? Say, in an hour or so?"

Shit! What was she supposed to do? "Yeah. Sure. See you in an hour." She said good-bye and hung up. *Why did I agree? Couldn't this meeting wait until after Steve got back from this trip to Toronto?* She immediately dialed the RCMP office. By now she had their number memorized.

"RCMP Investigations Department, Gloria speaking, how can I help you?"

"I need to speak to Ken. I mean Detective Groemann. Please."

"I'm sorry, but he's not in. Would you like to leave a message on his voicemail?"

*No, I wouldn't like to leave a Goddamn message! I need him now!* Beth thought before she spoke. "Is there someone from his team in today? I need to speak to one of them. It's urgent."

"Sorry, but the whole team is out of town. They are not in communication either. Can another officer or detective help you?"

"Um, let me think. Uh, I'll call back." And Beth hung up. She was shaking and couldn't think straight.

Within seconds her phone rang. She picked up the call, hoping it was Steve changing plans.

"Ma'am, if you are in any danger and can't speak, say the words 'Hi Dad' to me, right now."

"What?"

"Ma'am, are you safe? If you need police right now, I have the location of your phone. Just say 'Hi Dad' and they will be there in a matter of minutes. OK?"

"Oh my goodness! I'm so sorry. I'm safe. I am completely safe. Don't send the police. Oh my God! I have heard of things like this but never expected to be on the receiving end of a call like this. I am so sorry!"

"Ma'am, your voice sounds very shaky. Are you sure you don't want another officer to attend to this?"

"No, thank you. No. I'll be just fine. Sorry to bother you. And thank you for the concern. This is reassuring, let me tell you!"

They both hung up after the woman was convinced that there was no danger being posed to Beth. *But was there or wasn't there a danger?* Beth started to think about her meeting with Steve in a whole new light. Is there an actual danger being posed to her by meeting with him? The coffee shop was public, and it was broad daylight. Surely this is just her mind playing games with her now. There couldn't be any danger! *Could there?*

She got dressed, choosing warm clothes that also weren't very flattering to her body. For some unknown reason, she didn't want to appear attractive to Steve. Then she grabbed a scarf and coat and headed out the door. She knew she would be early, but she wanted to have her choice of spots to sit at. Just like the issue with the clothes, she wasn't sure why this choice-of-tables thing even mattered. It was helping her cope with her nervousness to just be doing something instead of simply waiting.

When she got to The Smiling Bean the place only had one other customer sitting at a table. It seems that she wasn't the only one who didn't like the idea of going out in the snow today. So much for being in a busy public space for safety. She ordered a double espresso and debated having a scone, but decided her stomach was in knots and wouldn't react well to any kind of food. She then chose a booth where she had a view of the front door. She sat nervously crossing and uncrossing her legs and had to make a conscientious effort to calm down. The strong coffee and loud music didn't help in her efforts. The soundtrack to Jesus Christ Superstar was being played. She wondered: *How did the young staff in this coffee shop ever became interested in this kind of music?*

The minutes dragged on. A couple of other customers did arrive, but only one elderly lady stayed to enjoy her purchase. Then she saw Steve walking toward the front door. He was with someone. Beth almost got up to search for a back door to escape from. It was Caroline that was with him! *What the* hell would Ken say to all of this? She wasn't supposed to see either one of them, let alone *both* of them! Her heart was racing.

Steve and Caroline gave her little waves as they entered, and they both proceeded to the counter to place their order. A moment later they were sliding into the booth, seated across from Beth.

"Hey Liz, great to see you." Caroline spoke first. Or was it Nancy now?

"Yeah. Hi Liz. Thanks for agreeing to this get-together. How have you been doing?" Steve was adding sugar after sugar to his coffee.

"I'm doing OK. How about you two?" Beth was tempted to correct them for still calling her Liz, but then she thought of the reason for the name change and that couldn't be explained without dancing around the fact that the two of them caused the need for it. She let it go.

"Same" Steve answered, while Caroline just smiled and nodded, then Steve continued; "Listen Liz, what I mentioned on the phone, well, it's complicated. I may need your help. Can I ask you a few questions though? Just so I know where I stand. OK?" Caroline just sat in silence beside him.

"Sure. What kind of questions?" Beth was already regretting this entire situation and wished she was back in her apartment, sitting in her housecoat and enjoying her coffee.

"The thing is, there have been some accusations people have made against me. I may need you to stick up for me. I think these accusations are totally false, but my character is at stake, and I may need help."

Beth's mind was racing: *Oh Jeez. He knows about the fraud investigation. He knows someone is ratting him out. But he doesn't suspect me? At least, I think he doesn't! What should I do? What should I say?*

Steve continued; "Here's the thing. When we were, you know, living together, you wanted to do that, right? I didn't force you to move in with me or anything, did I?"

Beth could hear the words of her counsellor ringing in her ears: "*You were groomed!*" But she answered "Yeah, I wanted to move in with you. Why?"

"And the whole time we were together, I never asked you to do something you didn't want to do, right?"

Beth's eyes moved to Caroline. Or was it Nancy? *Crap*, she thought, *three people here and five names to deal with! Is she Nancy or Caroline? And I'm Beth, not Liz*. She looked back at Steve. "No, you never asked me to do anything I didn't want to do. Why are you asking all of this?"

"Well, it's like this. Some women have come forward and accused me of doing something wrong. I think it's all bullshit. I think this whole 'Me Too' hype has got all their minds twisted about. It's all crap. They wanted to be with me. I didn't hold a gun to their heads, damn it." Steve's voice was starting to rise, and Caroline reached over and squeezed his arm.

Beth was thinking: *Women, as in more than one?* and *all their minds, again, multiple women?*

Steve continued, but in a lowered voice, "I didn't give these women date-rape drugs. I don't even know what that shit is. I may have had sex with them, that I'll agree with, but I'm not some kind of fucking Harvey Weinstein or anything. I'm just a local lawyer. And yeah, I like to have sex. But I'm not forcing anybody into it or anything." His voice was rising in volume again, and Caroline was now squeezing his arm harder and massaging his neck.

Beth cut to the chase; "How do you want me to help? What are you asking me to do?"

"If this goes to court, I may need character witnesses. People on my side who will tell it like it is. Like it was. To tell the fucking truth. Not some bullshit made-up stories about me grooming girls half my age or asking them to do kinky shit that they didn't want to do!" Once again, his voice was raised, and the other two customers in the coffee shop were periodically looking in their direction to see what was going on.

He carried on: "I think two or three of these bitches have gotten together over a few drinks and decided to make up some stories, and now I'm the guilty-looking one. If any word of this gets out, it would destroy my mother. She'd have an absolute heart attack or something. Why would these girls do this? What are they trying to prove? They're assholes!"

"OK. I think I can help. What do you want me to do?"

Steve seemed to relax a bit. "Thanks. I hoped I could depend on you. I just needed to know I could call on you if the need came up. I needed to know that you were on my side about this. Excuse me for a minute." With that he got up and went to the washroom.

Caroline spoke for the first time since she said "Hi." "He's really mixed up, Liz. Really stressed. The police came to his house two days ago and said that accusations have been made against him. He really flipped out at them, and things got intense, but I'm guessing they don't have any solid evidence. I think it's a case of 'he said, she said', and hopefully this will all go away. But let's talk about you for a second, how have you been doing? Is everything OK?"

"Just fine." Beth didn't know if she should have added a Caroline or a Nancy at the end of her reply. "What have you been up to? Where have you been working?"

"I don't work now. My husband has an import/export company and I make sure he is kept happy with our home. I do miss work though. It gave me direction, and some companionship with my co-workers. I do miss all of that."

Beth realized a lot of what was being said was lies, and they were getting dangerously close to the fraud issues Ken was investigating about Steve, so she tried to redirect the conversation. "I see you've kept in touch with Steve."

"Well, we're not very close. We just get together about some business things now and then. I haven't been close to him since university days."

More lies. Maybe she was caught up in Steve's fraud game and she was somehow trapped into this by Steve. *Was Steve blackmailing her?* He had bailed her out financially years earlier, so maybe he was holding that over her. *What other leverage did he have on her that allowed him to force her to do this?* Most importantly, *what can I talk about now?* There had to be a way to get away from this situation.

"Listen, I feel bad that I have to do this, but I do have to work today. We're all putting in overtime these days." *If Caroline can lie, so can I!* she thought. "I really should be getting going. Can you say good-bye to Steve for me?"

"I won't have to. You can say it yourself. Here he comes now."

Beth stood up and explained to Steve that she had to get to work. Steve thanked her for her support and said he would be in touch if he needed her to come forward with a testimony. They exchanged pleasantries and then left the coffee shop together, and Beth did her usual approach to this. After she saw which direction the two of them were going, she chose the other direction. Steve and Caroline waved their fingers over their shoulders at her. She didn't have to wave back. They were looking the other way and wouldn't have seen her anyway.

While standing at the bus stop, a little bit of paranoia set in. *What if they were watching me, to see if I was really going to work?* Beth decided to play it safe and took the bus that went to her office. As she sat on the bus, she asked herself; *Am I going mad?* She stayed on the bus and went to her office. She spent two hours there, then left the building through the back door to go home.

When she got to the apartment, she called the RCMP office one more time.

"Hi. Could I please have Detective Groemann's voicemail. I'd like to leave him a message." She left Ken a short message, just stating she had something new to share. She didn't say what it was. Then she got back into her housecoat and ordered in pizza for dinner, to be delivered at six.

She knew Ken would have to update her on the case now!

It was Wednesday before she finally received Ken's call. She was at work and was just about to go to the cafeteria for lunch with Donna. She hadn't slept very well the past four nights, and the lack of sleep was taking its toll on her mood. When she answered her phone, it was with a very curt "Hello."

"And a cheery good morning to you too. I got your message. You said you wanted to talk, but I still don't think we should, Beth. It is still too early in the process to bring you in."

Ken was very calm in his way of trying to dissuade her from getting involved with the case at this point. She knew she had to say something to get his attention. "Sorry for the tone of my 'hello.' I had coffee with Steve Gilby and Caroline Bottier."

"Gilby and who? Oh, Nancy. Caroline. Right. I told you not to be in contact with either her or Steve!"

"He called me. I couldn't avoid seeing him. He and Caroline, they met me for coffee. I need to see you. I need to talk to you about it." She held her breath while waiting for Ken to respond.

"OK. Come into my office right after your work is over for the day. Beth, do you feel safe?" His voice had gotten more serious.

"Yes. Of course. Why would you ask that?" Now Beth felt a little less safe.

"I just needed to hear you say that. I want to stress, no more contact with either one of them, you hear me. I'll be here until eight tonight. Come by when you're done there, OK?"

"OK."

Beth picked up her sandwich and went down the elevator to the cafeteria. Donna was waiting when she got to their table. "Hey Donna" she said as she sat across from her in her usual chair. After a few minutes, she asked; "Remember those names you looked up for me last fall? The list that I gave you. You said there was nothing unusual, right?"

"Yeah. Every name you gave me. All that was listed under Cause of Death was natural cause. Why?"

"Just wondering. I was worried that one of them may have been killed or something. I don't even know why. I guess my mind is still trying to put pieces together on this." Beth didn't want to disclose that she was now becoming nervous that she herself might be in danger. After all, this might just be her imagination and there may be no danger at all.

"You said that the RCMP detective guy wanted you to stay out of this. Then stay out of it! This is their job, Beth, not yours. Is that why you've been a little edgy this week?"

"I guess so." Beth didn't want to explain about the coffee meeting that had happened on Saturday. "I haven't been sleeping well either. I think I may have a flu or something."

"Well, don't go giving it to me, Typhoid Mary!"

"No, probably not a flu. Just nerves. I'd like this whole thing to be over."

"Let it go. Don't dwell on it. It's not your issue. You've done your part, leave it with the professionals now."

"Yeah, I guess. I'll try." She took a bite of her sandwich, and the conversation moved on to other things.

After work she grabbed her purse and coat and caught the bus to campus. Walking up to the RCMP office, she started to feel a little knot in her stomach. *Would Ken be mad at me for what had happened?* Surely even he could see how she was trapped into having a meeting with Steve. It wasn't herself that was trying to pry her way back into the case. She was the victim here! When she entered the building, she didn't have to ask for Ken. He was standing beside the reception desk, waiting for her. With a motion of his arm he then let her lead the way into his office. There was no offer of coffee or water either. He closed the door behind them.

Beth was immediately on the defensive. "Look, I tried calling you, but you weren't available. Neither were any of your so-called team members. I tried to do the right thing. You just didn't let me know what that right thing was!"

"I asked you to keep a distance, and that was for a reason. I need every 't' to be crossed, and every 'i' to be dotted, and every step taken to be documented without fail. If, and I am saying *if*, this goes to court, my team will be put through the ringer about these details. You could have easily said: 'Sorry Steve, I can't make it on such short notice. Can we try another time?' or even: 'No Steve, I don't want to see you. Ever.' Instead, you agreed to meet with him. Now, if he calls again, it will become very suspicious to him if you say no to a meeting. You've backed us into a corner here. One wrong step along the way and all the work we're putting into this case could be thrown out the window. Do you understand that?"

Beth closed her eyes and hung her head. A very soft "Sorry" was all she could offer.

"Beth, I get it. You want to know what's happening. I can promise you this, when all of this is over, I'll take you through it step by step. But not until then, OK?"

Beth's "OK" was just as soft as her "sorry" had been.

"Can you tell me exactly what happened now? I'm going to record this too, OK? Just tell me everything with as much detail as you can."

"Record this?"

"Yes. You're OK with that, aren't you?"

"Sure, I guess. Who gets to hear this?"

"Hopefully nobody. But if anything you say is needed in court or something, then it might be useful to record this rather than have you try to remember, at some future date, what you say to me today. That's the main reason. OK?"

"Sure. OK."

After he recorded some intro information about the date, the time, where they were and why they were making this recording, he turned to Beth. "So, tell me. What happened?"

Beth went through the whole episode. The surprise call from Steve. She made sure she mentioned her inability to get hold of him or anyone on his team. The appearance of Caroline with Steve. She tried to remember every detail that she could. She described the conversation between her and Caroline when Steve had excused himself to go to the bathroom. After about ten minutes, she felt she had covered everything and leaned back in her chair.

She looked up at Ken. He asked, "Did you ever feel threatened or coerced at any time during this meeting?"

"Why would I feel threatened? I don't think Steve would hurt me. And all those people that left their estates to his charity, they all died of a natural cause. He's not a dangerous man or anything."

Ken leaned forward and shut off the recorder. "Repeat that last thing you just said."

"What, about Steve not being dangerous? He isn't!"

"No, what you said about the people who left their estates to the foundation. What did you say?" He stood up and came around to Beth's side of the desk, perching on a corner of it and hovering over her.

Beth realized she had done something wrong. She wasn't supposed to know that fact, and now she could get Donna into a ton of trouble for sharing this information with her. She quietly repeated herself; "I said they all died of a natural cause." She waited in silence for a few minutes before Ken spoke again.

"I'm not going to ask you how you knew that. I don't want to know. But I want you to stay away from this case. Do you understand?"

*If he isn't going to ask how I knew, did that imply that he already knew that too? If Ken knew that, were they looking into more? Did they find anything else?* She looked up at Ken. "I understand." She knew she was blushing. She decided to push her own case a little: "But why did the police go to his house? What else is going on that I don't know about?"

Ken reached forward and started the tape machine again. "What do you know about the police visit?"

"When Caroline—Nancy—was alone with me, she mentioned he was anxious about a visit he had from the police. He was being asked questions about accusations some women had made. Steve called it all bullshit, but I think it really got under his skin. Otherwise, why would he have approached me about being a character witness?"

Ken turned the recorder off again and stood up, towering over Beth. "Here's the thing. We care about you, Beth. We—the team—want to make sure that if something like this meeting with Steve happens again, we are on top of it. We want to be by your side, in a way." He reached for a small box that was on his desk and opened it. There was a very stylish necklace inside, with a half-dozen turquoise gemstones embraced by ornate silver workings. At the lowest point was the largest piece of turquoise shaped like a teardrop. It was stunning. "I want you to have this." He reached out with both hands to hang it around her neck and fasten it from behind.

"It's beautiful! But why are you—?"

"It's a transmission device. If you simply reach up and squeeze the front and back of the gem right above the bottom teardrop, the squeeze will activate the transmission, and every sound will be automatically sent to one of our operators, who will then patch it through to either me or another team member. Possibly several of us. Everything will be recorded. The necklace also has a GPS locator, so we will know exactly where you are when you activate it. I've warned the operators that we will be testing this device before you leave today, so let's give it a try, OK?"

"What? This sounds like something from a James-freaking-Bond movie! Are you serious?" Beth's pulse was racing.

"Very serious. I am willing to bet Steve will be in touch with you again, and if that's the case, we are hoping to get him on record with something—anything—that might help shore up our case against him. Let's give it a try, OK? Squeeze that gem, second one from the bottom."

Beth reached down and squeezed it, and while she held it tightly she smiled and said "Testing, testing, one two three"

"You can let go of it. It isn't an old intercom system. One gentle squeeze and the whole thing is set in motion. Even the sounds from a phone call will get picked up." While he was saying this to her his cell phone started to vibrate. He answered and held it to his ear. "Yes, this was the test. You can shut it down. We're going to do it a second time, just to make sure, and then you can delete these two recordings, OK?" He hung up his phone and turned back to Beth. "Look, if he happens to just show up or something, I want you to be able to start this process very discretely. Let's try this again but be serious this time. Pretend Steve has suddenly arrived and is watching you. Just casually reach up and touch that stone, front and back, and then ignore the necklace entirely, OK?"

"OK," and Beth did as she was told, and gave a very natural caress to the second gem. Ken's phone started to vibrate and he answered it, but instead of placing it against his ear, he placed it against Beth's. He gently placed one index finger over her lips to signal that she was to be silent. He then walked to the far side of the office, turned, and clapped his hands together once. Beth had to move the phone away from her ear—the clap sounded like a hammer banging! It repeated itself again and again, slowly fading into the background. "Wow!" she said, and a split second later her voice came blaring through the phone, again, echoing "wow" over and over until it faded into near silence.

Ken walked back to her and took the phone away. Holding his finger over the speaker on the phone, he spoke once again to this mysterious operator, and then hung up. He sat back behind the desk and continued, "Look, this device has some of our best technology behind it. There is never a chance of feedback occurring, and when the software detects a sound loop like you just heard, it knows to reduce the volume on every repeat, which is why it fades away. I covered the speaker just now to reduce the looping effect. In regular use, that loop never happens. My phone will be with me, not with you."

"I see" Beth said, although she didn't understand most of what he was talking about.

"When you trigger the device, there may be as many as four or five of us listening in. We can all talk to each other during the transmission, but what is being recorded is only the sounds coming through the device that you are wearing, not our conversations. If there is any need, we will dispatch officers to your location immediately. Once we are satisfied that the reason for the trigger has ended, we'll contact you by phone, stop the recording, and reset the device. It's all controlled remotely by the operator.

"We want you to wear this necklace whenever you leave your apartment. Make sure you can always reach for that switch. If you need to cover the necklace up, for some fashion reason or whatever, do it with a scarf or something so you can still access it easily. When you are home, either wear it or keep the necklace right by your phone. Be ready to activate it if you get a call from Steve. Every month you will have to come back to this office. We will need to put in a new battery, and that usually takes about ten minutes. We'll also run another test each time you come in. OK?"

"OK. But why do you think Steve will contact me again? He said he just wanted to make sure I was on his team, and I think he knows that now. Or at least he *thinks* that I'm on his side. Why would he want to see me again?"

"There are possibly several reasons, but I would be guessing if I said I knew what he was thinking. And there's also the chance Nancy—your old friend Caroline—may get in touch with you too. I want you to treat that the same way. Touch the necklace as soon as you can. The earlier, the better."

"Again, why would she try and contact me? She barely spoke when we had coffee on Saturday. She let Steve do all the talking."

"Just like I said about Steve, I would be guessing if I said I knew what she was thinking. There's a very good chance all of this may be a fruitless exercise. Neither one of them may ever speak to you again. But if they do, I want to be prepared. I want *you* to be prepared. Got it?"

The meeting carried on for another few minutes, but the details of the meeting with Steve were just being repeated over and over. Beth was growing tired of the whole process.

"I think I'd like to go home, if we're done here."

"Yeah. We're pretty much done. Want a lift anywhere? I'm heading downtown."

"Uh, sure, thanks!" Beth hoped any extra time spent with Ken would lead to more details being shared about the case.

"Just let me get my jacket from the locker room. I'll be right back."

After Ken left, Beth looked around his office. It was the first time she had been left alone in it, and she was noticing things she hadn't seen before. The picture of Ken with a giant marlin, and another one with him wearing a bright orange shirt with yellow birds all over it and a bright green parrot on his arm. The framed certificate for a flying school he had completed. The football trophy on the shelf behind his desk. There was a lot to this man that Beth didn't know. She was just touching the shelf in front of his football trophy when Ken returned.

"I know, the shelves need dusting. The cleaning staff aren't allowed to touch a thing just in case they mess up some evidence or something. In the meantime, we all have to do our own basic cleaning, and I am lousy at it. C'mon. My car's out back."

Beth looked quickly at her fingers and realized there was a lot of dust on them. She wiped them on her coat and followed Ken through the door at the back of the office building. He walked up to an old green Toyota Prius and unlocked the doors.

"This is your car?"

"No. I make ends meet by moonlighting as a car thief. My specialty is stealing all the low value cars that the other car thieves ignore, because they're too busy grabbing BMWs and Porsches."

"I thought you'd have a company car, being that you're probably their best salesman." Beth said, pointing at the police cruisers. She felt she could give back the sarcasm.

Twenty minutes later, when Ken pulled the car in front of her apartment, something dawned on Beth. "I didn't tell you where I lived."

"It took some great detective work on my behalf. Maybe I should be getting that company car after all." Ken smiled, then added "It was the first information you gave us. Your name, where you lived, where you worked. The very first information. Beth, are you becoming paranoid?"

"Becoming paranoid? I *am* paranoid! This whole affair is so far removed from what I'm used to dealing with, I just want it to be over. I want to get back to my old life, as boring as it was."

"Well, maybe that will happen soon. You'll just have to wait for it, OK?"

Beth got out and Ken drove away. Without thinking, she found herself reaching up to fondle the necklace.

She stopped herself just in time.

# February 2019

Putting both the coffee she was carrying and her purse onto her desk, Beth took off her jacket and hung it on the coatrack beside the office door. Two of the employees from her department were standing close to her office door, and she paused to listen to their conversation. She did hear one of them mention "hump day—two more after this," but then they stopped talking and moved away. She was glad the days were flying by in her new position. Or was it the estate fraud investigation that was making it seem that time was going by very fast? But then again, the weeks with no contact from Ken felt like eons. Her phone started to ring. She closed her office door and got her phone out of her purse.

"Hello?"

"Hi Liz. It's me. I hope I'm not interrupting you at work or anything, am I?"

Beth gave the necklace a solid squeeze. "No, I'm just getting to the office. Can you hold on a second?" She counted ten seconds, hoping that would get the recording started, then continued "Sorry, I just had to put down my things. How are you, Caroline?" Surely, she should use Caroline. Nancy Cho was an unknown person to Beth, right? *God these things make me nervous,* she thought.

"I'm good. Real good, Liz. Listen, we really didn't get to visit when we were together with Steve. I was hoping we could see each other again. You know, to catch up. Would you like to get together?"

Damn it! After that long meeting and direction from Ken, and she now didn't know how to answer about an actual get together with Caroline! What should she do? "Um, Caroline, can I call you back? I've just had one of the employees from my office wave me over. I think it's urgent. I'll call you right away though, OK? Your number will be on my call display."

"It won't. My number is blocked. I'll call you back in what—ten minutes?"

"Sure." Beth couldn't get off her phone fast enough. She was about to dial Ken when her phone rang again. It was him.

"Great job Beth. I gather you stalled for the recording to engage too, but you don't really need to do that. It starts immediately. So, are you comfortable with the idea of a meeting with Caroline?" Ken had heard Beth use the name Caroline, so he tried to keep her thinking along those same lines.

"I guess so."

"Fine. Two things. Make it a public place. Lunch, dinner, coffee, whatever. Second, make it someplace where there will be some empty tables. I want to have officers on site for this. Less background noise would help too. I'll also want you to start the transmission as soon as you meet her. Sooner if you can. OK?"

"Sure. I think I understand. Is there anything you want me to get her talking about?" Beth's heart was pounding.

"Not at all. You don't hide things well, and I don't want to try to force any conversations that you may have into any specific area. That might raise suspicion. Just go have a normal visit with her, OK?"

"Sure. What's normal after not talking to someone for over ten years?"

"Just catch up. Let it come naturally. It will. Just relax." And with that Ken hung up.

A few minutes later Caroline called back. "Things under control there now?"

Beth squeezed the gem again. "What? Oh, that, yes, things are under control. So, what were you thinking? Dinner, coffee, or maybe a lunch?"

"Let's do a dinner. Remember the Gecko? I haven't been there in years. For old times sake, want to go there this Friday? Like, seven-ish?"

"Sure. That works." Beth found herself smiling when Caroline used the word "like" again.

"Listen, are you still bussing to get around? I could happily pick you up for this. Saves you from the bus ride. OK?"

Beth said "Sure" and gave Caroline her address.

"I know where that is. I'll call when I'm in front of your apartment block. Around seven. See you then!"

After hanging up from Caroline, Ken called again. "You did great. Did she say the Gecko? Is that place still around?"

"Yes, it is. We used to go there occasionally when we were students. I even worked there for a short time, when I was in my last year at university."

"I used to go there too. That was many years ago. So, just so you know, there will be somebody, one or maybe two officers, right there in the restaurant with you. They'll arrive ahead of you two. They'll be listening in to the recording system. If anything feels uncomfortable, we'll have a safe word. Something you say that will trigger an officer to come up to you. He'll pretend he knows you from the past, and you can strike up a conversation with him. Then he'll ask if you two can join his table, or if he can join yours. You can respond as you see appropriate. He will ignore any response from Nancy. Caroline. Makes sense?"

"Sure, but what word do I use?"

"You should pick it. That way you'll remember it. And don't pick something too obscure, or it will sound obvious. What word do you want to use?"

"How about Steve? If I mention his name—"

"No, that won't work. You might say it if you end up talking about him, and I'm certainly hoping you will. Pick something else."

"Um . . . how about snow. It's all gone now, but I can complain that we had too much snow or something, OK?"

"That's perfect. So, you'll say snow if you feel uncomfortable. Don't hesitate to use the word. We don't want you involved with anything you feel threatened by. I don't want that. Now, do you think we need to get together and review any part of this, or are you good to go?"

"I think I'm good. Thanks Ken."

Beth opened her office door and sat behind her desk. She hoped that none of her department's employees were watching, because she couldn't force herself to start working. There was too much going on in her head.

*Why did Caroline contact me? Was it only just to catch up?* When they had gone for coffee, she kept so quiet when Steve was at the table, and yet she talked as soon as he left. *What was the reason for that?* And this whole thing about women—girls—accusing Steve of wrongdoings. *Did he?* She was relieved when lunchtime finally came around. She needed a break, and

# A NATURAL CAUSE

not from work! Maybe Donna could find a way to get her thinking about something else.

The following forty-eight hours seemed like an eternity. Finally, that Friday after work, Beth bussed home. Her phone rang as soon as she got into her apartment. It was Ken.

"Now, are you sure you're OK with all of this? You still want to go through with the dinner meeting?"

"I'm fine with it. Caroline is an old friend. This will be OK."

"Don't say it out loud, but do you remember your safe word?"

"Yes, I do. Don't worry Ken. I'm all set."

They ended the call and Beth immediately went to her bedroom and lay down. "Why does life have to be so complicated? So confusing?" She hadn't really talked out loud in her bedroom before. The room made her own voice sound foreign to her ears. Then she thought, W*hat if this necklace is recording me now?* She got out of bed and showered. She spent a lot of time choosing clothing for the dinner, making sure the outfit worked with the necklace. She also chose a shawl that kept her warm but allowed easy access to the gem. For the first time in a long while, she put on make-up too.

Seven o'clock came and went. No Caroline. Minutes ticked by and still no call from her. Finally, at about twenty after, her phone rang. She gave the gem a gentle squeeze.

"Sorry Liz, I let the time get away on me. No excuse, I just didn't notice. I'm in front of your apartment now."

Beth moved Sneakers from her lap to the warm spot on the couch where she had been sitting and went down the elevator and out the front doors. There was Caroline, sitting in an old green Buick. Beth thought it was a car more suited to an old person. *What happened to the Mercedes?* she thought, but she knew she couldn't say anything. Caroline didn't know that she had ever seen the Mercedes. She got into the passenger side, and Caroline pulled away. But instead of turning right to go toward Main Street, Caroline turned left.

"Caroline, the Gecko is still on Main, y'know?"

"I know, but I've changed plans. I thought we could go to my place, open a bottle of wine, and we could relax more and be ourselves. Our real selves, not like we behave when we're in public. I've ordered food and I'll stop and grab it on the way. OK?"

"Sure. OK." Beth wondered if she should talk about all the snow that they had this year but held off. They drove about ten minutes when Caroline pulled in front of a Thai restaurant.

"I ordered everything vegan. I assume that is OK with you?" When Beth said yes, Caroline got out of the car and went into the restaurant. Beth's phone gave the jingle of a text message arriving, so she got it out and looked. Blocked number. All it said was "ALL GOOD." She had to hope it was Ken. She put the phone away and almost immediately saw Caroline approach the car holding a huge paper bag. "I hope you're hungry Liz!" She put the bag in the back seat and got behind the wheel again.

As she pulled the car back into traffic, Beth noticed they weren't heading in the direction of the North Shore. They were going toward the university. "Where do you live?" she asked, but she found herself having to strain to sound calm.

"I've got a little place in Kits, just off 4th. You'll love it, I hope. I've lived there for, like, seven years now, and it really is starting to feel like my permanent home."

Oh my god. Another house. Was she Nancy Cho in this house too? Or Caroline? Or somebody else even? Beth was once again considering talking about all the snow they had this year, but she held back.

Caroline drove down 4th and then turned right, but Beth didn't notice the street name. If there was a street sign, she didn't spot it. They parked and got out of the car. Caroline handed the take-out bag to Beth, saying "I'll get the doors for you."

When they went up the sidewalk to the beautifully kept old two-and-a-half story Edwardian style home, Beth noticed a plaque was posted on the front veranda. It was from the Vancouver Heritage Foundation, but the type was small and at a quick glance she couldn't read what it said. They entered the front door. On both sides of the door were stained glass windows, with vines, green leaves and red roses climbing an imaginary central pole.

Beth gushed "I love your home already, and I've only seen the front door! Is this all original?"

"About ninety-nine percent is. Anything new I've tried to stay with replacing the original as much as I can. This house was built in 1912, so it was exactly one-hundred years old when I bought it."

# A NATURAL CAUSE

Beth thought: *Bought it? You're my age. In 2012 you were in your twenties. You couldn't afford this! Oh yeah. Husband is a shipping magnate or whatever. Nice.* but she said: "Nice!"

"Let's go to the dining room. Here, give me that." And Caroline took the bag from Beth and went into the kitchen. She reappeared around a minute later and handed Beth one of the two full wine glasses she was holding. "Want a tour before dinner?"

"Sure!"

Walking through the home, Beth felt she was in a museum. The bedrooms were fully furnished, but they didn't seem to be in use. The two upstairs bathrooms looked like they'd been professionally decorated and had just been sanitized. Beth couldn't resist asking: "Do you have a maid?"

"A service, yes. Once a week. You've come the same day that they've been here, so I haven't made a mess of things yet. Our food is getting cold. Let's go eat."

Following Caroline down the stairs from the top floor, Beth noticed a desk with an envelope on it. She was dying to get a look at the address, but just as she was about to reach for it, Caroline turned around and said, "Have you ever thought of owning a home Liz?"

*Yeah, by stealing someone else's estate. I think of doing that every day.* She held those thoughts back. "I did at one time, but prices have become so crazy, I don't think it will ever happen."

"Never say never. I just got lucky on the hubby front!" And she flashed a huge diamond ring at Beth. They started down the second flight of stairs to the main floor.

"Will your husband be coming home tonight?" Beth thought that was a normal kind of question. Safe to ask. Reasonable, for sure.

"Unfortunately, no. He is based out of Singapore, but right now he's in India. His business is global, and he likes a very hands-on approach to running things. Have a seat. Are you OK if I just plate the food rather than put everything in fancy dishes?"

"Sure. Or even just bring the containers to the table and we can help ourselves. Whatever is easiest."

"Yeah, I can't do that. Huong—my husband, that's his name. He'd be stressed. Apparently, this table is worth a ton of money, and we can't put warm serving dishes on it or anything. Not that the food is still warm, for that matter. I'll go plate some food. You OK if I zap it a bit too?"

"Sure." And with that, Beth was left alone in the dining room. She looked at the artwork on the wall and at the beautiful dishes in the China cabinet that was covering one entire wall of the room. The entire room felt like, well, money. But not what a woman Caroline's age would want, she thought. Not what she herself would want, that was for sure. She sat in one of the chairs and waited for Caroline.

When Caroline entered the room and placed the plates on the table, she made sure that there was an insulated placemat under them. She then topped up their wine glasses and put the half-empty bottle in a special wine holder beside the table. *Apparently, she's serious about protecting the table* thought Beth.

Conversation centred on reminiscing about the lives they lived while working together for Steve but didn't hold much information about Steve himself. At least, nothing Beth wasn't already aware of. After the dinner, they moved to the living room. Beth sat on an overstuffed Victorian couch, maneuvering the pillows just to be able to find a place to sit. Caroline moved a large pillow out of the way and sat beside Beth. She was a little too close for Beth's comfort.

Caroline reached toward Beth and started to twirl a lock of Beth's hair in her fingers. "So, Liz, are you seeing someone these days?"

Beth became aware that she had drunk too much wine. She was definitely feeling tipsy. But she knew that their conversation was being listened to. And recorded. "Caroline, sorry, I have to use the loo." She stood up and went to the bathroom that was located on the main floor.

She stood there for two minutes, trying to regroup her thoughts. She had to find a way to keep talking. But she also had to find a way to not get into anything physical with Caroline. She searched her soul. *Did she still want to be together with Caroline? Physically?* She couldn't find the answer. She flushed the unused toilet, washed her hands, and left the bathroom.

As she entered the living room, she noticed Caroline was still in the same position that she was before. Then, out of the corner of her eye, she caught a glimpse of something she hadn't noticed earlier.

There, on a shelf on the far side of the room, was a sculpture. It was black alabaster. It was a bear, seated, and looking to one side. She knew that bear!

She walked up to the shelves, unaware that Caroline was focused on her every movement. She picked up the bear. It felt ice cold in her hands. A rush of thoughts immediately overwhelmed her. She became aware of something that she had missed the entire time she was reviewing the estate paperwork. Something that suddenly became very obvious. *How could I have missed this?* She placed the black alabaster bear back on the shelf.

"Look, Caroline, that trip to the bathroom was because I'm sick. It might have been something I ate, I don't know. But I just want to go home right now. Can I see you another time?" That last question was hollow. She was not sure if she ever wanted to see Caroline again. Ever.

"Yeah, no problem. I can understand. Let's do this again though, when you're feeling up to it, OK? I'll get my car keys."

"No!" Beth suddenly realized she sounded too panicky with that response. "Listen, a good friend of mine was killed by a drunk driver. I'll get an Uber." She was already fumbling with her phone. "The app says there's a car only one minute away." She fumbled a bit more. "It's on the way. Listen, thanks for getting in touch, I really enjoyed the evening. And I really love your home. You have my phone number, give me yours, and we can set up another time to meet, OK?"

"I'll text it to you when I get my new one. Huong is getting me another phone with a better international package, but he says it will mean I have to get a new cell number. I have yours, though."

Beth's phone vibrated, with a message saying her Uber had arrived. She went to the front doorway and hugged Caroline before leaving. Getting into the Uber, she didn't even notice the green Toyota Prius parked about three houses down the street.

As the Uber was driving down 4$^{th}$ toward her apartment, the driver suddenly swore and pulled over. There were red flashing lights in the green Prius that pulled up behind him. He rolled down his window, about to ask what he had done wrong, when a fifty-dollar bill was presented to him.

"I'll take her home from here. Go buy yourself a snack." Ken leaned down and spoke to Beth in the back seat. "Beth, you did great. C'mon. I'll take you home." Beth got out and went to the Prius, and the Uber driver simply drove away.

"Are you OK?" Ken asked as he pulled away from the curb.

"No. Actually, I'm not OK. Is this still on?" She was slapping at the necklace.

"No. I had them shut down the monitoring before I pulled you over."

Beth took off her seatbelt, turned to Ken and started punching him in the chest and shoulder. He pulled the car over so he could grab her fists and stop the pummelling.

"Whoa! Beth, stop. *Stop!*"

Beth's face was streaming with tears. She sat back and stared out the windshield.

"Beth, talk to me. What?"

"Take me home" was all she said.

Ken pulled away from the curb again. They were only a block further down the road when Beth turned to him and said, "No. Take me to work."

"Beth, it's almost ten on a Friday night. What work could possibly be that important?"

"I want you to see something. Come to my office with me."

Ken knew better than to press her with questions at this point. He knew what he had to do. He drove her to her office and followed her inside. They rode the elevator to the eleventh floor in silence. She sat at her desk and started typing on her computer.

"What are you wanting to show me Beth?"

By this time the new software was second nature to Beth. She continued to type for a few seconds more, then spun the screen toward Ken. "This" was all she said.

Ken stared at the screen for a minute. The screen was showing the estate settlement paperwork for someone named Grace Butler. Nothing unusual stood out to him. "What?" He stared at Beth.

"I'll tell you *what*! I want to be part of the team. That's *what*! You need me to be part of the team. And that means no more leaving me out in the cold. If you have information about Steve and the Aldbrecht Foundation, I want it. Either that, or you can drive me home right now and then say good-bye to me being helpful to you ever again." She folded her arms in front of her and stared back at Ken. His shoulders slumped.

"Look, if I'm going to give you some more information—"

"I have what you need. I think you call it the 'smoking gun' or something like that. I am holding it, and you need it. Either include me with *all* the information, or I keep what I know to myself."

"OK. OK, I get it. But there may be some things that—"

Beth cut him off gain: "Everything! All of it!"

There was a very long pause. Finally, Ken broke the ice. "OK. All of it."

"Get one of your team members on the phone, right now. I'd prefer Karen, that's her name, right?"

"What? Why?"

"Do it, or I clam up about what I know."

Ken thought for a minute, then dialed Karen. "Listen, Karen," Before he could say another word, Beth reached and grabbed the phone from his hand.

"Karen, this is Beth. Ken is going to give you permission to open up to me and fill me in on everything you know about this case. He wants me to be completely caught up, and it is urgent. We need to get this done now. Here is Ken again." She put the phone by Ken's ear.

"Karen, tell her everything we know about the Steve Gilby case. Don't hold anything back. And that includes what we know about Beth herself." He handed the phone to Beth.

*What did he mean about that last comment?* Beth wondered, as she put the phone to her ear and asked Karen to start. Ken sat and watched her. The call lasted about twenty minutes, with Beth remaining completely silent. She didn't change expressions, until the last minute. Then there was a look of shock on her face. She thanked Karen and hung up.

"You thought I might be involved in stealing estates? You thought it could be *me*!? I'm the one who brought this all to you in the first place. Why would I be a suspect?"

"Look, Beth, we'll be open with you, but be reasonable. There have been as many as thirty officers in six different provinces working this over the past six months. You got a twenty-minute summary. We could spend all night on this, or we could move forward. Which one is it?"

Beth thought for a moment, then she pointed to the computer screen that was still facing Ken.

"Tell me what you see?"

"I see somebody's estate being donated to a charity. We already knew all this, Beth. What are you getting at?"

"Look closely. Tell me what the charity is getting, and from who?"

"Somebody named Grace Butler. She left her house, her investments, her car, her insurance policy, everything. It all went to the Aldbrecht Foundation. For God's sake, we already know all this Beth."

"Keep looking, and keep thinking."

Ken was getting mad. "I've been looking at this and thinking about this for six fucking months Beth. What are you getting at?"

Beth gave up. "Where did her furniture go? Her jewelry? Her artwork? All of her possessions?"

There was a long pause before Ken reacted. "Holy shit! How could I have missed that? How could we all have missed that? I wonder if the others are like this too?"

"I'm willing to bet they are. Look at this." Beth changed to another screen. It was another Vancouver estate and again, all personal possessions weren't listed. "I checked a few others before I got to Grace Butler. Look!" Beth clicked her mouse a few more times, and with each click another estate came up, none of which had personal possessions listed.

"You did this in the two minutes while I was standing here?"

"I've kept these files on my computer for the past six months. The system didn't have to retrieve them. I've been losing sleep going over and over these records, but I didn't see this lack of possessions on these lists either. But, then again, I guess I'm not some fucking detective either. That isn't my job. What would I know. Why should I be told anything? I'm not part of the team." Her anger about being kept out of the case was returning.

"What triggered this train of thought Beth. Was it Caroline?"

"Not exactly," and Beth explained about the visit with Gracie and the black alabaster sculpture of a bear, seated and looking sideways. Gracie's bear. "I stood there, holding that black alabaster bear, and then looked around the house at everything else. I was standing amid items that old people owned, not somebody Caroline's age. I realized that I had missed seeing anything about general possessions in any of the estates that had been donated. Those things aren't broken down to every minor item, but they are listed at some point in almost every estate and have an associated value. These estates had nothing listed. Where did all that money go? And that money, by the way, is not exactly chump change. I know Grace Butler had first edition books worth tens of thousands of dollars, possibly hundreds of thousands, and artwork that was worth god-knows-what! And that is just one estate. How many more estates have there been where all their possessions were not accounted for?"

"Beth, this is gold. This is what we've been trying to find. I'm going to have to wait until Monday, when we can have team members check this out in the other provinces. I can tell you this, though, Steve is going down. It will all still take a little while, but this is what we needed!"

"What about Caroline? She's the one with all this stolen property, isn't she? What about her?"

"She's complicit, that's for sure, but Steve may have gifted these to her. Or she may somehow be in a forced situation too. Blackmail, entrapment, something. We don't really know her role just yet. Don't worry, we'll make sure she gets what's coming to her too."

They left Beth's office and Ken drove her back to her apartment. After he saw that she was safely inside, he pulled away. Instead of going home, however, he returned to his office. He had more work to do.

Hours later he pushed the laptop away and leaned back in his chair. He reached for his coffee mug, but soon saw that it was cold, and the coffee had evaporated a millimeter or two. There was an ugly black ring just above where the coffee now was.

"Christ, You're in early!" Karen placed a fresh take-out coffee on his desk.

"No. Not really. I'm here late."

"Jeez, you pulled an all-nighter?"

"Yeah. I'm bagged."

"What was with that call last night? Tell Beth everything about the Gilby case. Is that what you're working on now?"

"Yeah. I think we've now got what we've been looking for. Let me show you . . ."

While Ken was typing on the keyboard to bring up the screen he wanted to share with Karen, she asked: "With that call about Gilby, did I do OK?"

"I think so. I didn't hear everything you said, but you did tell her all about the Gilby case, and nothing more, right?"

"Yeah. Nothing more."

"Good. Now then here, take a look at this." Ken spun his computer screen to face Karen.

After several minutes, Karen was still staring at the screen and looking puzzled. "What?" she finally asked.

"That's what I said last night to Beth: 'what?' She's the one who pointed it out in each of the Vancouver estates. The list you're looking at is from all around Canada. And they all show the same thing. The thing we've been missing all along."

"Jeez Ken. Get to the point. What do they show?"

"Nothing." Ken waited a long while before continuing. "They show nothing. No furniture. No artwork. No coin or stamp collections. No jewelry. No valuable antiques. Nothing."

"Jesus H. Christ. You're right. Beth figured this out?"

"She did. Everything listed as part of the estate is the stuff one level of government or another would know about. Cars and houses? The provinces would have registered. Investments and bank accounts, that's the feds. But who the hell cares about their other belongings. No government audit would show up any missing items because they didn't know about them in the first place. We have over a hundred estates, none of which have any personal belongings to speak of. And we already knew these were estates of people who were well-to-do. I can't believe we all missed this. We owe Beth a lot. She's given us the evidence we've needed to take the next step and arrest this bastard. The other things we're working on can keep ongoing, but I think we should set the stage for an arrest in the next week or two, right?"

"You got it. I'll start the paperwork right away and make sure that by Monday all the detachments in the other provinces are on board. This will still take a few days, though, and there is no way we can consider this urgent enough to start getting warrants on a weekend. That will have to wait until Monday too. And Ken, can I make one more suggestion?"

"Sure. Shoot."

And Karen then suggested Beth should be allowed to witness the arrest. After all, she had been one of his victims, all those years earlier. Possibly one of his first. And she certainly was responsible for their being able to make this arrest.

## March 14 2019

### 1:30 P.M.

Beth looked down at the glove compartment in front of her. She wondered if there was a gun in it. Or had she just watched too many cop shows on TV?

"Want one?" Detective Groemann offered her a cigarette. His left hand was draped over the steering wheel, with an unlit cigarette in his fingers.

"N-no thanks Ken." Beth stuttered. She felt uncomfortable. The fact she was in a police cruiser was part of the problem. *Why weren't they in his Prius?*

"Look, you're nervous. Don't be. If anything ugly happens, I'll just drive away. The uniforms can handle all of this without me. I just thought, you know, that with all the work you did, you deserve to witness this happen. I'm doing this as a favour. You've earned that right. OK?"

Beth couldn't even bring herself to turn towards him. She had told him everything. *Everything.* And they were arresting the man who did those things to her. All she could do now was stare forward at the wipers intermittently working to clear away the light rain that was falling.

Her counsellor had encouraged her to be open with the detective. At this moment, she was wondering if that had been bad advice. But if this all led to an arrest, then she would be satisfied that she had done the right thing. She just wished that she had asked Donna to come along. She could use her comfort right now. Or Sneakers. Or maybe even Tiffany. Yeah, Tiff would have been a better choice for this.

Det. Groemann rolled down his window a small crack and cool air rolled in from the mist outside. "Look, Beth, this guy's gonna get exactly what's coming to him. I'll see to that. I promise."

From the very beginning, Detective Ken Groemann had fit the image of what she expected in a detective. He was huge, over 6'6", and built like he worked out every day. And his voice was deeper than anyone she had known. He was always calm. Always seemed gentle. But he looked like he could break a person in half if he really wanted to.

Beth stared ahead. Each of the three police cars had left their lights flashing, and combined with the misty rain they created a small light show on the windshield. Until the wipers once again swept the slate clear. That is what she needed. Another clean slate. Maybe this would be the start of it.

The uniformed police had forced their way into the house when they couldn't get a reply to their knocks. They had been inside the house for fifteen minutes now. What could be taking them so long?

She started to regret having agreed to this escorted participation. Maybe she should have stayed at home. Ken lit his cigarette and rolled the window down a little further to let the smoke out. Then she saw one uniformed officer approaching their vehicle. The officer knocked lightly on the driver's side window and motioned for Ken to lower it a bit more.

"What's up?" detective Groemann asked as he flicked his cigarette onto the pavement. It had just been lit. He had only taken one drag. He looked like he wasn't happy to be talking to the officer.

"Uhm. Uh . . . I'm afraid we can't follow through with the arrest, sir. We've run into a complication."

Beth just hung her head and closed her eyes.

# March 14 2019

## 6:00 a.m.

Ken went through the routine motions that defined his every morning. His alarm sounded at six a.m. sharp. He sat at the side of his bed and held the picture of Teresa. When she was still alive, she made him promise every morning that he would come home safe that night. He made a habit of promising that to her picture now. A hot shower was next, then toast with jam and a hot coffee. He put on his uniform, and then—the shoes. There was something about having to wear the shoes that didn't sit right with him. The rest of the uniform was no problem, even the badge and gun. It was the shoes that made him feel different than anyone else he knew.

He drove to the office and swapped out his car for a cruiser. He knew today was going to be the arrest, and he wanted the dashcam recording, just in case. Then he spent another four hours reviewing everything they had confirmed so far. He didn't want this effort to fail on a minor technicality. He called Beth to let her know he was coming by to get her in about twenty minutes. The approach for the arrest was scheduled for one p.m.

As he drove to pick her up, he thought about all that she had done. Before she reported this case to the force, she had done tons of legwork to ensure that she wasn't just wasting their time. After reporting it, she had kept helping, providing the paper records they needed, and even working with a wire to try and gather more information. That last step hadn't proven fruitful in the way he had anticipated, but that was also when she came up with the breakthrough idea that had sealed the need for an arrest. The estates were all missing the accounting for personal property. That arrest would come to fruition very soon.

He pulled up in front of her apartment and saw her approaching the cruiser. He just hoped that she wouldn't realize that the reason for today's arrest wasn't because of her work. *It was for a completely different reason.*

Driving to Steve's house, where the arrest was to take place, they barely spoke. Beth seemed to be in a very quiet mood. Possibly the greyness of the day was what put her in such a somber mood. When they pulled up in front of the house and parked, aiming the front camera to the area between the front door and the other marked police cars, he reached for his cigarette case. He had quit smoking after his wife passed away, but he still celebrated each arrest he made by having one cigarette. It was more a ritual than a habit. Pretty sure she would decline anyway; he offered one to Beth. She said no. He opened the window a little to help keep the windshield from fogging up.

He held on to the cigarette until he saw the front door of the house open and one of the officers emerge. He opened his window a little more, lit the cigarette, and waited. The officer approached his car and tapped the window, motioning for Ken to lower it further.

"What's up?" Ken was hoping it was just a snag in the routine that was holding things up.

"Uhm. Uh . . . I'm afraid we can't follow through with the arrest, sir. We've run into a complication."

"Why the hell not!?" Ken didn't suffer fools very well, and his temper rose quickly at any signs of incompetence. "What complication?"

"Sir, could you just step out for a second. I don't think she needs to hear this." The officer motioned toward Beth, who was sitting motionless, head hanging down.

"Officer, she's the main reason we're able to be here today. I'm pretty sure she can hear whatever you have to say. Why can't we make the fucking arrest?" Ken was getting more agitated by the minute.

"Sir, he's dead. We found him hanging from a rope in his dining room. From a hook in the ceiling, sir. It seems it was quite a while ago too. He left a note. Could you please come with me?"

"Shit!" Ken got out of the car and leaned toward the still open window. "Don't move a muscle. I'll get this handled in a few minutes and take you right back home. OK?"

"Sure." Was all Beth could manage to say. She was still frozen in the same position, staring at the floor of the car.

Ken started to walk toward the house and after a couple of steps he returned to the open window. "Hey, are you OK?" He knew she wasn't OK.

"I'll be fine. Go. I'll be OK."

He backed away from the window and ran a few steps to catch up to the officer again. When he approached the open front door, he could smell the familiar odour of a corpse that has been unattended for days. Several officers were now standing in the light rain outside the house. He guessed they were just trying to get away from the stench. Entering the house, he took a quick look into the living room and then crossed to where the body was hanging in the adjacent dining room. The officer followed him. Sirens could be heard in the distance.

"You called it in?"

"Yes sir. The ambulance and the coroner are both on the way. We've also called in the ID unit. One of those three might be what we are hearing now."

"Did anything get touched? Anything at all?"

"No sir. We found the suicide note but left it where we found it. We could only read the front page. This guy must have been a legal professional or a writer or something. The suicide note is pages long and it uses words that I don't see on many of these kinds of notes. Not that I've seen many. It's just—"

"OK. Officer Graham, isn't it?"

"Yes sir. Jason Graham."

"OK. Step outside and get some air that's worth breathing. I'll only be a minute or two myself. I'll stop out there with instructions for everyone once I've taken a look around. Don't worry, I won't touch a thing."

"Yes, sir." And officer Graham exited the house.

Ken walked through the rest of the house, taking a few pictures on his cell phone, and then returned to the dining room. Steve's body was hanging limp from a nylon rope that had been tied to a hook in the ceiling. The hook looked like it was freshly installed. The chair below the body was lying sideways on the ground. *Probably kicked over* he thought.

The body itself was dressed in a suit and tie, but that didn't help to make Steve look any better. He had soiled himself, which was common for people who die in this fashion. The lack of any colour in his face and hands made him out to be less than human. Almost mannequin-like. Ken was happy to see that the eyes were closed. He hated it when there was what he called "the death stare".

He went up to the table and saw the suicide note. He didn't read the first page, the only page visible. He knew he would have lots of time to read that later. He wanted to get back to Beth and get her home. He owed her that much at least.

Exiting the building, he stood on the front doorstep, so he was a head taller than the officers who had gathered by him. He issued the routine instructions but then added one more: "I would like a copy of the suicide note on my desk by the time I get back to my office. Treat it like usual for fingerprinting and DNA testing, but get me that copy asap."

He walked to the cruiser, where Beth was patiently waiting. She was still staring at the floor of the car. He sat behind the wheel and put the car in drive, but before he pulled away, he turned to Beth and asked again: "Are you OK?"

"Yeah. OK, I guess. But I don't get it. Why would he take his life over money? I mean, it was a lot of money, but no amount of money is worth losing your life over, is it?"

"People do strange things when it comes to money."

"But how did he even know we were onto this fraud? This scam? How did he find out?"

"That is a mystery at this point, but maybe time will tell. Let me take you home Beth, you probably need some time for yourself. Time to reflect." He pulled away from the scene. He couldn't bring himself to open up to Beth about the real reason they were wanting to arrest Steve. This fraud case was going to be the next step. She didn't need to know that yet. After all, she was one of his victims.

After dropping Beth at her apartment, and after making sure she was OK, Ken went back to his office. He filled his mug with coffee and sat at his desk, waiting for the copy of the suicide note to arrive. He mentally ran through the work they had completed over these past few months. His thoughts kept circling back to the day Beth first came into the office with evidence of what clearly appeared to be fraud. He thought of the follow-through that his team had done in cooperation with so many other RCMP detachments, all confirming what she had found. There was the revelation of where Caroline Bottier had disappeared to, and the follow-through on her activities now that she was posing as Nancy Cho. Again, Beth's work had led to this discovery. And the final piece of the fraud puzzle, the disappearance of any personal property. That was also Beth. She had definitely contributed more than any other civilian he had ever met.

Then his mind wandered to the young women. The girls. So many lives marred or ruined by Steve's acts. He felt a queasy churn in his stomach as he thought about it. His thoughts were interrupted by the sound of a ding from his computer. It was an email from Officer Graham. The subject line simply read "note."

Ken opened the email and read Officer Graham's brief statement: "ID unit has taken originals but allowed me to take photos of suicide note. Four pages. Attached." Ken read the "four pages" part and smiled a little. "Trust a fucking lawyer to be so verbose in a suicide note!" A clerk passing by his doorway asked if he was speaking to her, and Ken apologized and closed his office door. He hadn't realized that he had said those words out loud. He returned to his computer and opened the first attachment. It was page one of the note.

> "To whomever discovers my mortal remains, please serve this document to the officers who attend to my suicide."

*Fucking lawyer-speak. Whatever happened to a ten word note saying good-bye?*

> "I wish to advise of my decision to render myself guilty and have sentenced myself accordingly."

And on it went. Ken skimmed the main body, where Steve waxed poetic about what his life had meant to the elderly who needed care, and clicked forward to the second and third pages. He finally struck upon something of interest:

> "I have committed a crime, but I have also added value through this life that I have lived. I accept the wrongs of

my ways, and I know that my sickness, my addiction to young women, has caused pain and sorrow to many. I never involved an unwilling participant. But know that this illness is my one and only foible. To wit: I have started a wonderful charity that helps ease the elderly through these same gates that I am about to enter. It is my hope that this will be my lasting legacy, and it is in these pages that I leave my final request.

"My mother is about to join me, and that time is soon. Unfortunately, she is still of very sound mind. It is her body that will fail. I ask only one thing: please do not inform her of my passing, nor of any issues that have come forward due to my illness. Her mother was Alice Aldbrecht. She suffered a slow and painful death due to cancer and didn't receive the level of care she deserved. It was Alice's money that initially created our foundation, and my mother also was instrumental in the foundation's start. It was her dream that no woman should suffer like her mother had. My wish is that my mother will leave the world only knowing of the good that this foundation has done, and that I have done, and know nothing of my failing. My solitary failing. My illness."

It carried on. It mentioned the location of his will, and that the Aldbrecht Foundation would receive his entire estate. It even mentioned the contact person: Nancy Cho. There was a general apology to those whose lives he had negatively impacted, but it was a very shallow apology, if it could even be considered that. At the very end, it was signed. And dated. *Trust a lawyer to date a suicide note* thought Ken, and he turned away from the computer screen.

He was about to leave the office when Karen came through the door. "Sir, we have all the travel information for Vivian Simmons you were looking for. The airlines have confirmed all flights, and they fit right along with the timing of the deaths, just like Tim and I thought they would. The schedule lines up almost perfectly. With only a few exceptions, every death is around four weeks apart. That's not natural."

"Thanks Karen. Did you hear about Steve?"

"Yeah. It was all over the internals, and now I think the civvies are broadcasting it too. Sad news."

"I guess we won't be pursuing charges on that front now. Those poor women deserved better. I hope they get some consolation in knowing how this has ended, and that this bastard is now dead and no other woman will suffer from his wrongdoings, but I doubt it will make any of them feel much better."

"Yeah. I doubt it too. I don't know how I'd feel if I was one of them. What do you want me to do next with this travel information?"

"Just leave it here for now. It's almost four. I might take the rest of the day off. Let's regroup tomorrow, OK?"

"Sure. I'll see you then." Karen left the office and closed the door on the way out. She could sense that Ken needed a bit of time.

Ken knew that he needed to focus on the next steps to take, but today's events were still a little hard for him to process. He did know, however, it was time to pay a visit to Nancy Cho. Caroline. Vivian. Whatever she wanted to call herself. He knew two things: she was the driving force behind the financial dealings, and she was a murderer. First, he needed to review everything that they knew as fact as well as everything they were still guessing at. He got out a file and returned to his desk. This was going to take some time.

When he finally left the office and got into his car, ready to head home, it was eight o'clock. The activity of the day, combined with the load of information he was still trying to sort out, made for a weary drive home. It had been a very long day. He was only a few blocks from his own driveway when his cell phone rang.

"Hello."

"Hello sir. We have a new recording started. We are patching it through to you now."

He sighed. His day was about to get a little longer.

## March 14 2019

## 6:00 p.m.

Beth emerged from the shower and wrapped herself in her housecoat. The hopes that a lingering hot shower would help her relax and brighten her mood were not realized. She refilled the wine glass that she had been drinking from since she returned from the scene of the arrest. Since the scene of the attempted arrest. Since the aborted arrest. Since the suicide.

She had been contemplating crawling back into bed for the past few hours but knew that would just mean waking up at three a.m. and not being able to fall back to sleep again. Her erratic sleep patterns didn't help at all with her mood and her dark feelings.

She took her glass of wine and sat in the easy chair, looking out at the north shore. Sneakers snuggled up to her side. The afternoon rain had abated, and the sporadic cloud cover left some room for patches of sunlight to come through. Right now, the entire north shore looked sunny. A view that Steve would never see again.

*Why would someone take their life at such a young age?* Sure, the financial fraud was going to end his career, but he could have started over in some other kind of career, or even a basic job that didn't require a clean slate to do. He was capable of so many things. He was healthy and still very good looking. Then, *why?*

Her thoughts were interrupted when her cell rang. She got up and walked to the table to see who it was, hoping that Ken was giving her a call. 'Private Number' was on the screen – *it must be him* she thought. "Hello?"

"Hey Liz, whatcha up to?"

*Crap!* She panicked a little. It was Caroline. "I'm just relaxing right now. Not doing anything in particular."

"Great! I'm about ten blocks from your apartment, and I could really use some company. I just heard some bad news. Really bad news. I'd like it if an old friend could join me for a drink. Could you?"

*I wonder if she heard about Steve. How would she have found out? She doesn't know that I know. Or what I know. What should I do?*

"Hello, Liz, are you there?"

"Yeah, um, yes. I'm here. Sorry, this caught me off guard. I'm basically ready for bed right now."

"For God's sake, Liz. It's dinner time, not bedtime. C'mon, let's go for a drink."

Unable to come up with a good reason to decline, Beth just said "OK."

"Good. I'll be there in about ten minutes and pull up out front. Don't keep me waiting too long." And with that, Caroline hung up. Or was she Nancy now?

Beth quickly got dressed and made sure she had her wallet in her purse, then grabbed a light jacket and started toward the elevator. She was just about to lock her apartment door when she thought of one more thing. She went back into the apartment and picked up the necklace. She wondered if it was still active, or if she'd even need it, but she thought she would be a little more comfortable wearing it, so she put it on and left the apartment.

Walking through the lobby she saw Caroline outside standing on the sidewalk. She had two helmets in her hands *Oh god, she's on a motorcycle!* thought Beth. She was barely out the front door when Caroline tossed one helmet in her direction and then walked up and gave Beth a huge hug.

"What was that for?" Beth wasn't sure she wanted to know.

"Hop on the bike. We can talk when we get to my place."

"I thought we were going out for drinks?" Beth asked, but the question was lost in the noise as Caroline revved up the bike. Beth got on behind her.

They had only travelled a few minutes when Beth noticed that they were heading for the Lions Gate bridge. *She's going to West Van* thought Beth, but this helmet didn't have a microphone system and she knew that even if she yelled at Caroline with the question, she wouldn't hear any kind of answer. After another twenty minutes they pulled up in front of the house on Marine

Drive that Beth knew all too well. A remote control opened the front gate, and Caroline cruised down the short driveway and into the lower-level carport. She hopped off the bike and reached out a hand to help Beth dismount.

"This place belongs to a friend of mine. I'm helping her look after it, and it has way better views than my place in Kits. C'mon, I'll pour us some wine and show you around the place. Its views are spectacular!"

"I thought we were going out for a drink. I haven't eaten yet. Can we go someplace and eat?" Beth was not sure why, but she didn't like being so remote from other people right now. She also knew Caroline wasn't house-sitting for a friend, but she had to play along with that charade.

"I've already ordered Thai—totally vegan—and I'll make sure you get a cab home. I won't drive that beast after drinking. Like the new bike?" Caroline was good at deflecting the conversation away from places she didn't want it to go. She was nodding toward the BMW motorcycle. Beth didn't know a single thing about motorcycles. The black Mercedes convertible parked right beside it looked great though. And expensive.

"Yeah, nice bike." Beth couldn't think of what else to say.

"Come inside. Let's get that wine."

They walked into the house. Beth was almost breathless with an instant feeling of awe. The first thing you saw upon entry was the ocean through two-story tall floor-to-ceiling glass windows. The entire panoramic view of Burrard Inlet was right in front of you, with the towering buildings of downtown Vancouver on the far shore. The evening sun was shining through the windows both from the sky and from the reflection off the ocean, making the room electric with light. The entire main floor was white marble walls and glass fixtures, with designer furniture that obviously was built for this particular home. The whole space was an open-air concept, with a bar, the chairs, and wall system comprising the only functional things on the entire main floor. Four other sculptural pieces were non-functional and decorative only, but in a similar style to the furnishings.

Caroline walked to the bar and threw her leather jacket on the back of a bar stool. She took a Riedel wine glass down from a rack and poured it half full from an already uncorked bottle. She walked back to Beth and handed it to her. Caroline's wine glass had already been poured some time earlier, and she retrieved it from the bar. "I hope you don't mind my having made the decision for you, but tonight we're having a very wonderful vintage. It's an '05 Bordeaux that probably should have been left to rest a little longer, but tonight is special, so what the hell. I opened it before I came to your place to pick you up. It's had a little time to breathe. After all, it's for a very special occasion."

"What's the special occasion? You said special twice there." Beth was still trying to figure out where Caroline stood on today's events.

"I'll explain *special* in a bit. It's some very sad news, and also news of a great opportunity. First let me show you the upstairs. I need some wine in me before I get into any heavy conversation. Come with me." Caroline lightly grabbed Beth's wrist and led her to the spiral staircase that went up to the second floor. The second floor was only half of a floor, having no interior walls, with a view down to the front half of the main floor and a lookout that shared the same windows as the first floor.

The upper floor was split into two areas: a dining area that had the views you would want in a house located on the ocean, and behind it a kitchenette on the street side of the building. Beside both was a massive master bedroom that also had the same views. Both the dining room and the bedroom were open to the rest of the house, with no walls facing the ocean or between the two rooms. Both were decorated like you would if you were listing the home for sale, and neither one looked lived in. Just as they were going to enter the kitchen area, Caroline's phone vibrated.

"That's dinner. Check out the kitchen and then have a seat at the table. I'll bring the food up."

Beth took a brief look into the kitchen area, but then walked into the bedroom and looked around. On the street-side there was the largest ensuite she had ever seen, with a twin Jacuzzi bathtub and very large shower. One wall was entirely mirrored, with two sinks and a very long glass vanity in front of it. The bedroom itself was huge, but with no wall facing the ocean it looked even larger. She heard Caroline coming up the stairs and quickly walked back into the dining area.

"Dinner is served! I hope you're OK with eating up here. There's a little gazebo set up as a dining area down by the water, but it is a tad breezy tonight. This will be way more comfortable.

"This is absolutely fine. I can't imagine a place with a better view. This is great!"

Caroline placed the take-out bag on the table, which only now Beth noticed had been set for two. While Caroline transferred the various dishes from their plastic containers to stoneware ones she had previously set on the table, Beth finally got the courage to ask: "Why did you call me tonight? What was this special reason you were referring to?"

"You haven't heard the sad news today? I thought you'd be one to keep in touch with what's happening around town. It was on the TV and the radio. I'm surprised you missed it."

Beth could feel herself blushing. She hadn't listened to the news, but she damn well knew what had happened. That is, if Caroline was talking about the same thing that she was thinking about. "I had the day off and didn't listen to anything. What are you talking about?"

"I'm talking about our good old friend Steve. He decided to off himself today. Hung himself in his home. Well, he did it in the past few days, but the news said they just found his body today. I propose a toast. To Steve! Without him, you and I wouldn't have become friends." And with that, she held her wine glass forward toward Beth to initiate a toast. "May he rest in peace."

"Steve's dead?" Beth tried her best to sound like this was the first time she was hearing of the news. She touched her glass against Caroline's and added; "Oh my god! I'm without words. I feel so bad for him. May he rest in peace." They each took a sip from their glasses. Caroline sat across from Beth and smiled at her in a very knowing way.

"He was your first real love, wasn't he?"

"What? I mean, no! I dated a few guys in high school. And I had a short-term boyfriend in first year at university. So no, he wasn't my first." Beth felt this question was almost insulting.

"Hey, let's not let the food get cold. Dig in. What I meant was, he was the first man you really felt that you could get serious about. I remember you were moony-eyed when you were around him. Want some rice to start?"

"Uh, sure. What is the name of the place you ordered from?" Beth was hoping to divert the conversation away from Steve.

"Thai One On. They just opened in North Vancouver. Great food and all vegan, but the restaurant itself is nothing to rave about. Basic ugly décor. A sad statement about humans as a species, really, that someone would think that it's a treat to dine out in a place that's ugly. I only get take-out. So, why do you think Steve killed himself?"

"I can't imagine. Did you keep in regular contact with him? I wasn't in touch with him myself, so I wouldn't have any idea why he would do such a thing."

"Yeah, well, I saw him about three or four times a year. Mostly to do some things with this foundation he created. He seemed to be disassociating with everything and everyone. He was almost becoming a hermit. Try some of this Pad Ka-naa. It's delicious."

"Thanks. Can I pass you something? You're right, this place makes amazing food. I'm impressed!" Beth wanted to dig a little deeper into Caroline's involvement with the foundation. "What's this about a foundation?" She realized Caroline wouldn't know that she was aware of the foundation and had no reason to suspect it was the same one that had funded the research their summer jobs relied on.

"I'd love the Pad Thai please. So, the foundation is that one we were involved with at our summer jobs at university. He did something very tricky. His grandmother, Alice Aldbrecht, left him a pile of money and he had it put in a trust. He found a way to set the trust up as a nonprofit, get the nonprofit to fund research, and then tapped into the feds to add money for the research he was doing. Very clever, actually, but also not completely legal. I found that out, so I used it as a way to get him to hire me as the foundation's bookkeeper. Want some more wine?"

"Thanks" and Beth held out her wine glass. "So that's where the Aldbrecht Foundation got its name and its money, from his grandmother?"

"Yeah. And his mother. She donated everything she inherited to the foundation as well. He was totally fixated on his mother and his grandmother. His grandmother died without getting proper care, and both Steve and his mother felt that the work this charity did was a natural cause to support."

The hair on the back of Beth's neck stood straight at the words "natural cause." Something was stirring her thoughts around these words, but she couldn't quite place what it was.

Caroline continued: "I think the greatest joy in his life was getting to name the charity after his grandmother, even though by now her contributions to it are a mere fraction of the total that has been raised." She topped up Beth's wine glass and took a good-sized sip from her own, leaving her glass almost empty. "That brings me to why I wanted to see you tonight. This is the great opportunity part of the news I mentioned earlier. I may need your help."

Beth didn't know if it was the right thing to do, and she didn't even know if this would even do anything at all. It might no longer be active. But she lifted her hand to the necklace and began touching the various stones it contained, including the one just above the turquoise teardrop. She gave that one a generous squeeze. "What help do you mean?"

"Have you had enough to eat? Let's take our wine and sit in the bedroom sectional. It's way more comfortable." Caroline stood and grabbed both her empty wine glass and the bottle of wine.

Caroline left the dining room, and Beth automatically followed her, holding her wine glass as well. The front of the bedroom, the area closest to the handrail that overlooked the main floor, was set up like a lounge. There was a huge sectional wrapped around a coffee table in a semicircle, so any place you sat had a view of the ocean. It was after eight o'clock and the sun had already set. The lights from Vancouver's downtown offices were reflecting across the inlet, causing a flickering of sparkles on the water. Once they were both settled into the sectional, Caroline stood up and reseated herself closer to Beth.

"The opportunity I was referring to, well, it involves you. This foundation is going to have an opening for someone now that Steve is gone. I think I could put your name forward and get you involved. What do you think?"

"Jesus Caroline. Steve's just passed away. Isn't this something that you should take some time to consider? Aren't there others who've been involved that may be a better choice than me?"

Caroline reached to Beth's hair and started to twirl a lock of it around her index finger. "Here's the thing. Over the last few years Steve has relied on me more and more. I've gotten to know the other board members well enough that I can convince them to agree with almost everything I suggest. That house in Kits? –It's a foundation asset that I am allowed to live in because of the work I do for the foundation. I would be happy to set you up with something just as nice. You wouldn't have to live in that small apartment of yours.

"The position pays well. There is a little work to be done, but the income would be way better that what you currently earn, and you'd only have to work a few days a month. What would you say to that?"

"Um, tell me more. It sounds intriguing. Was Steve doing the work that you're thinking I could be doing now?" Beth decided to pry for a little for more insight and information, even if the necklace system wasn't active.

"Basically yeah. He was the executive director, and we need to replace him. The other board members won't have a person to put forward, and they'll both lean on me for a recommendation. I could say you were involved from the very start, which is true, and that you are currently in a management position with the province, which also is true. What do you say, Beth?"

"Why such an urgent need to refill Steve's position? He just passed away. Can't this wait a few weeks or even months?" Beth was not sure how far to push the questions. She noticed Caroline had moved from twirling her hair to softly stroking the back of her neck. She wasn't sure how she felt about that. It felt good, but it probably shouldn't feel good. She could also feel herself starting to blush.

"Beth, you never have found a partner to be with, have you? You've kept to a single life for all these years now. Aren't you lonely living that way?"

Beth suddenly realized: Caroline called her Beth, not Liz! She seemed to know a lot about her personal life that wasn't public knowledge. She was feeling less and less comfortable with this entire visit. "Sorry, excuse me for a minute. I need to use the bathroom." She got up and walked to the ensuite, only now realizing that there was no door to separate it from the bedroom, with only the positioning of a half-wall to allow for a modicum of discretion. Caroline could see her every move if she wanted, but instead Caroline stared out at the ocean.

Entering the bathroom, Beth felt she had to take a seat on the toilet, just to make sure that the sounds coming from the room were in sync with her words to Caroline. She sat and thought for a minute, then flushed and washed her hands before returning to the sectional. She intentionally sat a little further away from Caroline. Her mind was still spinning. The washroom tactic hadn't helped her get her thoughts organized at all.

"So, why the rush to find someone for Steve's position?"

Caroline reached for her empty wine glass on the coffee table, and as she sat back, she inched a little closer to Beth and put her hand on Beth's thigh. "Here's the situation. I mentioned that I'm the bookkeeper. It's my responsibility to ensure all the records for the foundation are properly kept, and all necessary filings are done for taxes, that sort of stuff. It's all very mundane and routine, but I know it's for a good charity, so I'm willing to do my part. The problem is this: certain cheques we write on the foundation's bank account require two signatures. I'm one, and Steve was the other. All our routine payroll and monthly expenses can still get paid, but nothing more. I had been calling Steve's place for a couple of days now because there are bills that need paying. Big bills. I need a person to come to the bank with me, tomorrow preferably, and get the signing authority switched from Steve to that person. I hope you will be that person, Beth."

Beth started to understand what the issue was: Caroline couldn't bring another board member to the bank. They were dead. The bank would need to verify the change with a living person who had photo ID. Caroline couldn't be both Caroline and Nancy at the same time if they wanted photo ID. Obviously, she needed access to the foundation's funds for something, and that something was urgent. Not knowing why, except possibly to stall for time, she asked Caroline: "tell me more about the Aldbrecht Foundation. What do they do?"

Caroline explained about the care homes that were operating in various provinces, and how the employees' salaries were funded by each province, provided the foundation was covering all other costs to operate the homes. She talked about how the surveys that were conducted helped Steve source candidates for the charity, and how each of their entire estates would have just gone to the government itself if these donors had passed away intestate and without relatives. "That would have been a shame. All these people wanted to see their estate money go to dignified end-of-life care. It was a natural choice. They could relate to the cause very easily."

She explained how the foundation had an operating account at the bank with funds that pay the ongoing costs, and a restricted account, with investment income that helped replenish the operating account. She went on to disclose how the foundation had sold some properties it had received in order to add money to the restricted account, and how it was now necessary to transfer some of the money in the restricted account to the operating account in order to pay some bills so that the charitable work could keep going. "Otherwise, all these palliative care homes will not be able to pay their bills for supplies, for food, for anything. It would seriously disrupt the great service they are providing. Do you see why I need you to come on board as soon as possible?"

Beth was about to ask if she could sleep on the idea for a day or two, but Caroline placed her finger over Beth's lips. "We could be friends again." She leaned in and gave Beth a long, lingering kiss. Beth's mind raced. She could feel her own pulse throbbing in her neck. Her ears were ringing. More of a whistle than a ring. She realized it wasn't a whistle. She was hearing sirens in the distance.

The sirens got louder as they got closer, and moments later they were right at the house. Before the sirens had even stopped, there was a loud pounding on the door.

"Caroline Bottier, this is the police. Open the door, Caroline. We have a warrant for your arrest!"

Beth pushed herself away from Caroline. She could only imagine how shocked she must have looked. Caroline herself seemed fairly composed. She slowly rose and walked toward the staircase. At the top of the staircase she stopped, turned toward Beth, and smiled. "Beth, this could have been wonderful." Beth rose to follow her as she went down the stairs. Caroline opened the front door. Detective Ken Groemenn was standing in the doorway with paperwork in one hand and his handcuffs in the other. Beth could see his green Prius blocking the gate to the driveway. Two uniformed officers were also approaching the house, each with one hand on their holsters. Half a dozen police vehicles were behind them, all with lights flashing.

"Caroline, please turn away from me and put your hands behind your back." As Caroline did as she was told, Ken took a moment to signal to Beth to be quiet.

"You are under arrest for suspicion of first-degree murder. There are several charges of this crime laid against you. You have rights, according to the Charter, to know your charges. You may remain silent. You have the right to counsel . . ."

Beth's mind had stopped processing after the first few words: "first-degree murder." While Ken carried on with the arresting process, Caroline looked at Beth and smiled once again. "This could have been wonderful, Beth" she repeated.

A half-dozen more uniformed police officers arrived and let themselves into the house. They started searching every possible location for something, though Beth didn't have a clue what they were looking for. She was still reeling at hearing the charge of murder. Was Steve the victim? Was he one of several? Ken had mentioned "several charges." For that matter, had she placed herself in danger with a murderer? Had Ken supported her visits to Caroline, wearing the necklace, knowing full well Caroline was a murderer? She wanted to ask so many questions but held herself back, not knowing what could or should be said.

A uniformed officer approached Ken. In his blue-rubber-gloved hand he held a glass vial containing a white powder. "I think this may be what we're looking for, sir."

"Good work officer. Treat that carefully. Make sure proper evidence recording is done. And for goodness sakes, even with the gloves, wash up after handling that bottle, OK?"

"Yes sir." The officer went outside to a van that had arrived and turned the bottle over to a man wearing a hazmat suit. Beth just stood and stared at the whole process.

"It must be nice to be innocent all your life. To look in amazement at all of life's wonders. I think that's what I've always loved about you, Beth. Your innocence." Caroline had chosen to not remain silent.

Ken spoke next: "There are also charges relating to procuring minors for sex. You are also being charged with participating in sexual acts with minors. Do you understand these charges?"

"Beth, how could you have worked with this guy? Yeah, I knew. I didn't know everything, but I knew you went to him." She nodded her head at Ken. "I had hoped that Steve was your target, but I wasn't sure. I was hoping it was some kind of delayed vengeance thing or something. I didn't know what you knew about my involvement. What you knew about me. I was hoping to discover that tonight."

Ken turned to another officer: "Please put this woman in the back of your cruiser. She is of no further use to me. And make sure her rights are repeated and recorded in the cruiser. Got it?" The officer nodded yes and took Caroline away.

Ken turned and looked at Beth. "The bottle they took away. Know what it probably was?"

"Her coke, I assumed. Why such a fuss about handling it so carefully?"

"It was sodium cyanide. Very lethal, even in small doses. It's a long story, and I'm going to be busy most of the rest of the night following up on this arrest. Have you eaten or drunk anything at all since you got here tonight?"

"Yeah. We had Thai take-out and some wine. What was…"

"There's an ambulance on the way. You're going straight to the hospital. You might be OK, but I'm not taking any chances. Not with you, Beth. Just hold tight. They should be here any minute."

There were so many sirens outside that Beth thought the entire police force had been called in, and before she could process what Ken had just shared with her, two EMT attendants were coming through the door with a stretcher. Both were wearing hazmat suits. Ken pointed at Beth and said, "That's her."

Beth was in a state of shock. "What's going on? What will happen to me?"

Ken tried to assure her. "Beth, this is just a precaution. You are probably fine, but we're getting you to a hospital right away, just to make sure. They'll be doing some tests, some bloodwork and stuff, but don't worry. They'll look after you. I'll come to the hospital myself once we're done here. OK?"

The ambulance attendants were asking her to lay down on the stretcher they had just opened beside her. One was wrapping a blanket over her. Within a minute, she was in the ambulance itself and the sirens were blaring as they were speeding through the streets on the way to the hospital. Most of what was happening, or what had just happened, was lost on her. She couldn't think straight at all. *Sodium cyanide? Have I been poisoned?*

At the hospital there was no delay in getting attended to. Blood was taken, and the ER doctor was grilling her with questions: "Are you feeling dizzy? Do you have a headache? Are you feeling confused?" The kind of questions that she could have said *yes* to mainly due to the wine she had drunk and the chaos that the evening had evolved into. Monitors were being strapped to her arm, and the nurse was placing an oxygen tube under her nose.

After about twenty minutes the doctor sat on a stool beside the bed and held her hand. "We think everything is OK. We are waiting on the blood results, but we are pretty sure you were only mildly poisoned. Are you feeling OK now?"

Beth didn't know how to answer. "I'm feeling OK. I'd just like to know what is going on. What does 'mildly poisoned' mean? What will happen to me? And will the police be coming by tonight?"

"The police? That I don't know. We got called that you were coming in, and the concern about what you may have been exposed to, but they didn't say if or when they would be by here to follow up. Would you like me to call them for you and ask?"

"First tell me about 'mildly poisoned'! Am I going to be OK?"

"We will first make sure it is sodium cyanide, then we can give you the appropriate antidote. With the short time that has passed since you've consumed the poison, there should be no problem in getting this treated and you should suffer no effects from the poisoning. Did you want me to contact the police for you?"

Before Beth could answer, she noticed a familiar figure walking down the hall toward her. It was Ken. Relief swept over her.

"How's our patient doing, doctor?"

The doctor repeated: "We're waiting on bloodwork to confirm, but I think there has been very little poisoning. Once we confirm the type, we'll administer the treatment. We think she'll be OK."

Ken frowned a little. "How long will that take?"

"Testing for cyanide is quite an involved process. It is usually only done with victims of fires and such. It takes a few hours at least. I can't in good conscience let her go until we know for sure that she has been treated with the proper antidote, and we will want to monitor for a day or two at least. You understand, right?"

"Of course, Doctor. We don't need her to leave here until she is one hundred percent healthy. That is our only concern. Thank you."

The doctor left the room and Ken took his place on the stool beside Beth. "You must be in a bit of shock right now."

"There are your masterly detective skills at work again, Sherlock. Well done."

"Beth, I'm sorry about how this played out. I had no idea that Caroline was going to contact you at all, let alone so quickly after the suicide. I think I am finally able to be completely open with you now. Not just about Steve Gilby but about everything. I left the crime scene early so I could come and see you. Can we talk? Or do you need to rest?"

"I'm not going to be able to rest for a long time. This evening has been insane. Did you know Caroline could pose a danger to me when you set me up to meet with her?"

"Not at all. I didn't put you in danger's way, not that I knew of at least. And I didn't think Caroline would have done anything tonight either, but I really don't know how she would have behaved if you had refused her offer to join the charity. That's why I was parked out front of that house on Marine for the last few minutes before I knocked. About twenty minutes earlier, as soon as you touched your necklace, I headed in your direction. I wanted to wait and listen to her plans with you, but as soon as I knew you were drinking wine, I had to act fast. We had warrants issued for her arrest and a search of her property at the same time we got warrants for Steve's arrest, but we were wanting to wait a couple of days before we acted on them. Then this visit with you came up."

"But you've charged her with murder. How could that make me safe?"

"You weren't the type she liked to murder. Let me explain. Can we go back to the beginning?"

"Please do. I want to know everything."

"When you came to us with the information about the Aldbrecht Foundation and the unusual estate information, we focused on that one item. You suspected something was not normal, and we assumed that there was a case of fraud.

"The further we investigated, the deeper the problems appeared to be. Then you came to us with information about Nancy Cho—the late Nancy Cho and the fact Caroline was using her identity—that opened up a whole new channel for us. We had old information about Caroline, mostly drug and gang related, but then she had disappeared. She assumed the Nancy Cho cover mostly to hide from a gang that she owed a lot of money to. That goes back quite a few years, and apparently, Steve was threatened by the gang. He had bailed her out of a debt with them some years earlier even, but this time he dug his heels in and refused to pay the latest debt, so the gang went after Caroline. They probably would have killed her if they found her."

Beth perked up. "When I was still in third year and working for Steve, he paid off a debt to some band musician Caroline had been sleeping with. She had taken ten grand of his money and Steve paid it off, but at the time he'd said: 'that's twice.' The first one must have been the gang debt."

"I'm guessing, but you're possibly right. Or it could have been a completely different debt. But here's where the situation gets messy, and some of this is still conjecture at this point. We're still working to prove some of this. Caroline had some sort of leverage on Steve, and we think it was because of his preying on young women. In some cases, even under-age girls. We think Caroline actually set him up with some of these women—especially these underage girls—and was using that to blackmail Steve into letting her run the foundation."

"So, Steve wasn't blackmailing Caroline! It was the other way around?"

"We think so. Earlier today when I read Steve's suicide note, he mentioned that his penchant for young women, which he himself called his 'sickness,' was his sole crime. He probably hung himself out of shame, the shame of what the exposure of his sickness would bring upon his mother and the foundation."

"So Steve wasn't the one committing fraud? It was Caroline?"

"Exactly, or at least we're pretty sure that is the case. But things get uglier. Once you connected us to Nancy Cho, we looked into the other board member, the other dead one that is, and we found out Caroline was also using her identity. Vivian Simmons was also Caroline. I guess I should say Caroline was playing herself to be Vivian Simmons."

"Why would she need so many aliases? Wouldn't Nancy Cho's identity be enough to hide behind?"

"Well, yes, and no. One identity was to hide from her past. The other was to hide from what she was up to now. Are you sure you want all of this tonight? I could come and see you in the next day or two and finish then. You have most of the picture now."

"No, Ken, I want to hear it all. I want to know what this all has come to. And what will happen to the foundation and all those people in palliative care in these homes?"

"Well, the last part I can't be too sure of, but there is another layer to the story. You haven't asked about the murder charges."

"Yes! What about the murder charges?"

"Well, one of our detectives in Winnipeg put some effort in and found a pattern with the estates being processed. It was the date of death where she noticed a pattern. There were a few exceptions, but each death seemed to occur about four or five weeks apart. That seemed unusual, especially since every autopsy listed the cause of death as a 'natural cause.' She then asked for the fifty most recent death certificates issued by Manitoba. There were only two that said: 'natural cause.' It struck her as unusual that for over one hundred donors to the same charity, almost every one of them had 'natural cause' as the listed cause of death. A few inquiries later, she discovered that for elderly people, unless the cause is obvious, say a heart attack or cancer, that kind of thing, well, they just don't do a very deep dive into why that person died. They are happy to just list 'natural cause' and leave it at that. And none of these people had relatives to question that analysis. They were all lone wolves, so to speak."

"So, you think Caroline killed them?"

"Yes. Well, Vivian Simmons was the suspect. We have flights from Vancouver to each city where the death occurred with Vivian as the passenger. About ninety percent of them at least. The others may really have died of a natural cause, and there were a few who died of known issues. Cancer, stroke, and other issues. But only a few. I am assuming this: I think Caroline saw the money to be made in skimming the personal property from these estates, and thought it was worthwhile to offer to run the entire charity for Steve. Then—and again, I'm mostly guessing, she became too impatient to wait for these donors to pass away on their own schedule. She started deciding on the date of death for them."

"But, how did she kill them?"

"You know that white powder they found in the house? You thought it was coke, and I told you it was sodium cyanide. It's a very lethal compound that is easily purchased and used for some valid reasons, but it can be used as a murder weapon as well. It doesn't leave an obvious trace and is only detected by some complicated and time-consuming tests on the victims. It can also be administered in its current form—dusted on food or whatever, applied to a person's skin when it's mixed with a lotion, or it can be dissolved in a liquid, like a glass of wine."

Just then another officer walked down the hospital corridor up to the two of them and held out some papers and what looked like a passport. "Sir, we've sealed off the site and have security on overnight. Forensics will finish with the place tomorrow, but I thought you might want to see these tonight. We found them just after you left the building." Ken put on latex gloves, took the items, briefly looked through them and handed most of them back to the officer.

Ken turned to Beth and said "You might want to see this too. Take a look at these." He held up one of the items the officer had just handed to him. "Please don't touch anything. We'll be needing to get these finger-printed and DNA tested. But let me hold them open for you to read." He opened the passport. It was for Caroline Bouttier.

Beth thought that this made sense for Caroline to have, but that she'd never need it. She could fly within the country using a provincial ID card, so she didn't need a passport saying Nancy Cho or Vivian Simmons. She would only need her own passport for any travel to another country.

"Now look at these." Ken took what looked like one folded document and opened it up to two pages. He faced them both at Beth. Beth's jaw dropped. They were two airline tickets booked for that Saturday. Both were direct flights: Vancouver to Ho Chi Minh City. One was made out to Caroline Bouttier. The other was made out to Elizabeth Grant.

"But—?" was all Beth could utter.

"When I was listening in tonight, she said she wanted you to be a co-signer for the foundation. That would have made you a criminal too. I'm betting her plan was to get out as much money as she could, and then convince you to join her in Vietnam. She could use the fact that you had committed a crime as leverage to convince you to go. Like some of the other things I've told you tonight, we need to do more work to prove this, but it seems pretty likely to be the case."

"Why Ho Chi Minh City? Why Vietnam?"

"Well, for one thing, they don't have an extradition treaty with Canada. The Canadian crimes would go unpunished. And with the amount of money that she had access to, she could have lived like royalty in Vietnam. She just couldn't ever come back to Canada, but I doubt that she'd ever want to."

"But what if I said no to her? What would she have done?"

"That will remain an eternally unanswered question. I wouldn't want to even make a guess, but I'm thinking the poison was part of that path. Now, have I filled you in enough to allow you to get some sleep? I'd really like to get back to work. I'll let one of our officers take you home when they release you in a few days, OK?"

"I still don't get it. She bought an airline ticket with my name on it, then she poisoned me? It makes no sense!"

"She would have treated you with an antidote somehow if you agreed to the trip – and she would have left you to die if you refused, I think. Again, Beth, these are just guesses at this point, but I can't think of many alternatives. Now try and rest. These good folks will make sure you're treated properly. Try and get some sleep."

"Sure, but I don't think I'll be doing a lot of sleeping tonight. I just can't believe all of this. I knew Caroline was a badass, but I never thought she would be a murderer. And why didn't Steve step in and stop any of this?"

"My guess is Steve didn't even know. She ran the books for the charity, and he just signed off on necessary paperwork as a formality. I'm willing to bet he really thought Nancy Cho and Vivian Simmons were alive and on the board. But again, I'm just guessing, and with him gone, well—"

"I get it Ken. Thanks."

Ken stood up to leave. "Can I give you a call tomorrow, just to see how you're doing?"

"Sure. I think I'm going to take some time off work. I think I need to get away. Maybe even go and see my dad in Mexico or something."

"Sure, Beth. You deserve a break. You know, I've never had a civvy work so much on a case like this before. I hope you know how much I appreciate the work you did. Actually, I hope you know how much I appreciate you." He smiled at her.

Beth smiled back. "I think I always wanted a cause to work for. Maybe for me, this was a natural one to choose. Right?"

# Epilogue

Beth did find the work she had done with the police to be greatly rewarding. She noticed that her own feelings were uplifted whenever she was doing anything related to the researching and investigating that the case had required. From the time she had received Steve's phone call in January of that year right up until the police arrested Caroline, she hadn't had a single blue day. She knew that couldn't just be a coincidence.

There had been a few days after Caroline's arrest where her mood had sunk very low, but she attributed that to the let-down of being finished with the case. Detective Groemann—Ken—had helped her a little during those times by visiting and updating her on the follow-up to the arrest.

Caroline was imprisoned immediately, and the prosecutors managed to convince the judge that not only were her crimes of a heinous nature, but they used the airline tickets to show that she was a serious threat to flee. She was denied bail.

In preparation for the trial, two traditionally buried bodies were exhumed and tested. Both tests revealed lethally elevated levels of exposure to cyanide. Beth was glad to hear that neither body exhumed was Gracie's. She was happy to know that at least Gracie didn't have to suffer that indignity.

Further investigation found that Steve had a lot of pornography on his computer, some even being child pornography. Included in that were also a few videos of Steve himself and some very young girls having sex. Caroline's voice can be heard in the background, possibly taking the video. Caroline herself refused to admit it, and Ken couldn't prove it, but he was certain that these videos were what Caroline was using to make Steve cooperate with her ideas about running the charity. They were her leverage.

# A NATURAL CAUSE

Prior to the trial proceeding, Caroline pled guilty to charges of identity fraud, financial fraud, real estate fraud, and murder. She must have known that there was no possible way to defend against the evidence that had been gathered. She has tried to convince the court that she was the victim of Steve's operations, that he was the devious mind behind the whole operation, and that they should be lenient with her. She is still awaiting her sentencing.

Steve's mother passed away shortly after hearing of Steve's death. She was never told how he had died, nor was she informed of his sexual transgressions. It was generally felt that she shouldn't be the one who suffered the indignity of his crimes.

The Aldbrecht Foundation has been allowed to continue, and many of the known assets that had been stolen were recovered and are now placed in the foundation's hands. Everything they had recovered except for one item, that is: a black alabaster bear, seated and looking sideways. It was presented by the foundation to Beth, as a thank-you token for the work she had done. It was Ken's idea.

The foundation is now in a better financial position than it has ever been, and the new board of directors is currently searching to appoint a new Executive Director. Apparently, thanks to the extensive groundwork done by both Steve and Caroline after the surveys were completed, there are still many more estates that have named the Aldbrecht Foundation as the sole beneficiary. Going forward, the personal belongings of those estates will not go unrecorded.

Ken did ask Beth out on a date. She consented, but after the one date they both agreed that just being friends was way easier. They continue to see each other on a regular basis. It was at one of those visits that Ken told her about the Civilian Criminal Investigators program with the RCMP. She applied and was accepted. She left her government job, and her introductory CCI training is starting soon.

Beth still drops by her old office building to have lunch with Donna at their usual table, and she also spends most Friday nights with her and Greg. Every few weeks she has dinner with Tiff.

And every few months, she calls her favourite "cleaning lady" and asks her to come for a visit.

Printed in Canada